NAMASTE TRUMP AND OTHER STORIES

NAMASTE TRUMP

TRUMP

& OTHER STORIES

TABISH KHAIR

Interlink Books
An imprint of Interlink Publishing Group, Inc.
Northampton, Massachusetts

First published in 2023 by

Interlink Books
An imprint of Interlink Publishing Group, Inc.
46 Crosby Street
Northampton, Massachusetts 01060
www.interlinkbooks.com

Library of Congress Cataloging-in-Publication Data
Names: Khair, Tabish, author.
Title: Namaste Trump and other stories / Tabish Khair.
Description: Northampton, Massachusetts : Interlink Books, an imprint of
Interlink Publishing Group, Inc., 2023. |
Identifiers: LCCN 2023016053 | ISBN 9781623717483 (paperback)
Subjects: BISAC: FICTION / Short Stories (single author) | FICTION /
Literary | LCGFT: Short stories.
Classification: LCC PR9499.3.K427 N36 2023 | DDC 813/.54—dc23/eng/20230403
LC record available at https://lccn.loc.gov/2023016053

2 4 6 8 10 9 7 5 3 1

Printed and bound in the United States of America

for Safia

CONTENTS

I
NIGHT OF HAPPINESS

THIS IS HOW IT BEGINS ...

You enter the room.

Who are you?

You could be anybody. Maybe you are a businessman or a CEO, passing through this teeming North Indian city and staying for a night in one of its five-star hotels. You could be a prosperous doctor attending an international conference, or an ordinary tourist from Denmark or the US, splurging on this room for a night or two after tramping the heat and dust of Indian streets. You could even be a writer, put up in this hotel—the sort you cannot afford on your own—by the organizers of a well-funded festival.

Or you could be a hotel employee, of the junior-management sort, sent in to check that the bar is fully stocked or that the cleaners have done their job—someone from another part of India, say, Manipur, or Kerala, or Bengal. But, no, you cannot be a mechanic, ordered to repair the air conditioner, or the cleaning lady. That is not a possibility in this time and place. You can be *almost* anybody.

It does not matter who you are—as long as you are the kind of person who can pause and read in English—or why you are here in this five-star hotel room. What matters is that you open the first drawer of the glass-topped teakwood cabinet next to the bed, the drawer in which copies of the Bible and the Bhagavad Gita are kept. There, under the copies of these two books, seldom read in this room, you discover reams of paper filled with a minute and neat handwriting.

You take out the sheets, perhaps only to throw them away. But your attention is caught by the first page: there is a title on it that intrigues you, partly because it has been crossed out. And then there is a stanza that you might vaguely recall from your schooldays.

It is a manuscript of some sort.

The writing reaches out and catches you by the sleeve. You feel its desperate tug. You start reading ...

THE SPECTRAL INFINITUDE OF SMALL DISTANCES

They groan'd, they stirr'd, they all uprose,
Nor spake, nor moved their eyes;
It had been strange, even in a dream,
To have seen those dead men rise.

Samuel Taylor Coleridge, "The Rime of the Ancient Mariner"

1

The sky had been a deep blue some hours earlier, but it was a gunnysack now, grimy and weighted with rain. Just Ahmed and I were left in the office, as was usually the case on such late evenings. And exactly when Ahmed was making the last of a dozen confirmation calls to our partners in Dubai, the storm, which had been a growl in the throat of the sky, burst with a deafening flash of paparazzi lightning.

I felt bad for Ahmed. Not only would he be late, he would get drenched too. I knew he never carried an umbrella. He never carried anything except that stainless steel tiffin carrier, wrapped in a clean cotton towel. He always spread out the towel on his desk and carefully arranged the three steel containers of the tiffin carrier on it before commencing to eat.

He carried nothing else. He did not even take work home. He simply stayed on and finished it, sometimes working after midnight. He was the only one of my employees who could be asked to work on any day, which he often was, as I ran an export/import business. The bigger it grew, the more we had to work according to the calendars of other nations and cultures. Holidays seldom coincide across borders. But if a deposit had to be made in Damascus during Diwali, I could count on Ahmed to stay back and take care of it. If a shipment had to be counterchecked in Iceland during Eid, Ahmed was willing to do so.

On any other day he would stay back without a murmur, without a frown. Any other day, that is, except this day.

It was Shab-e-Barat. Ever heard of it? I hadn't when I first met Ahmed, but then the only Muslim boy in class at my boarding school spoke English with an Oxbridge accent. It is not one of the Eids, the one with the sacrifice or the one with the *sewai*. Those I knew. Those my Muslim classmate celebrated too: One time his parents had come down and taken us all out to the house they would rent just outside Shimla, where they were throwing an Eid party that year. Friends and family had flown in and motored up from all over. It was like a Diwali party, minus the fireworks, plus the *sewai* desserts. But Shab-e-Barat?

Ahmed had told me about it during his first year with us. But I guess I should begin by telling you how I came to meet Ahmed.

I had just started the business, after a stint of teaching at an Indian Institute of Technology, based on my MBA from the same institution and then a Ph.D. in business communication from Columbia. Total waste. Teaching. Academia. What a load of bollocks! Babble, boredom and bad pay. I had had enough within three years. The missus quite liked campus life though; we had met at Columbia, where she had been sent by her Mumbai-based family to do a master's in creative writing. Those days she was still writing a novel and rebelling against her father's millions. I guess the two were the same thing.

Anyway, I took a loan from my father-in-law in Mumbai and a bank whose directors knew my father, and went into export/import, as they say. Best decision of my life, though my wife came round to it only after we started making very good money and she graduated from writing novels to organizing literary soirees. The money helped in the latter endeavor.

But in the initial days, before the moolah started rolling in, I had just three full-time employees. Ahmed was one of them.

I recall interviewing him. I had been surprised by his age. He was forty-two years old then; somehow, I had not noticed his year of birth on his résumé. That made him around a decade older than me, and I remember feeling awkward in his presence. He already had gray hair. Clean-shaven and with a way of looking at you directly in the face. Not hostile, but disconcerting. An austere face, deeply lined, with deep-set, almost unblinking eyes. Dressed in clean, well-ironed clothes, which were not entirely the cut or colors that were in, so that he reminded you of someone from an older generation. That was Ahmed.

I guess I had called him for the interview because of his name—he was the only Muslim applicant. Oh well, I thought, now I bloody well have to. But I was also prepared to reject him. Honestly, I had almost made up my mind to reject him. I did not want to feel prejudiced by not giving him a chance, but I had never known a Muslim intimately, and, well, you know how it is in such matters. One wants to work with known factors. First rule in business, first rule in life: work with known factors.

So I looked at him, a thin man, about four inches shorter than me—but then, I am a bit over six feet—and I prepared myself to go through the ritual of interviewing him before sending him a kind rejection slip. He was competent, not brilliant but evidently efficient. He had experience too, of the kind of work I wanted to recruit for, though not here—he had worked in other places, mostly at a multinational's warehouse and office in Mumbai and their branch office in Surat. He had moved here some months ago, he told me. Why? He looked at me without blinking: "I needed to move." I was taken aback by the terseness of his reply, and mentally ticked a box on the negative side for him.

But just as I was going to say thank you, we will get in touch with you, a small, previously overlooked section of his résumé caught my eye. "Languages spoken." Under it he had listed not just the usual English, Hindi and, in his case of course, Urdu, but also Marathi, Gujarati, Bhojpuri, Bangla, Arabic, French, German, Thai, Tibetan, Japanese and "a smattering of Chinese."

Initially I was skeptical. That many? So varied? How was it possible?

Ahmed had a story about it. He had grown up in a small town called Phansa, not very far from Bodh Gaya. In high school and all through college, he did odd jobs to help his mother. He was an only child and his father had died in a train accident when Ahmed was two or three. His mother, a religious person who strictly observed the purdah, had sent him to school, taking on all kinds of sewing, knitting, and embroidery work to supplement the small "widow pension" she got from the government. As soon as Ahmed could—which was when he entered secondary school—he strove to earn some money, mostly by running errands for neighbors.

One of the neighbors moonlighted as a tourist guide. There were not that many tourists coming to Phansa, but Bodh Gaya—you know, where Buddha attained enlightenment, when was it, some 2,500 years ago—well, Bodh Gaya would get tourists from all over. I should know. My parents had taken me there as a child and then I had returned much later, a fresh bride in tow, or maybe it was the other way around, for it had been my wife's idea to do the three main Buddhist spots of India that winter vacation.

Ahmed later told me that he even met Richard Gere strolling around in Bodh Gaya one day. At that time, he did not know who Gere was, but a friend had identified the self-possessed man in faded jeans as a "famous film star from America." That kind of place, you know; just imagine what would happen to Richard Gere if he walked down a road in this city!

At first, Ahmed had started working for the neighbor in Phansa, mostly because he spoke and understood English far better than others in the *mohalla*. He must have had an ear for languages, for he was going to a government-run zillah school, not an English-medium convent. Soon the neighbor started taking him to Bodh Gaya during the weekends.

The place opened Ahmed's eyes; an entire world was there, in that sleepy little hamlet. Of course, there were the Tibetan refugees and the Buddhist monks, but there were also tourists of all sorts: Thai, Chinese, Japanese, Sri Lankans, Germans, Danes, you name it. "The place also opened up my ears," Ahmed told me that day at the interview. "Some of the regular guides knew other languages, particularly Thai, French, German and Japanese. I found it surprisingly easy to pick up languages. I already had Urdu and Arabic from home. Ammajaan had insisted on my learning these two at the neighborhood mosque, and I had Hindi and English from school. But within weeks I was picking up entire phrases in other languages."

By the time Ahmed finished high school, he was spending all his weekends and vacations in Bodh Gaya. He loved taking people around. He had a studious bent, and read up on the history behind the place, its famous Mahabodhi Temple and the ruins around it. This gave him an advantage over many other guides, who often depended on hearsay or inspiration. The other advantage was his flair for languages; the more languages he picked up, the more tourists from those cultures sought him out. Soon he was earning more during a good weekend than his mother did in a month. People are generous when you speak to them in their language. They are nicer, happier; "Their hearts unlock a room for you in their distant homes." This very statement gave me reason to rethink, because of course it would also work in the export/import business.

But I was still skeptical during the interview. Did this man really speak all these bloody languages? His English was good, I could hear that, not convent-accented, but clear, correct and idiomatic. There was evidently a lot of reading behind it too. But Thai? Japanese? I was intrigued. I asked him to be prepared to come back another day. "I want you to speak to a Japanese acquaintance of mine who will be in town later this week," I told him.

I had not expected Ahmed to return. But he did, when I finally fixed the appointment, and he conversed with Mr. Kimura. I could see that Mr. Kimura started off warily, his impassive business face barely managing to conceal his amusement, but within minutes his guard was down and the two were chatting like old friends. I did not understand a word, of course, but I did not need to; it was evident that Ahmed was fluent in Japanese.

When Mr. Kimura came home to have dinner with us later that day, he joked about it. "Your interviewee," he said. "If you don't want him, I will take him. Why, he sometimes uses lingo that I never thought they taught in Japanese classes! I could use his linguistic skills."

But so could I. That is how I hired Ahmed, and soon he became my right-hand man.

As I watched it pour and Ahmed finished his last call, I felt a twinge of conscience. There was so little this man had asked of me—not even for a raise, though of course I had given him many raises over the years. He was still my right-hand man, even now when my business had sixty-seven full-time employees in more than a dozen cities and four countries. And he still stayed up or stayed on any time I asked him to do so.

The only thing he had ever asked of me was this one holiday. Shab-e-Barat. "It means the night of happiness," he had explained to me the first time we had spoken about it. That, as I told you, was in his first year with me.

We were in the old office, in the suburbs. I was in my shirtsleeves, peeling an orange. It was around ten at night. We were having trouble with a consignment in Germany. "Too late now," I told him. "Even the Prussians must have pulled down the shutters for the day. We will have to do it tomorrow."

That is when he said it: "Tomorrow is Shab-e-Barat."

I was still thinking of the consignment. "Something in Germany?" I asked him.

He gave his faint, slightly sad smile. "No, no, Mehrotra sa'ab, it is a Muslim festival. We celebrate it."

"But I thought you guys celebrated Eid," I said from my desk, automatically offering him an orange segment.

He accepted it with a nod and put it in his mouth. Then he chewed slowly. By then I knew him well enough to wait; he never spoke when eating. Actually, I suspect he never did two things at the same time. He was old-fashioned and slow in that sense, no multitasker. He always finished a task before moving on to the next one.

After he had swallowed the pulp, Ahmed finally answered me: "This is a smaller festival. It means the night of happiness: Shab-e-Barat."

The word "barat" caught my attention.

"Your wedding anniversary?" I asked him. I knew he had a wife. It was on his résumé: no children, but a wife.

He shook his head, looking bewildered. Then he understood. "Ah," he said, "Mehrotra sa'ab, because I said 'barat'? But you know, 'barat' just means happiness."

I did not know. So, the wedding processions we took out were called happiness? I had to remember to tell the missus later that night. It was the kind of thing she liked to know.

Ahmed continued: "Shab-e-Barat is a bit like the Jewish Yizkor, though we have it only once a year." He always had these bookish references in his conversation, not that I knew anymore about the Jewish Yizkor than I did about the Muslim Shab-e-Barat in those days. "During Shab-e-Barat we recall our ancestors, those who are dead, the ones gone before us to the realms of eternal peace and joy, the ones who made us possible on this earth. It links the past to the future through our present. That is why it is called the night of happiness. We visit the graves and burn incense there, though some Muslims are refusing to do so now because it is considered un-Islamic. And, of course, we make *halwa* at home."

Halwa I knew everything about, though I did not know that, like *sewai*, it was associated with a festival too. I guess every traditional dish is associated with one festival or another! Even the pragmatic Protestants at my alma mater had their turkey, though often it was dressed-up chicken for Christmas. Not to mention the Christmas pudding.

"Tomorrow, Mehrotra sa'ab," Ahmed was saying, "I would prefer to stay home. Shab-e-Barat is the only festival that matters to me."

Then, probably feeling he owed me an explanation—we were still new to each other—he added, "You see, Mehrotra sa'ab,

13

ever since Ammajaan passed away, my wife and I have always celebrated Shab-e-Barat together. We cannot go to Ammajaan's grave—she was buried in Phansa—but my wife makes *halwa* and we consecrate it, pray for peace as is the custom, and spend the evening together. It is a kind of family tradition between the two of us now: my wife makes this delicious *maida ka halwa* taught to her by Ammajaan. I grew up eating that *halwa*. No matter how poor we were, Ammajaan always made that *maida ka halwa* for Shab-e-Barat."

I am not sure I have managed to capture the tenor of his response. It was politely worded—Ahmed was always courteous, one thought of that Urdu word associated with the old city of Lucknow, "adab"—but for the first time I sensed something like steel under all that satin. What was it, the way he looked at me, unblinkingly, or the way he spoke, enunciating his words even more clearly than he usually did? It sent a sliver of unease through me—perhaps what you would feel if a loaded gun was pointed, playfully, at you. Then, being the obliging person he was, he relented. "I could come in the morning but I will leave around noon."

I had allowed him to take the day off that year—after all, the Germans could be expected to speak English—and every year after that. Until this year.

With the financial slowdown making all of us jittery and a truly huge order on the line, I had requested him to come in, promising to let him go around three. And we were now three hours over the deadline: it was after six in the evening. I would call him a cab, and he would reach home in half an hour, I thought. I had already resolved to give him a substantial perk for this day's work. He could still have joined his wife for the *halwa* celebration in the evening, but for this storm.

I called all the taxi services we used, but they were either booked or not running. The buses wouldn't be either. I cursed myself for driving to the office this morning, but the missus had needed a driver and the second driver had reported sick. I could see Ahmed looking worriedly at the sheet of water pouring down outside the windows, the roads filling up with rivulets. The wind was growing louder. Internet and phone connections were already unstable.

Then I thought, why don't I drive Ahmed home? He could give me directions, and I would still make it to the five-star hotel to honor some literary prize winner the missus had lined up for us. Who knows, maybe the literary dinner would be called off anyway. I could not imagine writerly types of the sort the missus associates with getting their embroidered sari edges and handmade trouser bottoms wet in a deluge.

In any case, I had time to drop Ahmed before heading home.

He did not object, though he looked distinctly uncomfortable. "If you can get through, tell your wife that we are on our way," I said to him.

"No need. She will be there," he replied. I glanced at him, surprised at the flat certainty of his words and tone. It was as if he was passing an ominous judgement, not making a simple statement.

Later, after I experienced what I did, I turned the phrase over and over in my head.

She will be there.

2

The rain spoke with greater harshness in Ahmed's part of the city. There were too many roofs, and no gardens or parks to soften the sounds. There were sheds, tin kiosks, and squatter shanties, seemingly abandoned on the sides of the roads. The billboards were many, and metallic.

It was a waterfall pouring out of the skies that evening. The wind was like an animal in pain; the thunder made me think of the voice of the gods. It was easy to imagine cavemen discovering the gods in such a storm! Branches had been torn from the few trees in the neighborhood. I had the wipers on at full but still had to clutch my steering wheel and peer over it through the windshield. I had not seen another vehicle on the road for the past five minutes or so.

Something that looked like a newspaper came flying toward my car—a new Toyota Innova, bought less than a year ago. I swerved just in time to avoid it and then realized it was a sheet of corrugated metal blown off some shanty rooftop.

"We are here," said Ahmed, pointing to a gate on the left. It had an asbestos-roofed guardhouse next to it, but no guard. The gate was open; its panels, chained to iron poles on both sides, were bulging and banging.

I turned tentatively through the gate toward the apartment buildings it led to; the level was lower there, and about a foot of water had accumulated in the driveway, making it look like a narrow canal. However, the parking lot was raised a foot or so above the driveway. Thin rivulets of water were crossing the lot, but it had not been submerged yet.

It was a typical lower-middle-class apartment complex, of the sort built by public corporations in the 1970s. A dark, cavernous parking lot on the ground floor, with insulated wires looping across pigeon-infested corners, and four or five stories of two- or three-bedroom flats, with pokey little balconies. It was the kind of neighborhood that makes me feel sad and uneasy. I once had an experience like that in the US. A large and foreboding man suddenly loomed across my path, stuck out a large paw with grimy fingernails, and asked for money. Two dollars, he was exact about that, a man dressed in rags, layers and layers of discarded clothing, his face raw and red. But he was a giant of a man, bearded and bristling with hair, and his gruff voice—two specific dollars—was impossible to read. Was he begging or threatening? I felt pity and fear, and dropped him a dollar, not because I could not afford two, but because I needed to find a way to maintain my self-respect. That is how I felt about such neighborhoods too; they seemed to exude a mix of sadness and threat.

I parked the car as directed by Ahmed. He had been looking worried all along the drive. I attributed it to his late arrival for whatever ceremony he performed with his wife for Shab-e-Barat. When he had first talked about the *halwa* made for the festival, he had mentioned something, somewhat apologetically, about consecrating it. "I am not religious or irreligious, Mehrotra sa'ab, but ceremonies are necessary to live in a fuller world than this one," he had said.

Now he got out of the car, his towel-wrapped tiffin carrier cuddled under one arm like a baby, and hesitated, a hand on the open door. There was a strange expression on his face, as if he was torn between contrary impulses. He bent down to look at me. "You should not drive back in this storm," he said.

The thought had crossed my mind too, especially after the car escaped being slashed by that metal sheet I had taken for a newspaper. But I did not want to be stuck here.

Ahmed added, as if reading my thoughts, "A storm like this at this time of the year—it cannot last more than another ten–twenty minutes."

Then he gave his slight, sad smile, his face clearing up. "Mehrotra sa'ab, come in for a while. The storm has reached its peak, it will abate soon. Have a cup of tea."

Why not, I thought. Even the missus can't blame me for being delayed by a downpour.

A narrow corridor, lined with tin mailboxes on one side, half of them broken, led to a narrower flight of stairs in Ahmed's building. His said his flat was on the fourth floor. There were two flats on each landing. Some had a potted plant, which had once been hopeful, next to the door; a couple had brass name plaques, others were bare and unadorned. It was obvious that there was no elevator.

Trudging up the stairs, which had a stream of water cascading down one side from a leak farther up, Ahmed apologized to me on behalf of his wife. "She observes the purdah. I will request her, but she might not come out to meet you. When I was younger I tried to talk her out of it, just as I once tried to talk Ammajaan out of it." He shook his head in recollection and added ruefully, "I failed."

"Well," I said, trying to be polite, though I was a bit taken aback by the revelation, "it is part of your faith, isn't it?"

"Depends," replied Ahmed. "Depends on how you interpret it, Mehrotra sa'ab. I have never heard of purdah as the sixth pillar of Islam!"

I knew it was something he felt strongly about, strongly enough to talk about it on occasion. He seldom talked religion otherwise. But I had overheard him discuss it in the office with some of the others. I had read about the five pillars of Islam in school textbooks, but it appeared to me, from the news that I read now, that the pillars had been multiplied by a few hundred in recent years. Wasn't jihad one of the pillars too, now? But I did not have to reply, as we had reached his flat.

Ahmed did not knock. He let himself in with his key. At that moment I thought nothing of it: Ahmed was the kind of person who never bothered anyone, never asked for favors—pass me this, fetch me that, please—and I assumed his wife would be busy cooking the *halwa* in the kitchen. Ahmed had told me that the main trick was to pour in the sieved flour, the other ingredients and milk, and stir them at an unhurried pace on a low fire before adding the melted cardamom-infused sugar while still churning the mix. Later, it struck me as unusual that he had not knocked or rang the doorbell, and that the door had been locked with a key rather than latched or bolted from inside.

The storm had already relented—I could tell from the sounds. But I could hardly turn back and leave from his doorstep. It would have seemed most impolite. I followed him in. Did I really feel that I was stepping into another medium, a denser, slower one, something more resistant, as when you dive into the swimming pool, or is it a thought I associate with my entry into the flat only now?

The door led straight into a sitting room-cum-dining room.

It was the usual sort, I guess: a sofa, two chairs, a low table in between, a couple of lamps with cloth shades on corner tables, and behind this section a small dining table with four chairs around it.

One window had been left open, and even though it was netted with wire to keep mosquitoes and flies out, and the balcony it opened onto was partly sheltered, the rain had washed in and pooled under the window. "You forgot to shut that window," I remarked. I could not possibly have said, "Your wife neglected to close that window," could I?

Ahmed looked at it and replied, after a moment of hesitation, "I always leave one window open. To seal a space is to shut out a soul." Strange sentence, isn't it? Like a line from a poem—cryptic, pithy, but what did it mean, what could it possibly mean? I did not pay attention to it at that moment—we knew in the office that Ahmed spoke like that at times—but later, yes later, the line came back to haunt me.

To seal a space is to shut out a soul.

With a courteous gesture, Ahmed invited me to find a place on the sofa and hurried through the curtains of one of the doors into what I presumed was the kitchen, telling me in English, "I will see if she needs help with the chai."

I looked around. There was a large laminated poster of puppies with the usual mushy slogan—I forget what—above the sofa, and two photographs on another wall. One of the photos was of an old woman, and I did not have to be told this was Ahmed's Ammajaan. The resemblance was clear, if difficult to pin down. Maybe it was in the eyes, the steady stare, the look that said, with resilience not hostility, "I know you, but I do not hold anything against you." Or so I remember thinking. Why did I think of it as "but," not "and"? I have no idea, but later, when I went through every moment and thought I experienced in that strangely bare sitting room-cum-dining room—and you will understand why when I tell you what happened—I always came back to this particular thought with that specific conjunction: "I know you, but I do not hold anything against you."

The other photograph was even easier to place. It featured a younger Ahmed and a woman wearing shapeless but colorful clothes. It was obviously a wedding photo, clicked in a small-town studio, as could be deduced from the false "Swiss" backdrop. What caught my eye was not the photograph or the fact that Ahmed could actually look happy, unabashedly happy, but the wife; she had a Mongol-like look. Not Chinese or Tibetan—they are usually fairer—but maybe Nepali or Manipuri. Dark, but with more Chinese than North Indian features. I was surprised. I knew Ahmed's wife was religious, even orthodox, unlike Ahmed, and I had assumed he had married one of his own community—maybe even a cousin, as Muslims are reputed to do. But this woman, with her round face, her high cheekbones, her slanted eyes, her dark but ruddy complexion: she could be no kin of Ahmed's!

At that moment, Ahmed came out of the kitchen and noticed me looking at the photograph. "The day after our wedding," he said. "But you have no idea how much I had to argue before she allowed me to put the photo out here. And to think she had never even covered her head until the day the photo was taken! But Ammajaan—I guess I have to blame her, I have to blame dear Ammajaan for the fact that my wife refuses to come out and sit with us even today."

He joined me on a chair next to the sofa. "'Another five minutes,' she says," he added. "Though you will excuse me for

21

serving you no *halwa*; it is not ready yet." Then he started, as if he had heard something, and said, "No, no, don't worry; Mehrotra sa'ab has to leave soon." Obviously, he was replying to his wife in the kitchen, though I had not heard anything, perhaps because the storm had not died down completely.

But as he sat there, ears pricked one would say, as if listening to his wife again, I tried to pay attention, and all I heard was the sound of the dying rain and a TV in a neighboring apartment. Ahmed shook his head seemingly in mild amusement and, excusing himself, went back to the kitchen.

Ahmed was a soft speaker, and I could hardly hear him as he conversed with his wife in the other room. But I did catch a few words of what he said to her: "No, not necessary … You don't understand, Roshni … Oh well, as you wish then, as you wish." All of it in Hindustani, of course. Strangely, his wife must have been whispering, for I did not hear her at all, not above the squabble of a *saas-bahu* serial coming from the TV set next door.

Perhaps she kept her voice veiled from strangers too? I tried not to give much thought to it, refusing to heed the murmur of doubt. And in any case, I was more intrigued by what Ahmed had revealed about his wife and their wedding, and I could not help questioning him when he returned, shaking his head slightly. "You mean," I said, "your wife had to convert to marry you?" I thought of what had been in the news recently: "Love jihad" is what those Hindutva lunatics called it, and while I disliked their fervor and terminology, I could not—deep in my heart— totally accept the fact that Muslim men married our women and converted them to Islam. The marriage bit I did not mind, but the conversion? That made me uncomfortable, maybe even a bit resentful. I won't pretend otherwise.

Again, that faint, slightly sad smile. "You see, that was the problem," Ahmed replied. "That is what finally forced us to move to Mumbai." But he did not really answer my question. He did not say his wife had to convert. I thought that was what he had conceded, but no, he did not say it—as I realized later.

Ahmed went into the kitchen again, this time to fetch two cups of tea in cheap flowery porcelain, of the sort you buy from general stalls with stuffed shelves. (I know; that is the sort of crockery my wife buys for the servants to use.) The tea was much sweeter than what we drink at home. Then, as we sipped the steaming hot brew, he explained, "Roshni—that's my wife's name—never really knew what faith she had grown up in, and I never asked her to convert. Everyone else around us did, of course; we lived in a *mohalla*. And when I married her nevertheless, everyone we knew put pressure on Ammajaan to get Roshni to convert. All those uncles and aunts, who had for years given us the occasional Eid gift but pretended not to really see Ammajaan's hardship; even her regular clients, the contractors, and affluent families for whom she had stitched and woven, all of them wanted Roshni to convert. All of them wanted Ammajaan to press me. But, for some reason, Ammajaan did not do so. She said to them, 'Roshni is a Muslim name, isn't it? She says her mother was Muslim. This is a Muslim girl. How can a Muslim convert twice?' Maybe that is why when Roshni came into our house, she imitated Ammajaan in her routines, even down to observing rigid purdah. At first I protested—she had never worn a veil, no, far from it—but how could I prevail against two determined women?" Ahmed laughed, a laugh that was little more than a grunt. "You see, when Ammajaan passed away, it made no sense for us to stay on in the *mohalla*. The neighbors had not accepted Roshni. Neither had anyone from my family, apart from Ammajaan. Mumbai made better sense. A big city. We could start anew there. Little did I imagine …"

Suddenly, as if a switch had been thrown, there was darkness on Ahmed's face. As if a curtain had fallen. His face closed; it simply shut down. It happened so abruptly that I almost looked around, expecting someone to have entered to have caused that change. But there was no one there, just me and familiar, transparent Ahmed, now worryingly opaque, as if something had come between us, something heavy and brooding, like a monsoon cloud.

I waited for Ahmed to resume, but his account had petered out, just as the rain was petering out too, and he seemed lost in thought for a few seconds. His face assumed more creases and shades, as if an invisible artist was reinforcing lines drawn in the past with deeper strokes. Then he shook himself out of his reverie and glanced at the curtain segregating the kitchen. "Ah," he announced, "it is ready now, and I have to do as I must. What do we all do but what we must, Mehrotra sa'ab? You know, Ammajaan taught this recipe to Roshni. Roshni makes it exactly as she used to. Can you smell it?"

He sniffed appreciatively—or was it anxiously?—and got up. It relieved the atmosphere of brooding expectation that had settled on us when Ahmed had abruptly discontinued his narrative. He collected our cups—we had finished our tea by then—and, placing them with his trademark slow care on the plastic tray, took them back into the kitchen. I sniffed discreetly. There were food smells in the air, but they could well have been from adjoining flats—there was nothing distinctive about them. I prepared myself to be enthusiastic about some insipid fare, which is the usual burden of being served a dish someone else has grown up with.

This time Ahmed was gone for longer. I squirmed impatiently. The rain had diminished to distinct drops now, and I could hear traffic on the streets again. There had been no thunder or lightning for some time. I texted the missus to say that I was on my way but delayed by slow traffic because of fallen branches and wires.

Ahmed came out of the kitchen carrying the same plastic tray, but now it held two small plates and two glasses of what, from the color of it, seemed to be Rooh Afza. I detest that nauseating drink and have never understood why so many people swear by it. Is it even real rose extract, I have often wondered.

Ahmed handed me a glass of Rooh Afza, and I accepted it gingerly, gazing dubiously at its contents and wondering how to get out of drinking it without offending anyone in the flat. Ahmed, I knew, would understand; he was not easily offended. Actually, I had never seen him offended by any incident or remark. But the rose drink must have been prepared, like the *halwa*, by his wife, and I did not want to seem rude and spoiled-rich to her. The best thing, I thought, would be to take a sip or two, and then just let it sit on the table, as if I had forgotten about it. I proceeded to bring the glass close to my lips, trying to block out its overly sweet and synthetic smell, and forced myself to sip from it.

So engrossed had I been in negotiating the Rooh Afza that I had not even glanced at the plate Ahmed had placed in front of me. He had gone back to his chair, holding his plate, and was eating from it. I put down my glass and picked up my plate. It was then that I noticed the plate did not contain any *halwa*. There was a pile of *nimkis* and a small spoon on the plate, but no *halwa*.

At first, it just struck me as an omission; in his hurry not to detain me longer than necessary, Ahmed may have simply forgotten to put *halwa*—that famous *maida ka halwa* he always talked about—on my plate! I was going to bring this to his notice with a joke, but as I glanced up at Ahmed, who was busy eating, my jokey remark was aborted by the sight of the plate was holding. There was no *halwa* on it either! Just as was the case with my plate, it only held a pile of *nimkis* and a stainless-steel spoon.

Can you imagine how taken aback I was? Yes, the sense of foreboding returned at that instant. It is one thing to forget to put something on a plate you are serving, and it is another not to notice its absence on your own plate! Time slipped back, just a few minutes, to that moment when I had seen a shade fall on Ahmed's face.

But still, I felt only discomforted, confused, nothing like what I experienced the very next second, when Ahmed, with the gentle tinkle of spoon on china, scooped "*halwa*" out of his plate and levered it, carefully, making sure nothing spilled, to his mouth. It was then that I broke out in a cold sweat: Ahmed was totally engrossed in "eating" the *halwa*! I felt as if a cold gust of air had entered the room and folded around my neck like an icy muffler. I stood up, half stood up anyway, and if Ahmed had not been so absorbed in eating the nonexistent *halwa*, he would have noticed it. I sank back into the sofa, eyes riveted on Ahmed.

He put down the spoon, picked up a *nimki*, dipped it in the part of the plate that was bare, and carried it to his mouth. He chewed, he swallowed. Then he grasped the spoon again, this time to scoop up empty air from the vacant part of the plate and "eat" it, his jaws and throat muscles moving exactly as if he was chewing and swallowing. I was struck with a sense of horror, a horror I had never experienced or imagined.

At that moment, Ahmed looked up from his plate and saw me staring at him, my plate inert in one hand. A vulnerable expression flickered across his face, some emotion raw and indecipherable. Then he gave his slow smile and said, "Go ahead, Mehrotra sa'ab; you have not touched it. I promise you, it is delicious. Exactly as Ammajaan used to make it. If anything, even a bit better!"

What could I do? What could I have done? How could I tell a person who was eating ghostly *halwa* that my plate did not contain that food either? I picked up a couple of *nimkis* and popped them into my mouth, that icy muffler strangling me now, my fingertips cold and numb.

"No, no," said Ahmed, "try them with the *halwa*. That is the best combination."

I picked up a *nimki* and dipped it in my plate, as though using it to scoop up some *halwa*. Then I carried it gingerly to my mouth, took a bite and chewed slowly, doubtfully. Ahmed probably took this for appreciation, for he looked pleased, relieved even, and nodded before returning to his plate. I could feel the *nimki* in my mouth, but of course there was no taste of *halwa*.

Ahmed's calmness, so domestic, so normal, must have defused my sense of icy horror. The chill that had gripped me, filled me with numbness, subsided. But now I felt bewildered, angry, and insulted. I did not then know the source of these emotions, especially the anger and feeling of humiliation, but I have since turned that moment over and over in my mind, and I comprehend these emotions better now.

Bewilderment, anyone would understand. But I also felt anger at the situation, at Ahmed, for turning out to be so different from everything I had taken him to be. Until then he had been the most reliable, reasonable, trustworthy, and easy person I had ever known. Now suddenly, he was—what was he—demented, superstitious, crafty, crazy, a fool? In any case, he was not the

27

person I had known. By not being what I thought he was, he had thrown my world out of gear.

The sound of a motorcycle being kick-started came from under the building.

And the insult? Yes, I was humiliated—because I felt forced; I felt I had to enact a role. What would happen if I were to say, Ahmed, you are crazy, there is no *halwa* on our plates! Would he go bonkers, start raving and arguing? Or would he laugh and say it was just a joke on me? Which would be disrespectful too, that sort of liberty taken with someone who paid his salary. Also, what if this was not just some hidden craziness, but a deeply subconscious bid of Ahmed's to humiliate his boss? I could not know. I did not wish to know.

Time had slowed down even further in that tawdry flat, with its pool of water next to the open window. The seconds and minutes were flies and tiny insects stuck on the edge of a cauldron of boiling molasses, which is one of the images that has stayed with me from the time I visited some remote villages while backpacking along the Ganges with my Columbia University classmates.

It had stopped raining outside. Entirely. I heard the water dropping from roofs, gurgling down pipes. It sounded ominous, as if the world had gone hollow. The place seemed filled not with real sounds but echoes, ghosts of dead sounds.

I decided to play along with whatever it was: madness or a sadistic game. I needed time to think. I swirled a few more *nimkis*—at least they existed and tasted good—in the empty *halwa* part of the plate and popped them into my mouth. I even drank the Rooh Afza in my distraction and hurry to finish off the *nimkis*.

Then I put the plate down and made my excuses. I was late; the missus was waiting for us to go to a dinner.

Ahmed looked slightly disappointed. "It was too rich for you, wasn't it?" he said. "You left most of the *halwa* untouched."

I made appropriate non-committal noises. I could not force myself to say something complimentary about the *halwa*, so I asked him to thank his wife for the "snacks."

Suddenly the place had filled with too much … too much of what? I could not make up my mind. I felt that each fat drop landing with a plop on the dingy balcony outside and the ledges of the windows was heavy with clouded significance. The water I could hear rushing down pipes and cisterns spoke a language both expressive and incomprehensible.

"I need to rush, Ahmed," I told him. I need to kick-start time again, Ahmed, I wanted to scream; I have to free the minutes from the molasses of your rustic cauldron!

Ahmed was polite as always. He insisted on accompanying me to the car. As we left the flat, I stole a glance at the kitchen, and the curtain moved slightly, as if his wife was standing behind it, watching us.

3

The missus was not exactly thrilled. The girls had been sent up to their room with the ayah almost an hour ago. I had ignored two or three of her urgent text messages while driving back. The fact that when I reached home the storm outside had ceased, but in my head it increased manifold, did not help. I was distracted, inattentive, trying to make sense of what had happened in Ahmed's apartment. Luckily, I did not have to drive us to the dinner—my wife had detained the other driver—and it was a short drive.

The dinner had not been canceled, and we arrived an hour late. We were by no means the only ones to do so. The storm had delayed many of the others, not least the deputy minister and the senior writer who were the guests of honor. Even the five-star hotel people were running late, righting the potted palms that had been knocked down in the driveway, mopping rainwater from the lobby, setting the hall. All this assuaged the missus, as did the fact that she was instantly surrounded by a group of young, aspiring writers, all dressed either like Bollywood stars just back from Hollywood or like models doing some kind of an ethnic cultural show.

It allowed me the time I needed to compose myself, put in place a face to meet all those faces.

The hall was set for a buffet, two sides lined with silvery containers, some simmering over small flames, some still being installed. On one side of the hall were high, round tables without stools, close to the food tables, and chairs and sofas on another side. In the sofa-and-chair section of the hall, against a wall bearing a large poster that featured the cover of a prize-winning book and exclamatory blurbs by famous writers, a microphone, bereft of speakers at the moment, stood on a low, purple-carpeted dais.

Uniformed bearers circulated with trays bearing elaborate snacks and drinks. The light from chandeliers, fashioned like strings of diamonds, reflected off the real and false diamonds adorning many necks. Not my wife though—she only wears pearls to literary events.

I had verified the dinner's raison d'être from my wife on the drive to the hotel. Evidently, a British writer of Indian origin had won a major award, and, as he was in town en route to a festival in Hong Kong, his Indian publishers had thrown this dinner "to felicitate a son of the nation," as the publicity pamphlets scattered around the hall put it.

The son of the nation was, as far as I could see, standing in one corner of the hall, surrounded by several admiring daughters of the nation (and a couple of other nations). This being only his second trip to the country, as the missus had informed me, he must have arrived on time, and was now waiting for the deputy minister and the senior writer to make their appearance. The storm was not the reason those two were late; they would have been the last to arrive in any case. The son of the nation still had to learn the national trick of arriving fashionably late, I thought.

All this provided me with the time to consider what had happened in Ahmed's flat and to regain a bit of composure.

Until then I had been filled with something like a sense of dread and gnawing distrust. It was the feeling of someone who had been walking on what he thought was solid ground and had discovered it was only a thin crust of ice over a deep chasm. Something had to be done. That much was clear to me. I have always been a man of action, and I take some pride in thinking logically. Success in business, believe me, depends a lot on thinking clearly and rationally. I took a pakora from a passing waiter, dipped it into the green chutney on the tray, and bit into it, thinking of what a relief it was when things were exactly what they seemed. The sheer solidity of this hall and the people in it pleased me immensely at that moment.

Yes, I knew something had to be done. But what? Should I confront Ahmed? Should I ask him to explain? Should I simply fire him? After all, I could not trust a madman to run my business, even though until now he had been my lieutenant. I knew that the success of my business owed almost as much to Ahmed as it did to me, but it would be foolhardy and bad policy to simply overlook what I had experienced in Ahmed's flat. A man so troubled as Ahmed obviously could go bonkers at any moment—mess up a major deal, or even walk into the office with a gun one fine morning. I could not ignore it. I owed it to my other employees, to myself. I owed it to my business.

And yet I hesitated to confront Ahmed, or summarily fire him. To dismiss him so quickly, so unthinkingly, appeared a trifle unjust to me. I am not an unjust employer. In Ahmed's case, moreover, I knew that I owed him much; I had come to care for him, as one would care for an older friend. As far back as I could think, in the old office and now in these larger, glitzier premises, I recalled innumerable evenings of the two of us working alone, in our shirtsleeves, late into the night. I could not think of lunch breaks without picturing Ahmed at his desk, the towel spread on it to prevent any spill, the steel containers arranged almost geometrically on the towel. He always ate alone in his cubicle, and almost never went out with the others for lunch in the neighboring South Indian eatery, yet no one considered him unfriendly. We just understood that the lunch hour was his moment to be by himself; for the rest of the time, he was the one person all of us could, and would, ask for help. I thought of those occasionally pithy sentences he would utter, lines that the others called Ahmedisms. Here's an Ahmedism from last week, one of my staff would say: "Rain is a relationship of the earth to the sky." Here's another, someone else would remark, as Ahmed might shake his head and give his sad, slight smile: "All distances are infinite, except those of the heart." No, I could not just fire him; I had to know more.

But I also shied away from confronting Ahmed: there was such an aura of vulnerable self-respect around him that one hesitated to say harsh things to him. He was not the sort of person anyone would jovially slap on the back or argue aggressively with. Ahmed never indulged in such acts—always treating others with the utmost decorum and old-world respect (always using "*aap*," never the familiar "*tum*," not even to the boy who fetched tea)—and only an outright boor would take liberties with him.

These were the thoughts occupying me when the missus wended her way back to me, accompanied by a couple of young writers she was championing that season. A cluster had entered from the main door, and I could spot the deputy minister and the guest of honor, a much-awarded writer from Delhi, in the thick of the throng. They were similarly broad-faced, heavy-girthed men in their seventies, fair and of medium height, dressed in almost identical ethnic garb with long silk scarves around their necks; from a distance they looked like twins to me.

My wife took me by the arm and hustled me to one of the sofas as the cluster gravitated to the dais. Florid speeches were made, but mercifully—perhaps because it was a function organized by a commercial publishing house and not an official institution—they were short. The son of the nation was presented with a heavy plaque by the deputy minister, who spoke more of the need for sports and health in India than of literature, perhaps because a cricket series was on, or perhaps because the cover of the novel—a collage of different images including a cricket bat—made the politician assume it had something to do with sports. The publisher spoke of how the book had again reinvented magical realism—that explained the collage, I supposed—decades after Salman Rushdie. "To explode the narrow reality of our world and fill it with a universe of worlds, what work of literature can hope to do more than that?" she demanded rhetorically, conferring the honor of such an intergalactic explosion on the son of the nation.

Much as I had enjoyed reading magical realist novels in the days when I still had time to read, I felt a prickling of irritation at this remark, as I was still obsessed with my evening at Ahmed's, and I could not help wishing no one had exploded the narrow reality of my world. I wondered how the publisher—or any of the other appreciatively nodding heads, coiffured and collared, including that of the missus—would feel if they were forced to eat a plate of nonexistent *halwa* after the speech.

We were neither the first nor the last to leave. As we were leaving, I turned and looked at the people still remaining in the hall, and the thought—strange as it was—crossed my mind: could I spot someone like Ahmed in that crowd? Yes, I was beginning to be obsessed with Ahmed.

I remember surveying the crowd for a full minute before hurrying to catch up with my wife, who was being charmingly escorted out by her writer protégés, and I remember saying to myself, but there is no one like Ahmed here!

It was not really true. There were people who were Ahmed's height; there were people who were dressed like he often was—in trousers and a light coat, sometimes with a carefully double-knotted tie; there were people with his close-cropped woolly hair, some who were as thin as him. Two or three even had his kind of face or his slow gait. But I remember thinking that not one of them resembled Ahmed.

I hurried out to the lobby, oddly disturbed by this absence of Ahmed in the crowd I had just left. What was I thinking of? Why did it make me sad? I did not understand it. Or if I did, I misunderstood myself at that moment, attributing the sadness to the insularity of all our worlds. The literary world has always reminded me of the academic world that I had dabbled in, or the corporate world that I frequent, large bubbles of talk unintelligible elsewhere, though of course my wife disagreed strongly the one time I made this comparison. Literature is about all of life, she had argued, and I knew she was right, but it never changed my impression.

As we waited for the car to be announced and driven up, I thought of the drive back: the distance to my house and the distance from my house to Ahmed's colony, and though the two were roughly the same in kilometers, they seemed entirely incommensurate to me. The car arrived. It was the Toyota Innova, which being the newer of our two cars, is the one the missus takes to such functions. I knew I was not thinking clearly and made an effort to pull myself together as a turbaned and mustachioed doorman held open the car door for my wife and me.

4

The next morning was clear, azure sky and all, sunlight falling through the gaps between the curtains like solid golden bars. By the time I went down, the girls—seven and ten years old—were already in their school dresses and dutifully spooning cornflakes under the watchful eyes of their ayah and the missus. Usually, I am the first person to get up in the family—apart from the servants, of course. I no longer need to; my business is a well-oiled machine, run on rational lines that enable all of us to see a problem coming and sort it out in time. I do not captain a business that lurches from crisis to crisis, and if we are hit by a small disaster then it is of the national or global sort, not anything of our own doing. Those crises—the national or global sort—do affect us, and they have been getting a bit thick on the ground in recent times, but we manage to cope with them. My staff has learned from the calm and level-headedness that I and my lieutenant in the main office, Ahmed, always display. So there is no reason for me to get up early, but it is a habit, and honestly, most mornings I almost leap out of bed. Even in the days when I read novels, I could never finish any by authors like Dostoevsky or Sartre.

There are people who take time getting out of bed. My missus, for instance; she lies morosely awake for at least half an hour before leaving the bed. But I wake up and am out of the sheets within a minute. I have always been like that. I cannot wait to get started. I believe it is because I run my life (and business) on clear lines; I have no reason to dread getting snagged by the unexpected during the day.

Not that morning. I had not slept well. The night had been full of dreams, mostly faded now, of which the one I still vaguely recalled in the morning (perhaps because it had recurred) featured a hand detaining someone—me, I thought—by the sleeve. There had been something familiar about that dream.

I lay in bed for almost an hour, well after my wife had gotten up. She asked me if I was well, and I mumbled that maybe I drank a bit too much at the dinner last night. It was a lie; I never have more than a glass or two. She gave me a quizzical look, but then went into the girls' room to supervise their school-going. We have been married long enough not to quiz each other too much.

I rang the bell and asked a servant to fetch me a couple of the day's papers and a cup of karak tea. We subscribe to all the top papers; it is on the office tab, and I believe in following the news, not just the business pages. Then I stayed in bed, pretending to read the papers and sipping tea. There was a great reluctance in me to get up, and I knew it had to do with a mix of repulsion and trepidation: I did not want to reach my office and encounter Ahmed again. I wanted to forget what had happened last evening. I knew I could not. And I knew I could not ignore it either, especially when confronted with Ahmed's presence in office.

Would I detect signs of madness in him, a glitter in the eye, a fervor in the voice, a grasping of the hand, or would he still be as he had been for so many years: polite, considerate, orderly, reliable?

As you can imagine, I reached my office late. Ahmed had already held the morning briefing in our meeting room—it was his job in any case, though I usually liked to be present—and all the staff (except one who was on leave as she had a wedding to attend in Kolkata) were back in their cubicles.

As much as I wished to steer clear of Ahmed that day, I knew it was not possible. But I tried to avoid meeting him, and kept the door to my office closed. I am the only person in the place to have a separate office, but I always leave my door ajar unless I am having a meeting. By leaving the door ajar, I think I signal my availability to all my staff: anyone can walk in with a matter to discuss. When the door is closed, the assumption is that I am holding a meeting or, for other reasons, do not wish to be disturbed.

The closed door gave me a bit of breathing space. I switched on my computer and checked my email, answering a couple. I checked on shares and other matters. I perfunctorily read the reports sent in from other offices. But all these were mechanical acts. What I was really thinking of were the dreams, half-remembered, from last night and, inevitably, the plate of *nimkis*—without *halwa*—at Ahmed's flat. The more I thought of the plate, the more unreal it seemed to me. If someone had walked in and said to me, "Ah, you are back from Toronto—how was your trip?" I would have welcomed it as the real explanation and slotted the experience at Ahmed's flat as a bad dream I had while flying back! I was that desperate to wish it away.

Then the thought struck me: this was so uncharacteristic of me! I was trying to hide behind stories, to construct fictions, instead of facing facts. I asked myself, How are facts faced? I knew the answer: facts are faced with evidence, with data, with numbers. Fiction cannot be numbered; it cannot be proved. But facts, yes. I have known it all my working life, I have built my business on it: facts can be proved.

In Ahmed's case, I argued with myself, I could not get the evidence myself; there was too much between us, too much humanity, too much reciprocity, and I needed someone else to collect the evidence for me.

I knew exactly the person for it—Devi Prasad of the Prasad and Sons Private Investigations Agency.

Why hadn't I thought of it before? Maybe because I did not wish to get Ahmed investigated? But I had used Devi Prasad and his agency on numerous occasions, often to check out potential business partners, once to pin down a corrupt employee. And then, in a flash, I could place the familiarity of that dream of the hand reaching out and detaining me by the sleeve. It was nothing. Just the shards of a memory jogged by a discussion of Coleridge at one of my wife's literary dinners some weeks ago, lines from a poem I had once memorized for an elocution contest in school. It was the ancient mariner detaining the wedding guest. I laughed aloud with relief.

I wonder whether you smile at this because you recognize the compulsive nature of the account I am penning down here, how it ignores everything else for just one story?

Devi Prasad's agency is not one of those cubicles in the wall you might associate with private dicks. It is swanky, like a multinational corporation's showroom, its reception staffed by a beautiful Northeastern woman dressed in impeccable corporate gear, down to the tie, and it is in one of the more expensive parts of the city. Not everyone gets to meet Devi Prasad, who looks more like a prosperous CEO than a private investigator. But I had no trouble getting admitted to him: I was an old client and we played golf together. Or rather our kids did—we had children about the same age, though Devi was a bit older than me—

as our respective wives had decided the kids had to play golf. So, once a week, we took them to the club, where an instructor put them through their paces while we reclined, drink in hand, on wicker chairs outside the club restaurant. This was expected of us, as fathers. The mothers took care of the chore on the other golf-training day of each week.

Devi Prasad was surprised I had come to see him in his office. He was an astute man and understood it must be something vital. Motioning me into one of the plush leather chairs against his mahogany desk, he closed the door behind us, after instructing his peon not to let anyone disturb us. Then he returned to his swivel armchair, seated himself in it and simply looked at me, the fingers of both hands touching at the tips and gently fluttering. He was wearing a waistcoat—Devi has a penchant for them and two-tone shoes, season permitting—and his clipped goatee gave him the look of a solicitous dentist. Why a dentist? Perhaps because I could imagine him extracting information as cleanly as a dentist would pull out a tooth—and sending off just as elaborate and large a bill!

Faced with his fluttering fingers, I was a bit lost for words. I could not possibly tell him about the invisible *halwa* and Ahmed's incipient madness. Devi knew Ahmed, having met him during functions, the last time when we celebrated my company's tenth anniversary at the Radisson. I had also sent Ahmed to Devi's many years ago, when I was getting another business checked out. I never sent him again, as it was the only time Ahmed had explicitly disagreed with me.

"It is not something for me, Mehrotra sa'ab," Ahmed had told me after the visit.

"What's not for you?" I had asked, quite uncomprehending.

"Suspicion, maybe," he had replied. "I am not the suspicious

41

type. I do not want to be involved in suspecting others."

"But, Ahmed," I had reasoned, "we need to know everything in order to trust our collaborators."

He had smiled his sad smile. "What does knowledge have to do with trust, Mehrotra sa'ab?" he had almost murmured in reply. "There is no *need* for trust if one has knowledge."

I had not understood his reluctance, but I respected him, and I never sent him for similar jobs to the agency. I took care of future cases myself, and as such built up quite a close relationship with Devi, further cemented by the last few years of paternal golfing.

Yet, I could not force myself to tell Devi about the evening at Ahmed's flat. It was partly because I was afraid of sounding stupid; Devi, like me, was a highly practical person. I also felt I owed Ahmed—who was so careful of his own space—a degree of reticence, at least until there was concrete reason to abandon it.

I had brought a copy of Ahmed's résumé. It had been updated over the years, as was my policy with all senior employees. I instruct them to make "all relevant changes" in their résumés every March and resubmit them to me using encrypted files.

I put the printout on Devi's desk. I could not bear to mention the name, so I simply said, "I would like to have this person's domestic and personal circumstances investigated."

Devi took up the file and opened it. Then he glanced up at me, surprised. "Ahmed?" he asked, and then added, inevitably, "Ahmedji?"

I nodded.

He put the file down and looked straight at me. "I thought he was your right-hand man," he remarked.

"He is," I replied.

Devi frowned. "Embezzlement?" he asked.

I felt embarrassed and guilty. "No, no," I hastened to assure him, "nothing like that. Ahmed will never do anything like that, you know. It is just that ..."

But I couldn't really tell Devi, could I? What would he think? Wouldn't he just burst out laughing and perhaps regale all of us at the club with a wicked account of it some New Year's Eve?

I made up a story instead. "Ahmed's been distraught. Not acting like his usual self. I think he has problems at home. Maybe his wife is ill or something. I want to know what his circumstances are so that I can help if necessary. I cannot ask him directly. You know him; he has so much self-respect. I just want to find out. I don't want him to find out about it though."

Devi laughed. "You are an even better employer than I thought you were," he said. "If I cared half as much about my people, I would go crazy." Was there a touch of irony in his words because he only half-believed my explanation?

He dropped my file in a drawer and added, "No problemo, boss. Consider it done." He liked to say "No problemo, boss" to all problems; I suppose it was his version of "Elementary, my dear Watson."

Devi Prasad and his people are nothing if not efficient. That is why they have the reputation and the clientele that they do. He called me five days later, on my mobile as we had agreed.

"You don't really have to see me, boss," he said on the phone. "There doesn't seem to be anything much, apart from one discrepancy, but I suspect you will want to follow it up."

We agreed to meet at the golf club that afternoon. It was not one of our chaperoning-the-kids days.

There was a time when one could sit in the restaurant of the club and hold a private conversation. My father had been a member, and I remember coming here with him during the two periods he was posted in this city. Only a few members and the occasional guest would be there, and members mostly left you alone with a nod. It was a very British atmosphere, even in the 1980s. Then the Indian economy changed, and more Indians started feeling the need to belong to elite clubs and swing a golf club. Membership exploded. As the restaurant continued to be one of the best and cheapest places to eat, members began bringing in guests. Soon the place was congested. And as the members and their guests wanted to meet and greet people— the club's restaurant was no longer a place where you avoided the undesirable over a whisky or met the chosen over a meal—it became impossible to hold a table without being greeted by all kinds of acquaintances all the time. The only way one could speak privately now was to go golfing, which is what Devi and I did. We selected a discreet caddie.

Devi waited until the second hole. Then he began out of the blue, "The subject, you know … nothing remarkable. A reserved man, respected in the neighborhood as he seems to be helpful despite being quiet, lives alone."

That's the kind of stuff I had been expecting. What kind, I did not know, but something like that, something normally odd or oddly normal that could explain the unexplainable. I looked up; I tried to appear surprised. Devi was preparing to swing. He did not notice the expression on my face.

"You had asked me to find out about his family circum-stances, but there aren't any. His résumé mentions that he doesn't have children, and that is the case. No child. Also, no wife living with him."

"The résumé ..." I said helpfully, restraining myself. The explanation, give me the explanation, I wanted to shout at him.

Devi swung and the ball described a perfect curve, settling down three meters from the hole.

"*Tchah,*" he said, beaming with satisfaction. He continued, "I know his résumé mentions a wife. One name only. Roshni. But she does not live with him. No one has ever met a Roshni. No one has seen her. People consider him a widower. No woman has ever been seen with him in any case."

It was my turn now. I selected the right club and waved the caddie back.

"Divorced maybe?" I asked. We were getting there, I thought.

"We couldn't find out, boss. No evidence here; he doesn't even get guests. Never been a wife in this flat, say the neighbors. This is confirmed by the part-time maid, who goes in for two hours every day to clean up and wash dishes. Dishes and clothes for just one man, she says, nothing else. If you wish, I could have it checked out in the places he has been to, that town he was born in ... what is it called ... and Mumbai and Surat. But it will cost much more."

"The expense does not matter," I replied. The explanation would have to await another incursion into Ahmed's past, it appeared, but I was hopeful; I thought that in due course I would have an answer I could comprehend. Devi was the man for it.

Devi nodded. "No problemo, boss," he mumbled, a bit doubtfully.

I practiced my shot a few times. I could see that Devi was thinking about something.

"There is something else?" I asked him encouragingly.

"Well, I don't know. Most of it is gossip. You see, the subject is seen as harmless but idiosyncratic. He almost never invites anyone into the flat, though he is always willing to help neighbors; he sometimes talks to himself when he goes shopping."

"So do I, trying to remember what to buy." I laughed.

"The subject does more than we do. He talks as if he was addressing someone else."

I paused in my swing and raised an eyebrow at him. I had never heard Ahmed talking to himself or an invisible interlocutor.

"There's something else," Devi added. "You see, we do not go around shadowing people most of the time. Maybe that is what private eyes do in the West, where no one seems to know his neighbor or second cousin, but this is India, where everyone knows everyone else." He grimaced funnily and jerked his head toward the restaurant. "So the best way to find out in India is to go through contacts. What we do first of all is try to see if one of us knows someone who knows the subject. I have a staff of twenty-seven and each one of them has roughly 227 contacts, each of whom have ... well you know, it's like that Chinese legend of the grain doubled per square of a chessboard, and at the end you have more grain than the earth can hold. You would be surprised how often we end up knowing people close to the subject. We call it 'getting the family lore.'"

I took my swing, got the angle of approach wrong and did much worse than Devi. We started walking again.

"As you can imagine, this time we could not get the family lore directly from around the subject. He keeps to himself and does not seem to have relatives in the city. But we got an indirect connection—recycled family lore, the boys call it. The flat adjoining the subject's is occupied by an old couple; they are known to one of my men: Sen. Mr. Sen's a retired headmaster. Mrs. Sen's a retired schoolteacher. Their only son is posted in Hyderabad. Mrs. Sen has arthritis and Mr. Sen has other health complications. The subject often looks after them, does their shopping, fetches the doctor. You know. They love him as a son. They probably know him better than anyone else in the building. But they also said something that I am not even sure I understand ..."

"What was it?" Maybe I spoke too sharply. Devi hastened to assure me that it was nothing to worry about—"No big deal, boss." He was not even sure it was worth mentioning.

Devi broke off to concentrate on the shot, sank the ball, raised a fist to the sky and then continued: "You see, boss, they are an old, lonely couple: Mrs. Sen is so big she waddles; Mr. Sen is thin and neurotic. Both are full of conspiracy theories, according to my man, who is actually a kind of nephew of theirs: JFK, Netaji, you name it. They probably have nothing to do but imagine all kinds of stuff."

"But ..." I encouraged him, practicing my swing. Then I handed the golf club back to the caddie and asked for another. I rotated my arms, limbering up; suddenly, a chill seemed to rise up in the breeze.

"But they seemed to suggest that the subject keeps his wife shut up in the flat for some reason. Or so my man gathered, as they were highly vague and guarded in their wording. They spoke of her as if she existed and did not exist at the same time. This is what made my man assume that the wife was there in the flat in some way. Just a hunch, he claims. It doesn't make sense though, as someone, at least the part-time maid, would have spotted her. Mr. Sen might have said more, but Mrs. Sen shut him up with a look. My man says that Mrs. Sen's looks are not to be denied."

I pursed my lips, trying to keep a faint hammering out of my head, hunching up against the chill that I suspected only

I could feel. The caddie handed me a new club. I concentrated as deeply as I could. I told myself golf is a sensible game, golf makes perfect sense. But this time my shot was even worse than the last one.

Sense was what I had wished to make of this investigation. Answers—I had expected reasonable answers.

I was disturbed. But more than that I was irritated: I felt as though Ahmed had played a dirty trick on me. You know the feeling when life seems to have stuck out a leg and tripped you without any cause? You want to kick something, scream into the void? That's how I felt.

So irritated was I at this intrusion that had upset my ordered life that, for the first time, I "unfriended" some Facebook friends. These were not people I knew personally, and they had not posted anything particularly offensive—or not more offensive than what they had written in the past. But for various reasons—a posting on politics, some remark about Bangladeshis, a derisive comment on Obama or the Indian cricket team—I simply "unfriended" them. A tap and they were out of my life forever!

As I did so, I regretted the fact that people were not as easy to unfriend in real life.

My way of life has fallen into the sere, the yellow leaf. I recall that line from one of those plays we read in school and college. *Macbeth*, I think. Yes, *Macbeth*; I have a good memory.

I had always liked Shakespeare in school and college. I was tickled by the way critics—and sometimes our teachers—interpreted him and discussed all his ambiguities and paradoxes, when actually, to my mind, Shakespeare was just finding ways out of the contradictions and impasses that he got his characters

48

into. In his tragedies, he usually resolved them by killing off people. I thought, then, that I could see through his tricks. One of his methods was to distract the reader, or the viewer, with some powerful poetry, so that when the lazy resolution of the crisis came by—the chap in the play was blitzed by something or the other—the viewer, or the reader, was still too bedazzled (isn't that a word Shakespeare would have loved?) to notice or complain.

That line is one of those. Or was it two lines?

Anyway, the line came back to me again and again over the next few days. My way of life has fallen into the sere, the yellow leaf. I could feel—honestly, for the first time—the full power of that line. I do recall that this is when Macbeth has committed his crime and knows that honor and peace will be denied to him in his old age. I had committed no crime. But I felt that a crime had indeed been committed and I had been dragged into it. I did not fully suspect Ahmed of foul deeds, believe me, that was not it. I could not even believe Devi's man's wild goose theory of a woman hidden in that flat in some devious way.

The crime was more like an existential disturbance; it denied me the peace and calm I had hoped for. Someone was guilty, and I wanted it to be proven that it was not me, because what had happened in that flat had somehow, in some vague, weird manner, imposed a burden of guilt on me too. Something *had* grasped me by the sleeve.

I wanted my days to be golden, not yellow.

5

Ahmed's father was a low-grade municipal employee, and he died in a train accident when Ahmed was between two and three. That much I already knew. Ahmed was not garrulous about personal details, but he was not overly secretive either, and given a genuine context, he would tell me things.

The context, on this topic, had been in his second year with me, when we were still a business of just four or five people. I had told him he would have to take care of our appointments the next day, as I would not be coming in. Then, because it was a day rather heavy with work, I explained to him, "My father is flying through, and I have to spend time with him. You know, alas, the sort of thing one has to do."

In those days, my father was on his last diplomatic posting—in Paris. My mother had already moved to the house they had bought for their retirement in Goa. She was setting it up, and writing—as she has done all through her life—colorful travel pieces for various publications. My father was on his way to spend a week in Goa, before returning for his last three or four months in Paris.

Ahmed thought about it and said, "Mehrotra sa'ab, one is lucky when one has to do such things." He added, "I sometimes think of it."

"Think of what, Ahmed?"

"I think of what it would be to have a father visit you, to talk about your small worries and joys with a father. But I am not sure I even remember what my father looked like. He was very religious and did not get a portrait done. I have only seen him in group photos, and maybe just a dozen of them. Small, stained black-and-white photos, or photos in faded color. He could be anyone. Ammajaan never referred to his accident or death. She only said *he never came back.* Sometimes I think of what brings people back. Love perhaps? Not hate, I am sure of that; hate has the power to take away, not to bring back. But love surely, not love as in films, but a conversation of hearts across distance. Who knows? I suppose a point comes when no one comes back. Ammajaan did not come back either. We are rags being blown by the wind in a light drizzle. We get heavier with time. And one day we stay where we are."

As was occasionally the case when Ahmed went into his soliloquies, I had ceased following him. He would, at times, speak in shifting ideas, as if using a few pieces of a jigsaw puzzle that only he could visualize.

So, I had known for some time that his mother had brought him up. Devi's printed report from the two men he sent to Phansa filled in the missing bits.

Ahmed's father belonged to the Tablighi Jama'at. "This is a small but thriving society among religious Muslims, which is best understood in terms of evangelism," the report explained. "These are Muslims who believe that the message of the Quran has to be spread, especially among other Muslims who, in their opinion, have forgotten it. In secular terms, one can describe the society as fundamentalist, but it is both pacifist and, unlike organizations like Jamaat-e-Islami, not political. They see themselves as modern, not as traditional or fundamentalists. Their stress is on education and living an ethical life defined by Islamic precepts. While they insist on strict purdah in public, they also encourage women to get an education and seek respectable work."

After being widowed, Ammajaan was not abandoned by the local members of the society. She was provided with support, mostly in the form of work such as knitting, stitching and weaving, some of which she had done in her spare hours in the past too. While she paid for Ahmed's education in the zilla school, society members took care of teaching him Arabic and Urdu. He went to a local mosque for his lessons. He was brought up as a proper little Muslim in the *mohalla*.

I can imagine Ahmed at eight or nine, a skullcap on his head, scampering along the narrow alleys of the *mohalla*—it was called Maruganj, said the report. I can imagine Maruganj. (Is it a gift that I have always had, or has it come to me, come to me after …?)

I tell myself I can imagine Maruganj because I have been to Muslim *mohallas* in bigger, older cities—Old Delhi, Agra, Lucknow, Hyderabad—mostly as a tourist, inspecting the old mosques and forts, being taken through long, winding, filth-filled alleys, avoiding the eyes of the beggars or hurriedly dropping them a coin.

Maruganj in Phansa must have been dingier, dirtier, its alleys narrower, its sewers uncovered and overflowing, bearded men sitting in corners, children in skullcaps, shrouded women, the stench of decay and filth everywhere except when, suddenly, a different smell would drift by—the fragrance of burning incense or an appetizing whiff of one of the many kinds of kebab being skewered over an open fire. I have no objection to beef—neither did my father, though my mother was and remains a vegetarian. I can appreciate the smell of beef kebab, and its taste.

Strange, isn't it, incense and kebab—those are the good memories that I associate with my cursory incursions into Muslim colonies. Smells, memories that travel in the wind, as if they carry, encapsulated in themselves, the history of a people who have moved, and moved, and moved. The missus would wax eloquent on this; she discovered Sufism—through a translation of Rumi—at Columbia and has ever since been an enthusiast of that branch of Islam, ignoring my, at times, provocative remarks that Sufism seems to have little to do with Islam as practiced and enunciated by mullahs today. "What do you know?" she would say. "Well, I read the newspapers," I would reply, holding up a sheet and pointing to some report of an Islamist atrocity or terrorist attack. There was always one handy. She would throw up her hands half-comically, as she knows I am only half serious when I make such remarks, before going back to whatever she was doing.

Those smells, and then suddenly, through devious, grimy alleys strewn with filth on the ground and caged by electricity and telephone wires overhead, a sudden glimpse of some exquisite dome or gateway. That is how I imagined the Maruganj that Ahmed grew up in—but, of course, I knew it would have no exquisite dome or gateway. Those are to be found in the old imperial cities. Phansa wouldn't have them. Maybe a whitewashed dome with pigeons fluttering around it, maybe a decaying brass-studded door in what was left of a *haveli*, and the smells—that was it. Phansa was a taluk town in a godforsaken state. It was not Lucknow or Old Delhi.

I had been reading the report in bed. I did not want to read it in my office, and I knew the missus never looked at any of my business files. The only time she inquires about the business is when she needs sponsorship for one of her literary events: that is when she asks about my "close" business associates. It is a small price to pay for privacy.

My wife came in, having checked on the kids. She was wearing a silk kimono; she had taken to wearing kimonos as nightdresses this year. Last year it had been a *ghagra choli* set, adapted as a nightdress by one of her designer friends. I sometimes wonder how she can fall asleep in some of these dresses. But I guess women like to be dressed well even in bed, and the missus has retained her figure despite two pregnancies.

Don't misunderstand my tone; we have the best of marriages. A sensible one, a marriage that works. We do not bother each other with deep existential issues; just as I would not discuss the matter of the missing *halwa* with her, she would never moan about approaching menopause to me or the fact that she once wanted to be a novelist. We talk of small matters: the girls and their schooling, the dinner next weekend, where to go next summer. That is why I appreciate her and she appreciates me. What is far more important, we leave each other alone at times, coming together when required to maintain a sane household, bring up balanced kids. We have different interests, but both of us know how to live life sensibly. That is the trick.

The missus got into bed, looked at the file lying on the bedside table and said, "Bringing work home again?" Just for a while, I assured her.

She smirked, playfully. "When is the last time you read a novel?" she asked.

"Just seven months ago," I told her. It was true. I had picked up a thriller during a vacation.

"I don't believe you."

I named the novel.

"Well, you used to read real books when I met you," she added, a bit ruefully.

"I used to be poor too," I replied.

"Neither of us was ever poor." She laughed.

"Everything is relative, ma'am," I noted.

She prepared to fall asleep, but I propped myself up on an elbow and looked at her. She noticed. "What is it?" she asked me.

"You have a Muslim relative, don't you?" I asked her.

"You mean my cousin's son?"

"He married a Muslim girl, didn't he?"

"Yes. Why?"

"I just need to find out a bit about Muslim cultures. Could you ask them?"

"When did you start getting interested in culture—Muslim or Hindu?" She laughed again.

I assured her this was strictly business.

"They live in Canada, Anil. And the girl is just as much Muslim as you are Hindu."

"Of course, I am Hindu."

"Beef eater!"

"So did the ancient sages," I argued back.

"How do you know?"

"I have read a news report on a history book on it, by a chappie called, what was it, Jha. Yes, Jha. Very Hindu name, isn't it? Brahmin name, I dare say. Your *chaddi-wallahs* had the book banned. Or tried to."

"Name an ancient sage," she challenged me.

I thought. "Aryabhatta," I said.

She giggled, "That was a scientist."

"There were no scientists in the past, only sages," I argued back, and then added, "Viswamitra."

"Well," she conceded, "everyone can name one or two."

"The matter that concerns me, ma'am, is not our sages but their mullahs."

"Whose mullahs?"

"Muslim mullahs."

"Never heard of any non-Muslim mullah." She laughed. She was in one of those teasing moods she gets into when her literary events are going well.

"Anyway," I said, seriously, "I need your help. I need to speak to someone who knows Islam from the inside."

"Not that poor girl in Canada. I will get you an expert."

I knew what she meant by an expert: either a scholar of Sufism or a Muslim novelist. I did not object. Either would serve my purpose.

My purpose was simple: I wanted to know more about the society—Tablighi Jamaat—Ahmed's parents had belonged to. I thought it would answer my questions. It would enable me to solve the mystery of the secluded or missing wife, the invisible *halwa*. I was beginning to see Ahmed as a member of some cult. But I had read only a third of the report from Phansa, and by the time my wife got her "expert"—it was a novelist—to come to our place for dinner, I had managed to read the rest of the report. And that had changed my impression of Ahmed—and my questions—once again. Actually, as you will find out, more than just once again.

You recall my image of little Ahmed with tattered notebooks, a skullcap perched on his short-cropped hair, scampering down festering, murky alleys relieved by a flash of brilliance from an ancient doorpost or a whiff of kebab from a roadside stall? Well, as the report specified more pedantically, this image was valid only up to a certain point.

Until secondary school, Ahmed played the part of a studious lower-middle-class Muslim boy, mugging up math tables in school and Arabic at the mosque. In his spare time, he ran errands for his mother—mostly delivering and fetching her work (saris to be mended with fine raffoo work, pullovers to be knitted, salwars or trousers to be repaired) from other houses in Maruganj, and especially from the houses of members of the Tablighi Jamaat, who made an effort to provide Ammajaan with work and Ahmed with tutelage.

Ahmed was popular in school, for he was good at both English and Hindi, and popular at the mosque, where his recitation of the Quran was held up as an example even to older and full-time madrassa boys. He was not talkative even then, but he was not reclusive either—and in that description I recognized Ahmed as we knew him in the office, a man who would speak when required but would not gossip, a man who was always friendly but did not seem to have any special friends.

But Ahmed was growing. He was a boy with not just a sense of responsibility—always thinking of what he could do to help his Ammajaan—but also, hidden under those layers of mature responsibility, a childlike sense of wonder, of excitement at life, at new things, at people. In class eight—when he must have been thirteen or fourteen—Ahmed started helping out a neighbor who was neither a member of the society nor particularly religious. The neighbor's name was Hanif, and he was often called Hanif Ustad, as he was a bit of a neighborhood goon. Hanif Ustad was not considered admirable by the Tablighi families that patronized Ammajaan and Ahmed, but he was not ostracized either—partly because he went to the Friday namaz and partly because he had good contacts with the kind of people who can "get things done." This, in a place like Phansa, I gathered, means petty government officials, policemen up to the rank of thana-in-charge, minor goons of various persuasions (and some of none), and municipal councillors. Also, the good members of the society reasoned that Hanif Ustad could hardly avoid being lax in certain matters—he was said to drink, for instance, though never on Fridays. After all, he earned his livelihood as a tourist guide in neighboring Bodh Gaya.

The season Ahmed started working for Hanif Ustad was a bad one economically. A vague global crisis, like some jealous invisible god, had blighted businesses and salaries in Maruganj too: many members of the society had less to spare, and hence they gave less work to Ammajaan. It was this that might have induced Ahmed to start working for Hanif Ustad. Hanif had been asking Ahmed to join him for some time. "I am very busy in Bodh Gaya during the season," he had told Ahmed. "You could take on those of my tourists who want to see Phansa and we will share fifty-fifty of whatever they pay."

"Does anyone want to see Phansa?" Ahmed had asked seriously.

"Not many. But there are some loonies. I thank Allah for the loonies. They make better sense economically." Hanif had laughed, chewing vigorously on his *paan*.

"Why me?" Ahmed had enquired.

"Ingliss," Hanif had replied shortly, spitting a thin stream of *paan* juice six feet away into a nullah. Ahmed looked on admiringly. Ammajaan did not allow him to chew *paan*. Most of the society members frowned on the habit too.

It wasn't just English that helped Ahmed when he started working for Hanif. At first most of the tourists who came to Ahmed, via Hanif, were from other parts of India; very few foreign tourists diverted to see the 200- or 300-year-old temples that existed in Phansa, and rarely did a European detour to the colonial graveyard where some ancestor lay buried, having survived the Crimean War but succumbing to malaria in Phansa.

Observing Ahmed's success with the Indian tourists— which, he was canny enough to realize, depended a lot on the boy's ability to pick up phrases from their languages in just a few days—Hanif started asking him to help out in Bodh Gaya and sometimes even escort tourists to Rajgir and Nalanda.

Ammajaan felt uneasy about this, mostly because some of her Tablighi acquaintances warned her against Hanif Ustad's "influence." Did she bring this up with Ahmed? The report did not say anything about it, but I suspect she did not do much. Maybe just a word to warn him against "bad society," I could imagine that. From the way Ahmed spoke of his Ammajaan, on the few occasions that he did, I was convinced not only of the love between mother and son but of an unusual degree of trust—the kind of confidence in the other that is built up through years of mutual support and dependence.

"Next Friday?" the missus asked me at breakfast two days later. "Are you free next Friday?"

"Why?"

"Shuja Shirmali can come over for dinner that night."

I must have looked mystified.

"He is a well-known Muslim novelist and journalist. Just last year he published a novel, *The Lamp of Delhi*, based on the life of Nasiruddin Chiragh-Dehlavi."

"Who is this chirag–lamp of Delhi?" I asked.

"A Sufi saint, seventeenth or eighteenth century, I think. You can ask Shuja your questions on Islam."

"Ah," I replied. "Sure, though my questions have changed."

My questions had changed because around eighteen or nineteen Ahmed started changing, according to the report. The Tablighi people later associated it with Hanif Ustad's influence. This might not have been the case. According to the report, by then Ahmed and Hanif Ustad had parted ways, amiably but irrevocably. Ahmed was now working as a guide on his own, and Hanif Ustad had quit the field to move on to bigger matters—an auto repair shop in Gaya, his own taxi service and municipal politics. If they met now, it was when the tourists who employed Ahmed rented a taxi driven by Hanif Ustad or one of his stooges.

Ahmed's reputation had grown, along with his knowledge of languages. He was now being booked even before "parties" reached Bodh Gaya, sometimes even when they were still in Bangkok or Tokyo. He was earning enough to enable Ammajaan to quit stitching and weaving for her Tablighi patrons, though she still took on work sent her way; she felt it would be vain of her to refuse now that she did not need the money.

Ahmed did not object to it: he had not changed outwardly. He had passed the Intermediate with respectably high second-class marks and had accepted the results uncomplainingly, though many people remarked that the only reason Ahmed did not get a first class was that there was no one to do "pairvi" with the powerful on his behalf. He still dressed the way he had, in cheap, clean trousers and shirts that seemed just a bit out of fashion, and even the most critical of Tablighi patrons could not accuse him of "putting on airs." Many of them even sent their children to him, especially to get their English and Hindi compositions corrected, and Ahmed always found time for them.

There had been only one visible sign of change. Like most of his peers, when he finally could, Ahmed had started cultivating a small beard and a mustache. Now, at the age of nineteen, he shaved them off. This might have gone unnoticed, but Ahmed also started being irregular in attending the weekly Friday prayers. Some of the stricter Tablighi members brought this to Ammajaan's notice, who ticked Ahmed off, but lightly because she knew his time was not always his own—he could not ask tourist parties for Fridays off, after all! Moreover, she trusted her son and, never having been allowed by society to go to the mosque for regular prayers, focused more on ordinary signs of faith and virtue: courtesy to others, respect for elders, care for the weak and children, lack of bluster about one's achievements. She could see that Ahmed remained a paragon of virtue in such matters, without even—which was just as important—considering it a virtue.

The years passed like that. The report had little to say of them, and my imagination balks at filling in the gaps. Of course, I can imagine Ahmed conducting tourists through the vast, desolate remains of Nalanda, that ancient Buddhist university destroyed for perhaps being a fort by invading Muslim hordes, looted so many centuries ago. And though I wondered what Ahmed must have felt recounting that history, as a Muslim, to Hindu or Buddhist tourists—his unspoken unease, their unspoken accusation—I could imagine such scenes and even narrate them to you.

But I cannot really talk of how mother and son lived, or even what Ahmed did in his spare time. I know—the report notes it—that he had become a voracious reader. I know of this also from my experience of Ahmed. But what did mother and son talk of when they were in their rented two-bedroom section of a house in Maruganj—Ammajaan had refused to move—or when, say, Shab-e-Barat was being celebrated and Ammajaan was making the famous *maida ka halwa* that Ahmed had often mentioned and that, finally, was the reason for the report and my questions? What transpires in the small spaces between people covers such vast distances that it is often impossible to measure. That is what I think now, and perhaps I unconsciously echo some forgotten Ahmedism. But then?

Then, as I read the report, the questions I wanted to ask the Muslim novelist changed from page to page. Had I met him a week ago I would have asked him about the Tablighi society, about fundamentalism and such matters—in the hope that it would help me understand Ahmed's actions that Shab-e-Barat evening when he had served me a plate of non-existent *halwa*. But I had read on, and I had discovered another person in Ahmed.

It was this person that created the second biggest crisis of her life for Ammajaan—the first, I assume, must have been the death of Ahmed's father.

At the age of twenty-four, while finishing his master's in commerce at a local college, Ahmed announced to Ammajaan that he wished to get married. This was an unlikely announcement where Ahmed was concerned. He had never said anything so decisive to his mother. The old woman, who was probably stitching a torn pocket back onto a pair of jeans, put down the garment. Then she removed her spectacles and put them carefully in their case. She was astounded and overjoyed. Astounded by the tone of Ahmed's request—it was so unlike him—and overjoyed because for the past five or six years she had been prevailing on Ahmed to get married.

"I will find a nice girl for you."

But her joy quickly turned to consternation: Ahmed had himself found the girl he wanted to marry. How had it happened to a boy as shy as Ahmed? Ammajaan probably never got the full answer, but Devi's report sketched a meeting that I could easily flesh out.

Imagine Ahmed a few weeks before he made his announcement to Ammajaan. He is a thin young man of average height, dressed in trousers and a checked shirt, sometimes a blue blazer or a green-yellow pullover (knitted by Ammajaan). He speaks various languages fluently. Imagine him walking down the roads of Bodh Gaya. It is early December, so he has his pullover on, and a cheap scarf. No, the pullover and scarf are my inventions, for the report simply mentioned that "the following account, as reported, is ascertained to have taken place in early December." I can imagine early December in Bodh Gaya; I had taken my wife—or perhaps vice versa—to Bodh Gaya in the winter.

True, when I think of Bodh Gaya, I cannot always distinguish between my memories of the time I had visited it with my parents—I had been twelve or thirteen then—and the time I took my wife there, in the third year of our marriage, when newlyweds still go sightseeing, unencumbered by children. I had noticed a difference: the place was more crowded during my second trip, and it had a greater preponderance of bussed and chartered tourists, urbanized cafes and air-conditioned hotels, which had largely replaced the *dhaba* joints, with benches and charpoys on the pavements or under flimsy awnings, and the hippie-like backpackers I recalled from my first trip. The Tibetans were still there though, the monks with shaven heads and long saffron yellow or dark red robes, the laypeople in even more colorful dresses, traditional ones, a reminder of the fact that they had slowly followed the Dalai Lama into exile after

1959. On both the trips, I even saw some newcomers (or so I supposed they were) wearing sheepskin *chubas* and heavy boots, as if they had just tramped down snow-lined passages.

That is mostly how I imagine the place with Ahmed walking up its main street, every bit a small-town Indian from the plains, dressed in western clothes and a knitted pullover, a scarf wrapped around his head and neck, rubbing his hands to keep them warm in a winter that is almost summer for the Tibetans. The tourist season is at its height: small shops teeming with souvenirs, statues of stone and wood, scarves, carpets, inlaid boxes; the pavement sellers hawking their spreads of Buddha heads, bead strings, incense sticks. Incense is in the air, as well as a faint stink of defecation. Further up, the Tibetan colony—a network of tents in a field—has been thriving for two months now. The Tibetans are yet to flee the heat of these plains for the Himalayan foothills, which most of them do every March in order to return after monsoon. Their return marks the beginning of the tourist season, their evacuation its end.

Ahmed is heading for their colony. He passes the many temples—all built in distinctive national styles—that line the road. Bodh Gaya is full of such temples. He catches just a faint glimpse of the Japanese temple, spare and neat, for it is a bit off the road. But he passes by the elaborately gilded Thai temple, turns left with the road, which shows a slight incline and crosses the Tibetan temple to his left. There is a greater crowd here. Air-conditioned buses are unloading and regurgitating them. It is early evening, and a slight chill is in the breeze. A pack of street dogs run across the street squabbling; they are shooed away by two shopkeepers. Ahmed skirts the fracas.

He turns off the road, into the field where the Tibetan tents are pitched. Some of them fly banners and flags. There are mostly

Tibetans and western tourists in this area, not many Indians. They are the cheaper kind of tourists: students, backpackers, some appearing to be left over from the time of the flower power era. I wonder how Ahmed sees them: as "hippies," as "addicts," which is how I remember the locals referring to them on my second trip, or as students and ordinary jobholders out on that once-in-a-lifetime trip, a vacation in the exotic difference of India shaped by nostalgia for their own past, that time of Bob Dylan, the Beat Generation and Vietnam protests.

That is what I had found most of them to be: students out on a lark, as I too had been with my backpacking American friends when we trekked along the Ganges for three weeks, or people with insecure jobs, traveling on a shoestring. Many of them pay to sleep in the tents and eat in the Tibetans' impromptu cafes. Then Devi's report mentioned something that surprised me: Ahmed ate there too at times, though surely the meat could not have been halal. It was not just the non-halal aspect that surprised me, it was the fact that he ate there at all, for when I was in Bodh Gaya I was often warned by the locals to stay away from the "stinking" restaurants of the Tibetan quarter. Tibetan places serve dog meat, they often appended as explanation. That is when they did not offer other, more personal, explanations.

But "the subject had Tibetan friends," the report stated. Devi either trains all his detectives to write like him, or he has an editor working on all the reports. The latter option would not surprise me, knowing how immaculate Devi is in his waistcoat and goatee, his creaseless patent leather shoes, his way of speaking. "It has been reliably ascertained that this was not unusual practice by the subject, as Indian guides in the said hamlet always cultivate Tibetan contacts."

In the tourist season, the Tibetans know everything about foreigners in Bodh Gaya. It was his Tibetan friends who tipped him off two years ago when Richard Gere was in town and looking for a guide to show him the remote and unfrequented Buddhist caves across the dry Phalgu river. Ahmed got the job, and was handsomely tipped, though he recalls with some chagrin—because even as he said it, he knew he was being stereotypical, being forced by something deeply unconscious and against his better judgement to speak in an alien manner—that Gere could not help laughing when Ahmed approached him and said, "Mr. Richard Gere, I presume?"

It is one of the very few anecdotes from his days as a guide that Ahmed had ever recounted at the office, chuckling drily over it.

Ahmed goes up to a tent and pulls aside its flap. His friend Thubten lives there with his family, whose exact composition and number Ahmed has never been able to ascertain. There are two sisters, sturdy, rosy-cheeked young women whose eyes Ahmed does not dare meet. They are sitting at a table—the first section of the tent is a kind of café, with a brick-and-mud platform running around its outer circumference. The platform, piled with quilts and cushions, serves as a bench—there are tables and folding chairs facing it—during the day, and can be rented as sleeping space for the night. A woman with dirty blonde hair is asleep in one corner, a book on yoga lying half open next to her.

Thubten's two sisters are drinking tea, made the traditional Tibetan way, with butter blobs floating on the surface. They say something to each other, and then shout into the tent for Thubten. Ahmed understands Tibetan, but they often speak too fast for him or use unusual dialect words. He knows they make good-natured fun of him.

Thubten peers in, waves a half-plucked chicken at Ahmed to indicate what he is doing and disappears again. He is bare-chested, dressed in a pair of jeans. One of the sisters pours out butter tea for Ahmed and hands it to him. He accepts it with mumbled thanks, without looking at her. He does not sit down. He sips the tea, standing by the entrance of the tent. The girls know he won't accept their invitation to sit with them unless Thubten is there too. They giggle.

Thubten comes out in a few minutes, wiping his hands dry and then buttoning a cotton shirt. He likes going around in Bodh Gaya without warm clothes, as if to reiterate his origins, for otherwise he wears western clothes, prefers to speak English and swears a lot in it. He tosses the rag at his sisters, and they exchange a few light remarks that Ahmed does not overhear, for he has finished his tea, put down the glass on the nearest table and gone out to stand by the tent.

When Thubten joins him, he slaps Ahmed on the back jocularly and says in Hindi, "Ahmed yaar, why are you so bloody rude to the poor girls?" Thubten is active in the Tibetan Youth Congress and speaks Hindi fluently, though he insists he was born in Tibet.

"What do you mean?" asks Ahmed. He can see his friend is ribbing him, but Ahmed has a horror of being rude.

"You never even look at the girls."

"In my community that indicates respect," Ahmed replies defensively.

"I suppose in my community it would be considered rude. The girls think so, anyway." Thubten laughs.

"I never look at women unless there is a proper reason to do so."

Thubten is in a teasing mood. "I thought you lot solved that problem by putting your women in those blasted burkas," he quips.

Ahmed has a sense of humor, but this witticism is wasted on him. By the time he came to work for me, he had mostly lost the desire to defend or justify his people. He never got into the occasional arguments about Islamist terror that I overheard erupting in the cubicles of my office, answering only with accounts of personal experience—like what he did for Eid or Shab-e-Barat—when asked. It was as if he did not make any connection between abstract discussions of his faith and his own personal experience of it. At a certain point, these had become two different things for Ahmed. But in those days in Bodh Gaya, according to Devi's report, he still felt compelled to explain and defend.

Thubten, Devi's man had noted, still laughed at the recollection. (Thubten is now a prosperous middle-aged businessman, with a restaurant in Dharamsala, the report specified.) "It was hilarious how old Ahmed would get into the intricacies of such matters," Thubten had recounted in English over a beer to Devi's man. "The guy was a walking encyclopedia on his fucking faith. Oh sorry. You are not Muslim, are you? No? Thank God! I just tend to swear; I have nothing against any faith. I have a good relationship with all faiths: I leave them alone and they leave me alone. But Ahmed, my God, the man did go on and on. I think he gave me a long, rambling lecture on that occasion, quoting the Quran and—what's it called—the Haddis or Huddis or something, it's like a reference book on their prophet's activities, and I had just been pulling his leg. The gist of it was—I have forgotten the fucking details, oh sorry again, me and my foul mouth!—that the purdah was not a veil put on women but a curtain between private and public spaces. He had looked it up, and the veiling of women was basically just one interpretation.

Another interpretation was modest dress and behavior—and the separation of private and public spheres, which evidently had to do with something that happened to his prophet during one of his marriages, the prophet's that is, keeping in mind that the Arabs in those days were only a partly settled people. Like us, I had lightly remarked, living in tents. He had looked nonplussed and then nodded absentmindedly. Yes, tents, he had said. I had teased him a bit more by adding that, tents or no tents, if any of us tried to veil a Tibetan woman, he would get a clout that would send him reeling for three days. That set him off again, and you know, the funniest thing about this episode is that I was accompanying him because of a matter to do with a woman. That is why he had come to me. He needed support. A woman was way beyond his ken."

Ahmed had known her for more than a year. She worked in Jogi's restaurant on the town side of Bodh Gaya. This was not the side Ahmed had crossed on his way to Thubten's tent. That had been the tourist side, which started soon after the half-desolate campus of Magadh University ended and a few large hotels appeared; beyond these, to the right, could be seen a massive outdoor statue of Buddha, towering over all the buildings. This relatively open side of Bodh Gaya spread around a main road with its temples in different national styles, curio shops and small restaurants with ambitious names, even a small public park. The road then ascended slightly and reached the Mahabodhi Temple, the intricately carved seventh-century stone structure—now smothered with cement in a bid to "restore" it—marking the spot where Siddhartha, the prince who left home to ponder suffering, death and life, became the Buddha, the enlightened one, under the foliage of a tree. Then the road grew narrower and descended on the other side of the temple, where it finally split into two even narrower strands.

This was the native town side of Bodh Gaya. Behind it lay the mostly dry banks of the Phalgu River. This side had fewer and dingier shops; its restaurants had less ambitious names. Jogi's restaurant had no name; it was known by the name of its owner, who was a short, rotund man in his sixties. He was no mystic; Jogi was just what his parents had named him.

Jogi's restaurant—or Jogi's *dhaba*, as it was more often called—was a three-story brick building, mostly unplastered. The upper stories contained rooms that Jogi rented out, some for years, and some for a day or two. The ground floor contained rooms used by Jogi and his family, and a large hall, with a kitchen behind it. This hall was Jogi's *dhaba*, though the board propped outside at the entrance gave it no name. It just said in Hindi: "Food Made of Pure Ghee Here."

The first time Ahmed went there, almost three years ago, he was with a bunch of other guides. These were young men who hung around the shops and restaurants of Bodh Gaya, offering to exchange foreign currency or show you sights. Ahmed did not like going out with them—their talk was mostly of money, booze and women, and they often joked about taking advantage, monetary and sexual, of the tourists they had recently guided—but it was a close-knit band and Ahmed could not avoid them. He had known most of them from when he used to stand in for Hanif Ustad, and he often tried out his foreign languages on them—for many of these young men, mostly high school dropouts, spoke Thai or Japanese with greater fluency than they spoke English. Despite the years together, Ahmed remained wary of them, their physical jostling, their lewd jokes and the "side businesses"—such as selling weed or procuring women—some of them also ran. On the other hand, they took to Ahmed with unexpected respect, seldom making him the target of their jokes.

They had been celebrating that evening. One of the guides was getting married next week. "Beginning of wife, end of life," they told the prospective bridegroom, and dragged him to Jogi's *dhaba* for dinner. Ahmed was sitting with them, smoking over cups of tea in the square outside the Mahabodhi Temple— for the season was dying and tourists were few—and could not refuse to go along.

Jogi knew all of them except Ahmed, who was elaborately introduced as the most brilliant of all guides and a great scholar from Phansa and, for it proved his unproven greatness, a man who did not touch alcohol. After that, the men ordered beer— Jogi did not have a permit to sell alcohol but would procure it for reliable patrons—and a woman who had been working in the kitchen came over to get their order.

The men obviously knew her, and she knew them, for one of them said to her, after she had plunked metal plates down and taken their orders, "Ah, what a ripe fruit." The remark, though it made Ahmed flush and the other men smirk and nudge each other, was descriptive: there was something of the luscious fruit about this young woman, ruddily dark, with high cheekbones and slanted eyes, a tightness, a fullness, a ripeness that her sari could not hide. The woman was not flustered at all. "Well beyond your reach, shorty," she told the man. At which another of the men sang out, "Fall into my hands, O ripe fruit." The woman scoffed on her way back to the soot-blackened kitchen, "You are not strong enough to hold me, twiggy." All the men—except Ahmed, who was staring at his metal plate—laughed uproariously.

"Who is she?" he later asked one of the men. He was given a name, a Hindu one. But another man corrected the first one and gave another name, a Christian one this time. A third man offered a third name.

She was a woman of various names. One of them was Roshni.

The basic facts of Roshni's life were commonly known, and the men took turns narrating them to Ahmed, though in a hushed voice. She lived upstairs with her mother, who was said to be Muslim and was Jogi's keep. They used the English word "keep." The mother was ailing now and surely it was generous of Jogi to let her stay on, as she could not be of any further use to him, could she, and there had always been friction between her and Jogi's rightly wedded wife, who lived downstairs with him.

Then the girl was Jogi's natural daughter? No, the men laughed. Do you see any resemblance? Everyone knows that Jogi keeps pestering her, but she won't let him dip his stick in her creek. Though it is not a creek that has remained unfished, the men laughed. Not by any means. She is said to have a penchant for the *goras*, but of course only if they pay her in dollars.

Whose daughter is she then? No one knows. Jogi half-pretends she is his daughter—so that he can keep her next to him, now that her mother is an old crone, good for nothing—but look at her, yaar, look at her when she comes by next time. There is nothing of Jogi in her. She is as dark as her mother, true, why I have never heard of a Muslim woman that dark, she looks like a Munda, but look at her legs, those sturdy calves, look at her cheekbones, those chinky eyes, don't you see it? Her father has to be a chink, probably one of those Tibetan monks who got a heatstroke meditating in April and went for her mother!

When Roshni—that is the name Ahmed decided he liked best—came back to their tables with the bill, scratched on a chit of paper, and as they debated who was paying what, the bridegroom being exempted on the condition that he would treat all of them after his wedding, Ahmed stole a bolder look at her, almost despite himself. She noticed it and smiled back at him. "You are new," she said. Then she added, "I have seen you before in the square. You are always reading a book." One of the men hastened to inform her that Ahmed was a great scholar from Phansa. She laughed as she counted their money. "What is he doing with you empty-heads then?" was her parting shot as she flounced back.

Ahmed started going to Jogi's *dhaba* regularly. He had to eat somewhere on his days in Bodh Gaya. But he must have realized that pragmatism was not his only reason, for he never went there with any of the men.

I can imagine the relationship as it developed, though Devi's man had put it in only a few sparse words: "In due course, Ahmed started helping Roshni with her homework, and with medicines and doctors for her mother." It says everything one needs to know, but what one needs to know seems insufficient in such cases, doesn't it? Even a pragmatic businessman like me can do better: Imagine … the clanking fan under which Ahmed sat as the year got warmer, Roshni just serving him first, maybe with a flirtatious joke that would leave him flustered and tongue-tied, then joining him at the table, despite Jogi shouting at her to get on with it, and slowly a conversation flowing between them—first a trickle blocked by the minutest of chores, then the many trickles uniting into a river that could sweep any interruption aside. I can imagine Ahmed's surprise when he realized Roshni was preparing for her Inter exams. He must have computed her age then and thought, Roshni might be just seventeen years old, but surely that is unlikely, for she could not have studied without many interruptions, and she must have lost at least a year or two in the process. I can see her bringing him some mathematical theorem or language problem, perhaps with a joke first—"Say, Mr. Great Scholar, can you solve this?"—and then seeking more and more help from him. I can see Ahmed, naturally inclined to help others, offering to fetch a doctor when her mother had one of her collapses ... I can imagine all this spread over the next year or two, though, as I have already confessed to you, this ability to imagine large segments of Ahmed's life leaves me shaken too. I ask myself, Did you always have this hidden ability to speak about things that you have not witnessed, not *seen*, or has it been bestowed, a gift or a curse, on you by the very events driving you, here and now, to confess to a stranger?

Around the same time, the report specified, Ahmed had his falling out with the religious Muslims of his *mohalla*. This had to do with Shab-e-Barat.

As I had learned from Ahmed, there is a tradition in many Muslim families to visit the graves of the dear departed, clean them, light incense sticks and pray at the graves during Shab-e-Barat. Ahmed had been accompanying Ammajaan to his father's grave year after year. That year, mother and son got ready as usual—each took a longer bath and put on fresh clothes, Ammajaan fumbled in her rusting Godrej almirah for the box of incense sticks she kept there—and set out on a rickshaw for the graveyard, which was a couple of kilometers from their house. They had greater reason this year to look forward to this annual ritual as the graveyard had been finally enclosed in a boundary wall under a new management. It had been modernized, it was said. Ahmed had been there once after the changes were made, the wall built, and he had come back and given an enthusiastic report to Ammajaan, who was now too old and infirm to go to the graveyard more than once a year. "The walls prevent goats and dogs from entering, and there is even a gateman to keep loiterers out! Taps have been installed at regular intervals to wash feet and hands, Ammajaan, and to water the flower plants and pomegranate bushes at the graves. Garbage has been cleared away, paths laid out. The new management is finally doing some managing!" Ahmed had told Ammajaan.

As their rickshaw pulled up at the gate of the graveyard, Ammajaan pushed aside her face cover—with age she permitted herself some leeway with the purdah—and said in appreciation of the developments, "*Subhaan-Allah. Bahut accha kaam kiya hai management ne! Dil khush kar diya!*" Do you understand that? No? Well, it means, "God be praised. The management has done excellent work. It pleases the heart."

Then she waited for Ahmed to get off the rickshaw and come around to her side to help her alight and hand her the walking stick she needed. All this took some time. The sun was shining. Sparrows were fluttering on the wall next to the gate.

Ahmed helped Ammajaan to the gate, which was slightly ajar, but just as he held it open for her, the gateman came running. He had been sitting at a nearby kiosk. He knew both Ammajaan and Ahmed. "Ahmed sahib," he shouted from a distance as he ran toward them, "Khalajaan cannot go in."

The sparrows took off with a whirr, like the sound of pages turned by the wind.

Both Ammajaan and Ahmed were surprised. "Why not, *mian?*" asked Ammajaan, a trifle brusquely.

"*Manahi hai,*" said the gatekeeper. "Women cannot enter the graveyard, Khalajaan."

"What errant nonsense," replied Ammajaan. "I have been entering it every year for longer than you have lived on this earth!"

"It was wrong. It has been prohibited." The gateman was obdurate.

An argument unfolded, with Ahmed pitching in to support his mother and a crowd gathering. Two management committee members also came up. One of them had worked with Ahmed's father before quitting and getting a job in Saudi Arabia; he had retired and returned home only a couple of years ago. He was clear about it: "Women are too weak, too soft-hearted to enter graveyards. They cannot bear it. It is for their good that they are prohibited from entering."

"It has been confirmed by reliable sources that the subject was not a man to get angry," the report put it in Devi's register. "But that day he got excessively angry. This surprised the crowd, which had been neutral until then, recalled three of the witnesses interviewed." I wondered if Ahmed's anger was provoked by the new rule or by the fact that no one in the crowd supported him.

"Witness Number 3, also quoted above, recalls the culmination of the episode in these words, translated verbatim: You do not just start shouting at a Haji, telling him, a member of two mosque and one graveyard committees, what the Holy Quran says, do you? The old gentleman had worked with his father too. And the Haji, he is dead now, Allah bestow peace on him, honored that association; he kept addressing Ahmed's Ammajaan as *bhabhi*, which is the proper way. But Ahmed? He was stubborn, quoting from this and quoting from that, as if he was a sheikh, not a lowly guide who everyone in the *mohalla* knew ate with Tibetans and in Hindu hotels. We did not like Ahmed's attitude that day. No, I did not. He had become too big for his boots, having earned easy money and been with unbelievers too often and too long. There was some mumbling. The hotheads in the crowd would have roughed him up had his Ammajaan not been there. And it was his Ammajaan who pulled him away, literally by his sleeve. Let's go, son, she said. Let's return home. The day will be over soon and there are things to do."

The elder who had worked with Ahmed's father was very proper. He apologized for hurting *bhabhi's* feelings, and said to Ahmed, "Son, you can go in."

"Not without Ammajaan," Ahmed replied. It was known that he never entered the graveyard again, except once. This too turned many of the *mohalla* people against him and perhaps led to the problems he had over the matter of Roshni later on.

I was reading this part of the report late in the night, sitting at the dining table. It was after midnight. Even the servants were sleeping. The house and the streets outside were quiet except for the occasional car and a faint yapping of street dogs from different directions.

I had woken up to read the report. I had not been able to fall fast asleep, my mind returning to it in sleep, with that dream of the hand clutching at a sleeve recurring. It had returned three or four times that night, and finally my half-awake mind had identified a new element: I had recognized the hand clutching at what I had thought until then was my sleeve. It was not an unknown hand, not the ancient mariner's. It was not even Ahmed's hand, as you might have assumed. It was my own hand—I had recognized the scar that I have carried from the time I fell down and cut myself while running hurdles at school. It was *my* hand. And the sleeve? I just could not tell whose sleeve it was!

That had chased all sleep from my eyes. At first, I had lain there, spread-eagled, staring up blankly at the ceiling. Then I had stolen out of bed—my wife is a sound sleeper—and returned to reading the report on the dining table.

Now I put it aside because a memory had returned to me. It was from some years ago. Some of the staff, including Ahmed, were taking a tea break. The office has a nook with tea and coffee machines and a few chairs. Once in a while, when staff members take a break, I join them too—it serves to add the human touch to the business and also ensure that the pauses are not too long. It was one of those occasions.

When I joined them that day, they were talking about the old tragedy queens and kings of cinema, discussing who was better—Guru Dutt, Dilip Kumar, Meena Kumari, Nargis, Rekha—at playing tragic roles. They were discussing the great tragic scenes. Ahmed was there too, listening but not saying much, which was his usual way, unless asked.

One of the men turned to him. "Ahmed, you have not told us what the most tragic scene is in your view."

Ahmed had said, almost instantly, as if the words had burst out from deep within him, as if from a scene framed forever in his heart, seared into his mind: "An old woman hobbling on a stick along half a kilometer of a railway track, a hazardous, shit-infested track, to catch one last glimpse of her husband's grave."

"What film was it?" the colleague asked.

"It wasn't a film," Ahmed replied, and withdrew from the company, back into his own cubicle.

Can't you imagine it? It might have happened the same day or some days later.

I see it this way. Ammajaan and Ahmed return to their section of the house. Ahmed is angry; Ammajaan is silent. They go through the other rituals of Shab-e-Barat; they eat the *maida ka halwa*. But Ammajaan is unusually silent. Then she says, perhaps only to herself, but aloud, "If only I could have seen him once more."

Attentive Ahmed, now preternaturally sensitive to his mother's mood, overhears and inquires immediately, "Seen whom?"

"Your father's grave," Ammajaan replies.

Ahmed is immediately ready to go out and argue with the graveyard management committee again. But Ammajaan does not want that. She forbids it. Instead, she suggests they could walk along the railway tracks behind the graveyard; she knows from previous visits that her husband's grave is on that side and would be visible from the railway tracks.

Can you imagine it? The old woman, unstable, balancing herself on the tracks and between them, the tracks that contain so much disposed from the trains, the tracks that are used by poorer Indians to defecate, the tracks that can, at any moment, bring a train rushing at her. And her son, supporting her, keeping an ear open for the slightest sound of an approaching engine, restraining himself from hurrying her and still wanting her to move as fast as she can ... And then they reach the spot, and she identifies the grave from a distance, cups her hands and offers the usual prayer. Then they turn back and return the way they had come.

It made sense now, what Ahmed had said then in my office: "An old woman hobbling on a stick along half a kilometer of a railway track, a hazardous, shit-infested track, to catch one last glimpse of her husband's grave."

You might think I have forgotten about that walk with Thubten, that my story has gone off in other directions, become involved in an intricate past. But that is not the case. Because, you see, that day when Ahmed asked his Tibetan friend Thubten to accompany him, he had made up his mind. He was going to ask Roshni to marry him.

He had known her for three years now, during which she had completed her Inter, with second-class marks. Two months back Roshni's mother had died. A few weeks ago, Roshni had complained to Ahmed that Jogi had tried to come into her room one night, drunk, and after she had physically thrown him out, he had given her notice to vacate. She had asked Ahmed to help her find "safe lodgings," but Ahmed had other ideas. He could have asked her himself, but of course he wouldn't.

"Imagine Ahmed asking a woman to marry him?" Thubten told Devi's man. "It is so damn funny! No, he wanted me to ask her on his behalf. Matchmaker, matchmaker, find me a match! I think he would have wanted his mother or some old woman to do the job, but that was not possible. And tell you what, it fucking worked. I was a bloody good matchmaker. I don't want to take too much credit though. It had been clear to everyone for months that the girl was totally in love with Ahmed. Clear to everyone except Ahmed, that is!"

Devi's Phansa report had fewer details about what happened next, except that Ahmed and Roshni were married by a mullah in Bodh Gaya, and Ammajaan accepted it. Not everyone else did though, as I think I have told you. Some *mohalla* people wanted Roshni to be converted to Islam and the *niqaah* to be performed again. They did not believe Ahmed's claim that Roshni was a Muslim. "She doesn't look like a Muslim," said those who did not know anything about her. And those who had heard about her from Bodh Gaya said, "Who knows what her father was?"

But Ahmed refused, and—what disappointed the deeply religious in particular—Ammajaan defended him. "How can a Muslim be converted again to Islam?" she maintained stubbornly. It isolated Ahmed from many in the *mohalla*, but he did not seem to care. His world was his mother and now Roshni, who imitated her mother-in-law's dress codes despite Ahmed's objections.

"They will never accept you no matter what you do," he told her.

"Do you think that is why I am doing this?" she answered him. Then she added, "I only want to be seen by you."

6

Devi's second report—the report on Ahmed and Roshni's years in Mumbai and Surat—must have reached him around the same time the missus told me she had asked Shuja Shirmali over to dinner, because three or four days before the dinner I received a phone call from Devi. Once again, my discussion with Devi changed my questions. Ahmed's realities, it appeared, shifted with every new inquiry into it, as if he was not a solid human being but something amorphous, imaginary, ghostly.

I was in my car, being driven to office when the mobile buzzed. Devi's opening words took me by surprise. "Are you alone?" he asked. I told him I was on my way to work.

"Boss, can you come to see me today? The other report has arrived."

"Why don't you just send it over by courier, marked confidential like last time? That way I will have it sooner."

I could sense Devi hesitating. Then he replied, in a lower tone, "I can, but … it is just that not all the information is there in the written report. I can give you a verbal summary."

I was surprised. "Why isn't all the information in the report, Devi?" I asked.

There was a moment of silence on the other end. Then Devi chuckled. "My innocent friend," he replied, "as governments tend to put it, some of it is sensitive."

"Sensitive?"

"Or classified. It cannot be written down."

As I was not too busy that day, I arranged with Devi to see him immediately, and asked the driver to take me to his office instead of mine.

It was only when Devi shut the door to his office and locked it that I noticed something I had not really heeded on my previous visits. His walls and door were padded. What I had seen as a kind of 1970s decor—the sort found in some Delhi and Kolkata restaurants in particular—was insulation and padding meant to make the room soundproof. Once the door was closed and the shutters pulled, I could not hear a sound from the outside, and obviously no one outside could hear us.

Devi returned to his plush revolving chair and sank into it. He noticed me looking around. "Part of the business," he explained.

"You make me nervous," I said, and I partly meant it, even as the other part of me felt amused at this cloak-and-dagger scenario.

"Mostly for show, boss. But sometimes we do work for people who want more secrecy than you do, my friend, and they have enemies who can be hugely curious," he replied. "This time it is best to be careful in your case too."

I laughed. "What can be so hush-hush about Ahmed's days in Mumbai?" I asked, even though old fears were again surfacing in my mind. Mumbai has a huge underworld; it is known to have terrorist links. Was Ahmed involved in stuff like that, after all?

"It is not really his days in Mumbai. It is the way they ended." Here is the story he told me, minus the interruptions I made and the innuendoes Devi employed.

Roshni and Ahmed left for Mumbai within a week of Ammajaan's death—"of old-age-related complications," as the death certificate put it. She was buried next to her husband, and Ahmed entered the graveyard for the last time. But after the body had been laid down, Ahmed scandalized the gathering once again by not saying the required prayer by the graveside. Instead, he left immediately; he was seen walking out of the graveyard and up the railway tracks behind it. Then he stood at the point closest to the grave, on the railway tracks, covered his head with a handkerchief and said the prayer for the departed.

With Ammajaan buried, what reason could Roshni and Ahmed have had to stay on? There was nothing connecting them to that community anymore, as Ahmed's gesture indicated. And they appear to have settled into Mumbai quite easily. That huge city which has accepted so many strangers also embraced them.

Ahmed had used one of his contacts—a rich businessman from Mumbai, whose family and friends he had guided around Bodh Gaya and Nalanda on different occasions—to get a job. This said a lot to me. Devi's man could not know it, and hence Devi's narration did not mention how unusual it was for Ahmed to make such a request. I had seen Ahmed working in our office for years, and he never asked anyone for anything if he could do it himself. You know how one asks a colleague to pass a pencil or a sharpener? Can you pass me this? Will you toss me that? Ahmed never did so. He would get up and fetch things himself, no matter how minor, moving in his usual unhurried manner. So, the fact that he asked someone for a favor—a job—indicated to me the intensity of Ahmed's desire to leave his *mohalla*.

The businessman might have initially thought he was doing Ahmed a favor, but he was astute enough to realize Ahmed's potential; within two years, he had moved Ahmed from being a warehouse supervisor to a more responsible desk in his main office. And then, in 2001, he put Ahmed in charge of their Surat office.

Devi covered Roshni and Ahmed's years in Mumbai in a few prosaic lines, reserving the bulk of his words to describe how they ended. "They were happy, I suppose," he told me. "They rented a flat in the suburbs, and Ahmed commuted about two hours every day to work. They were liked by their neighbors and participated in neighborhood activities and festivities—you know, the usual movie show or puja. It was a mixed neighborhood, mostly Hindus, but also a smattering of Muslims, Christians, Sikhs, one or two elderly and impoverished Parsis. Roshni still observed purdah, but less rigorously, going out in public with her face uncovered, participating in neighborhood gatherings without Ahmed, sometimes even going to the cinema with the two or three female friends she had made. Ahmed and Roshni often went out during vacations and weekends, either to the cinema or to one of the beaches. Nothing to distinguish them from a thousand other newlyweds."

Isn't it sad how easily we skim over happiness? I have done it all my life too, inadvertently, ignorantly. It is only now I realize, dimly, that I have been doing so for years. I recall entering the girls' room sometimes at night, just to check if they are sleeping, and observing their blanket-covered forms lightly breathing. The soft heave and fall of the sheets in that room of toys and posters. A feeling of calm and joy washes over me, but I do not tarry to savor it; I rush back to whatever worry or nonsense or TV show engages my attention downstairs. I think of my wife talking about some vacuous literary event—banter over a cozy family dinner—and how, instead of appreciating the simple moment,

I try to contain my irritation at the missus going on and on about something that does not interest me at all. What did Ahmed say once, during one of those office discussions? Yes, this was it, an Ahmedism if ever there was one: "One need not search for happiness; one needs to stop for it."

It is only now that I am beginning to understand what he meant by it. We skip happiness, as Devi's report did, we don't pause for it. The report had nothing to say of Roshni and Ahmed walking the sands of Juhu Beach, eating *bhel poori* out of the same paper plate, the breeze blowing Roshni's face cover over her head as if it was a cloud following her. The report had nothing to say of Roshni riding pillion on the motorcycle Ahmed had bought, either to go shopping or to the cinema. The report had nothing to say of the two sitting next to each other, watching the rich and handsome hero and the accomplished and beautiful heroine singing out their larger-than-life-happiness across a dozen locales on three continents, and feeling not the slightest trace of envy, for Roshni's hand has slipped into Ahmed's in the darkness of the theater and this little space between them is more than all the continents can offer.

Happiness! Who has time for happiness? Definitely not people like Devi—and me.

I interrupted Devi's narrative. "Did they join any society?" I asked him, "Ahmed, especially."

"Society, boss?" he asked, surprised.

"I mean"—and I felt embarrassed to spell it out—"is there any indication that Ahmed might have had Islamist sympathies or met people like that?"

"No, nothing. Quite the contrary. He does not seem to have gone to the mosque any longer, and only turned up for the open-air Eid prayers."

I was relieved. Despite the suspicions I had harbored soon after the evening in Ahmed's flat—suspicions that, I confess, did return to me occasionally—there was little to associate Ahmed with fundamentalist Islam. True, he did not drink alcohol, but then he did not seem to insist on halal meat either; he ate the meat served to him during parties and restaurant outings, and he allowed the tilak mark to be put on his forehead when we held the usual, rather perfunctory, puja in the office. And yet, it was difficult to slot him—yes, I think that was the root of all these suspicions that returned to me despite my better self. That is why I had to ask Devi the question.

Take, for instance, this episode from Ahmed's fifth year with me, or maybe the sixth year. By then the business had expanded. We had just moved into bigger premises, the one we occupy now. In tandem with all these developments, I had decided to issue company credit cards to my top four employees, and of course Ahmed was one of them. These were people who took clients and partners out for lunches and so on, when I was too busy to do so or the guests were not big enough for me to bother with. It would be simpler for them to put checks directly on the company account, instead of filling forms to get a reimbursement.

But Ahmed, I was informed by the accountant, had refused to accept the credit card. He had said he did not use credit cards. He used only debit cards or paid with cash.

Of course, I had to take this up with Ahmed on the first opportunity. And I did. I asked him, as soon as I found him alone, "I am told you do not use credit cards, Ahmed?"

"I have never had one, Mehrotra sa'ab. I would prefer not to."

"Why? Is it for religious reasons?" (Even I was aware of

Islamic banking and the reputed objection that religious Muslims have to charging or paying interest.)

"Not really, Mehrotra sa'ab. But who can stand security for the future? One either has debt, or one has time."

"That is Greek to me, Ahmed. And Sanskrit too," I had said, laughing. "Can't you put it in plain English or Hindi?"

He had thought for a second and then said, "Debt is a slap in the face of time. I don't have debts; I have all time."

It had made even less sense to me, but I had pointed out the obvious: "All money is debt today, Ahmed."

"You can make your own money, Mehrotra sa'ab."

"It is called forgery, Ahmed," I had joked.

"Not that kind of money!" and he had uttered the grunt that passed for a laugh with him.

But now Devi was leaning closer to me, across the desk, and his voice had become a loud whisper. His look had changed, turned wary and secretive, and it accentuated his heavy jowls, which he hid behind the goatee, and the deeply furrowed brow he usually lightened with his standard jovial demeanor. He was obviously back in cloak-and-dagger mode.

"Do you remember 2002?" he asked me.

"2002? Let me see. Wasn't that the golden jubilee of Queen Elizabeth? Did the Iraq war begin then?"

"No, no, think of Mumbai, of Surat."

"Mumbai?" I shrugged. "Nothing comes to mind."

"The Gujarat riots," Devi said.

"Ah! That was the year?"

"That was the year."

"It affected Surat, didn't it?" I asked, a horrific suspicion crossing my mind.

"Yes, it did," Devi looked grim, "Roshni and Ahmed had just moved into a new flat in a part of the city a few months ago."

Then he handed me some sheets, obviously from the report that he did not want me to have in its entirety. "Read these," he said. "My man does not want me to include this in any report to be given out officially—to you or anyone else. I can understand why. We are businessmen, boss—professionals, not activists."

It began many kilometers away from Ahmed and Roshni's beloved Mumbai, which they must have been reluctant to leave for Surat. Why did they leave? Ahmed might have been ambitious in those days, or he might just have been too polite to refuse a promotion by his benefactor and employer. Or, perhaps, they had missed living in a smaller town—and Surat is a relatively small place in Gujarat.

A train was set on fire in Godhra on February 27, 2002, and the fire spread across Gujarat.

Violence, Ahmed had once said, is a virus; it spreads by contaminating others. Ahmed had been trying to defend Gandhi's philosophy of ahimsa, which was being criticized by a couple of his colleagues who claimed to support the Hindutva ideology of the Bharatiya Janata Party for intellectual and not religious reasons. That is when he had said these words. I think his point was that the only way to resist violence is to refuse to harbor it, or you become a carrier of the virus and it spreads further through you. But what if the virus is injected into you? What if the doctors of your society infect you with the virus?

You look bewildered, and, to be honest, I had to dredge up the facts of the Gujarat riots on Wikipedia too, so deep down in the swamp of my consciousness had the tragedy sunk. It was not something that was discussed much in my circles, except when some major accusation surfaced in the newspapers, and even then, fleetingly. It did not belong to my world. I know that now.

The sheets from Devi's report kept the information to bare facts, always carefully attributed to public sources. It had started neither in Mumbai nor in Surat. A trainload of Hindutva activists, returning from the site of a mosque in Ayodhya, destroyed by Hindu fanatics some years ago because it was said to have been built on the site of a temple marking the birthplace of Lord Rama. Do you know of it? You do? Well, then, this train was set on fire. Muslims were accused of doing it, though later investigation suggests it may have been an accident. More than fifty Hindu pilgrims died in the fire. The fire spread to various towns and cities of Gujarat, then governed by our new and great prime minister.

As I said, the sheets I read in Devi's office, after which he took them from me and put them through the shredder on a side cabinet, were taciturn about the details. This is all they said, as far as I can recall, about the main tragedy:

"Based entirely on what the newspapers reported (see Appendix 3A) and not any evidence obtained or sought by this investigator, the riots that followed led to the death of 790 Muslims—some put the estimate at double that number—and 254 Hindus. Thousands were injured and rendered homeless. It was reported in national newspapers (see Appendix 3B) that women were raped and impaled on spears; children were burned alive. The government of Gujarat was accused—and later absolved, it has to be noted—of purposefully dragging its feet, to give vigilante Hindutva groups, some supposedly led by politicians, a chance to teach 'those Muslims a lesson' (see Appendix 3C)."

Roshni, as Devi told me, was one of those Muslims.

But the sheets said more about what happened to Roshni and Ahmed. I suppose they had to; after all, Devi's people were known to do a thorough job. And I think that is why they had to be shredded.

The fire came to Ahmed's part of Surat when he was not there. He had gone to work. Roshni was alone in their small flat.

At the office, when Ahmed heard of riots in town, he was not overly worried. They had settled in well, and by now Roshni knew many of the neighbors. Ahmed trusted them. He was confident the neighbors would not harm Roshni.

It was not the neighbors who harmed Roshni. A mob came into the neighborhood from outside, led by minor politicians belonging to the ruling party. It had a municipal list of houses belonging to Muslims, and another list of flats rented by Muslims.

The mob went about its task methodically. In that sense, it was surely not a mob. When it banged on Roshni's door, she did not open it. They broke it down. Then they dragged Roshni out of the flat. Only one neighbor tried to protect her. (I would like to believe this was so because all the men, like Ahmed, were away, stuck in the places where they worked.) It was an old South Indian man, who tried to tell the crowd that Roshni and her husband were part of their community, that they were not "bad" Muslims, that they even participated in neighborhood pujas. The leaders of the mob were in no mood to listen. They had not been able to catch many Muslims; most of the others in this locality seemed to have fled. They needed to kill.

When the old man continued to protest, he was shoved aside by one of the leaders, and cuffed and kicked back into his flat by other men. There he was restrained by the frightened women of his household.

It was this organized mob that dragged Roshni down the stairs. They ripped the veil off her. They mocked her. "Where is your God?" they shouted. "Where is your bastard man?" they mocked. "No one can save you now, you Pakistani whore!"

Roshni, the neighbors reported, said nothing. She just sat in the dust, head bowed, as if lost in deep thought. She did not even react when the South Indian man, in one last attempt to help her, screamed that she was not Muslim. "Look at her," he shouted, from his doorway, where the women held him back, "Look at her. Does she look Muslim?" But Roshni did not ply this sliver of doubt inserted in the mob by the old man. She did not claim she was not Muslim. She did not say anything. She neither cried nor remonstrated; she never pleaded.

In that description, I see her as I now see Ahmed: people with deep and mysterious sources of strength and calm, men and women of a kind we fail to recognize in the crowd, because we no longer pause to look, for we associate strength with violence, or at least with action. Was that why, when I had looked back into the hall of the literary party on the evening of my fateful encounter with the invisible *halwa*—the party my wife had dragged me to, the one thrown to honor an award-winning "son of the nation" on his second trip to India—I had failed to find anyone resembling Ahmed in that crowd of movers and shakers?

Roshni's calm frustrated the mob. They were men on the move in a nation on the move, and all she did was sit immobile on the ground, her head bowed, neither defiant nor submissive. Would weeping and pleading have saved her? Should she have grabbed the feet of the men, supplicated them in the name of their gods or hers? Should she have abased herself, done violence to her own self, torn out her hair, slapped her cheeks, beat her head, before they could do violence to her, and thus appeased their blind craving for action, for change and movement?

Who knows?

It was one of the leaders of the mob—easy to identify but never arrested, of course—who poured kerosene on her bowed head. The crowd around her withdrew, as the sweet smell of the fuel spread. They were ordinary people: they knew the smell from domestic situations. Suddenly a space opened up around her. She was there in that space, with the leader next to her. Then the leader took a step back. And then another. He struck a match and threw it on Roshni.

Some in the mob erupted into shouts of glory to the divine nation. Some started walking away in silence.

I cannot imagine it anymore. Or I can only imagine it as its opposite: a stone thrown into a lake, how the stone sinks, and the ripples spread, and then there is nothing.

Then—in *my* world—there is nothing.

When Devi finished narrating Roshni's fate, there was at least a minute of silence in his padded room. I did not know what to say.

Then I said, "So, Ahmed's wife is dead?"

Devi nodded.

"There is no chance she might have survived, perhaps badly disfigured?" I asked.

"No, boss," replied Devi. "Ahmed claimed and buried her charred remains in a Muslim graveyard, three or four days later, when such things could be done."

You do realize that knowledge of Roshni's fate did not make matters any easier for me? If, on the one hand, it left me with no choice but to face up to Ahmed's basic insanity—his traumatized refusal to accept the death of his wife—on the other hand, it added to the sympathy and affection I felt for that quiet, peaceful, almost entirely self-contained man. I could not even blame him for refusing to accept the death of a woman he had obviously adored.

But could I ignore his madness? Did I not owe honesty to him—and to myself and my business? Was I not responsible for the others who worked for me—and with him?

I was still turning these issues over in my mind when the Friday dinner with Shuja Shirmali finally came around. My questions had changed yet again, but of course I did still have questions for the Muslim novelist.

Shuja Shirmali was in his sixties, a large man with a short, bristly beard. He had a deep voice, tailored for audiences, and an appropriate couplet—culled from all the great Urdu poets: Zauq, Ghalib, Faiz, Iqbal—for every topic of conversation. The missus and the two younger writers she had invited for company lapped up his every word.

Even I, despite a degree of skepticism (he made Islam sound like it was Dalai Lama's Buddhism minus the idols), was entertained and almost distracted from my obsession with Ahmed.

But I did manage to insert a question unobtrusively into the conversation, just before dessert was served. It was *gajar ka halwa*, the only kind of *halwa* we make at home.

You see, all my questions had finally boiled down to this one, and its answer, I was convinced, would help me do right by my company. I felt the proper thing to do, as far as my business and other employees were concerned, was to let Ahmed go. But I still hesitated, for I did not want to be unfair to him as a Muslim.

What did I know? Perhaps belief in cohabiting with ghosts was a feature of Islamic beliefs?

But Shuja was conclusive about it when I asked him. "There are really no ghosts in Islam. Souls, yes, but they do not wander about on earth like ghosts. Of course, many Muslims believe in ghosts, but that is all local beliefs. In Islam, Allah placed only two kinds of reasoning beings on earth: humankind, made of earth, and the djinns, made of fire. There is no rationale in Islamic thinking to explain ghosts, though I quite like the idea. Spiritual power, as in some saints, at least we Sufis believe in—but that is not a matter of ghosts. The Sufi saints do not walk the earth as ghosts, they simply have the spiritual power—accorded to them by Allah—to intercede with Allah on behalf of ordinary human beings. There are actually no ghosts in Islam. It might well be the only religion in the world without ghosts!"

Everything was unresolved. All those reports, all that thought, and nothing was a jot clearer. All the explanations seemed wrong. But what I could not avoid facing was the fact of Ahmed's discrepant behavior: he pretended that his dead wife was alive. What was more, after years of this private pretense, for some reason his fictional world had spilled into our factual one. He had inserted me into the fiction of his wife the evening he offered me that plate of *nimkis* and the invisible *halwa*.

Facts have to be faced. I have strongly believed this. And whatever the fiction behind Ahmed's existence, the fact was this: He was living a fiction, and that fiction was gradually living him. He was not reliable. There was no avoiding the matter; he had to be relieved of his responsibilities in my business. I had to protect myself and the others.

Now I knew that in believing his dead wife was still co-habiting with him, he was not even being very Muslim. That knowledge lifted a burden from my soul. It would not be unfair to act as I should—even his religion did not permit belief in ghosts.

It still took me all weekend to gird myself up to the endeavor. I had to face Ahmed. There was nothing else to do.

On Monday, I called him into my office and I told him, point-blank, "Ahmed, I have the highest regard for what you have done for us in all these years. But businesses change, and I am going to begin a process of restructuring. This will involve some transfers and layoffs. I am afraid we will have to let you go soon."

If Ahmed was surprised, he hid it well.

"Is it something I have done wrong?" he inquired passively.

"No, not at all."

He gave me his faint, slightly sad smile. "Mehrotra sa'ab, you know you can be honest with me."

"Nothing to do with your work in any case, Ahmed," I replied. "We need to restructure, as I said."

"Ah," replied Ahmed, "it was that evening at my flat. I had told Roshni the *halwa* wasn't something for you, but she insisted ..."

"There was no *halwa*, Ahmed," I broke in, a bit angrily.

"But there was, Mehrotra sa'ab, my wife had made it ..."

"Your wife died, Ahmed. She was murdered," I broke in again, this time with genuine sorrow in my voice, I would hope. "I was sorry to learn of it, and I wish such saffron ruffians are brought to justice. Lock them up and throw away the key, I say. But you have to face it, Ahmed. Your wife is no longer with you."

Ahmed sat in the chair, a smile still fixed on his face, looking down into his lap. The sudden silence in the room made me hear all kinds of noises: the air conditioner, people talking outside, a phone ringing. Then he muttered something I couldn't hear.

"Beg your pardon," I said.

"Roshni is always with me, Mehrotra sa'ab," he repeated, a bit louder.

I took a risk. After all, I was convinced I was dealing with a deeply disturbed man. I stood up, went around the desk and put one hand on Ahmed's shoulder.

"You are a rational man, Ahmed, a practical person. You need to face up to it," I said.

He looked up in surprise. "But I have always faced up to it." There was something chilling about the calm and stubborn manner in which he responded. I felt repulsed, almost threatened. I struggled to keep my voice even.

"This won't do, Ahmed," I said, returning to my chair. "It is bad for you, it is bad for business. I am giving you one year's leave, fully paid. If you see an expert and come back in a state that I feel is good for you, you can ask to have your job back. Otherwise, well, you have a year's paid leave to find something else."

Ahmed thought about it. "I won't need more than a year," he said, as if to himself. "No, I don't think it will last more than a year now."

"I am glad you agree, Ahmed," I replied. "You need help."

Ahmed smiled again, this time more broadly than he usually did.

At that moment, his very assurance and smile revealed him as irrevocably demented to me, and one part of me finally wrote him off as a reasonable person. Had he raved or argued, had he revealed a nervous tic or a shaking hand, I would have hoped for him, as one hopes for a suffering fellow being. Had he even been angry at me—after all, I was a Hindu!—I told myself I would have reached out and grasped the hands of the man who had buried his beloved as a heap of charred bones and blackened flesh. I told myself I would have shared his tears. But this? Can one pity suffering that refuses to show? Can one comfort someone who remains calm? Can one hope for the healing of a patient who refuses to acknowledge the chasm between health and illness, sanity and madness? Answer me those questions, before you judge me!

"Thank you for your generosity, Mehrotra sa'ab," Ahmed said, smiling, and moved toward the door. Then he turned and added, "I have all the help I need."

He closed the door softly behind him, and I discovered that, despite the air conditioning, my forehead was beaded in sweat, my heart thumping so hard that I thought everyone could hear it.

7

Roughly a year must have passed. I had stopped thinking of Ahmed; he never contacted me after clearing out his cubicle. Oh no, he did once, indirectly; we had given him a farewell gift, a new laptop. A week after he left, he sent us a thank-you card. The staff pinned it up in the coffee nook, and it is probably still hanging there, though, to be honest, I no longer join the others during coffee or tea breaks. But that was it: just that card. Nothing more, and honestly, I was relieved.

Do not misread me. I am not a stone-hearted man. But I try to live a sensible, useful life, and what Ahmed had done by presenting me with that non-existent plate of *halwa* was, what can I say, it was deeply disturbing, if not totally inconsiderate as well. The half-explanation he had given was not much help either. Could I absolve him of madness or serious psychological troubles by beginning to believe in ghosts—and a *halwa* I could not even see? Though I felt for Ahmed and had many fond memories of our years together, building up the business brick by brick, rationally, systematically, when I thought of the plate, I was filled with repugnance, resentment, yes, even rancor against him. Why did he have to plunge me into his delusions and problems? And our last interview, the way he left, calm and smiling, demented beyond redemption, with his total refusal to acknowledge the world of sense and caring?

As the months passed, my dream of the familiar hand clutching an unknown sleeve stopped recurring. I started sleeping soundly. It was back to business as usual.

I thought less and less of Ahmed, and that day, when his name came up, I was almost surprised to hear it. I had not thought of Ahmed at all for weeks, maybe months, before that. His name popped up because the sub-accountant, a young man who had been appointed only six months ago, walked into my office with a ledger and inquired, "Sir, this Mr. Ahmed, who has been given his full salary in absence for a year—his year comes to an end next month. I suppose we should instruct the bank to stop paying him, shouldn't we?"

"Has it been a year?" I asked.

"It will be after next month."

"Well, then, unless we hear from him, in which case I am to be consulted before any action is taken, instruct the bank to stop making the payments after next month," I said almost unthinkingly, like reading out from a book. And I was pleased with the fact that the recurrence of Ahmed's name did not seem to cause me any ghostly agitation. I had distanced that evening from my life. I was behaving as I should: like a sensible businessman.

It must have been a day or two after this episode that I returned to office from a lunch meeting with some visiting businessmen and found something wrapped in a clean white towel lying on my desk. I was surprised. I unknotted the towel and its folds revealed a steel tiffin box—exactly like the one Ahmed used to bring with him. A bit smaller though, containing only two compartments: a small top one and a deeper bottom one. A delicious smell was emanating from it. There was cinnamon in that fragrance, and cardamom, and half a dozen other minute herbs and seeds I could not identify for they grow on an earth I have seldom stopped to observe.

The smell had a physical presence. It swirled out of the tiffin box and filled the room in waves. It evoked a strange feeling of longing and peace in me, and I could feel my mouth water. In the light of what happened, I have thought of this moment again and again, and I assure you, what I felt at that moment was peace and longing—not the longing of unrequited desire but a longing that came with a feeling of trust in its fulfillment. Had I felt terror then, or even doubt, I would have understood it better.

So there I stood, on the side of my desk where I seat visitors. The towel—white cotton—lay unfolded on my desk. In the middle of it sat the tiffin carrier that reminded me, once again in two days, of Ahmed, who had been gone for almost a year.

I opened the first compartment. It contained *nimkis,* exactly like those Ahmed had served me in his flat. I took it off and put it aside. The deeper bottom compartment contained *halwa*: it was of a consistency much denser than a dip but not solid; its color was that of rain clouds in monsoon, a dark, pregnant gray. The fragrance filling my office came from the *halwa*.

I took a *nimki*, dunked it in the *halwa* and popped it into my mouth. It was delicious. It was heavenly! I ate a bit more. Then I looked around for a note. There was none.

I tapped the buzzer to call my peon. "Who brought this?" I asked him. He looked at the tiffin carrier and shrugged. "Must have been during my lunch break, sahib" he said.

"Don't you lock my door when you go?" I reprimanded him.

"I always do, sahib," he pleaded.

I did not retort that he was contradicting himself. He had not been appointed for his capacity to think clearly. That was not his job. I waved him away, sat down in one of the visitor's chairs and ate a bit more *nimki* and *halwa*. There was enough for three or four people. I was sure the missus would love it. She loves these Muslim dishes in any case, and, honestly, this was the best *halwa* I had ever eaten.

Then a thought struck me. I called back the peon and asked him if any of our Muslim employees was working today. We had only two, after Ahmed had left. The peon said they were not.

"Why not?" I asked him.

"They are on leave today," he replied.

"Why?"

"They have a festival, sahib."

"Shab-e-Barat?"

"Yes, sahab, I think that is what it is called, sahib."

He looked relieved. I dismissed him again. Then—as I said, I am not an insensitive person—I started feeling guilty about Ahmed. I did not regret letting him go. He had left me with no choice. One runs a business—and life—on certain principles. That is the way it is. That is how to live a sensible life. Ahmed had left me with no choice but to ask him to leave. But I felt guilty about not even sending him a new year or Diwali or Eid card. Surely I could have done that much!

It was this thought that made me detour to Ahmed's flat on the way back from the office that evening. I could have sent him a card, but I thought I would call and give him a box of chocolates. I bought the best box I could from a fancy department store. When I re-entered the car, I put it down next to the tiffin carrier on the front seat, close to the driver. I was taking the *halwa* and *nimkis* to the missus. As I reclined at the back and the driver revved the engine, it struck me that the chocolates had no smell. What a contrast to the *halwa*! I remarked jocularly on this to the driver: "Isn't it funny, Hari, that the sweets the *firangs* make hardly smell of anything, and the ones we make are so fragrant? I cannot smell these chocolates at all next to the *halwa*."

Hari said, frowning slightly, "I had a cold last week, sir. I think my sense of smell has not come back yet. I cannot smell anything."

I did not give much thought to his response and recommended a potion to him.

It took us a while to find Ahmed's apartment complex. My memories from that stormy night were of little help once we reached the area. But I had the address, and Hari knew the area better than I did. We did find it after stopping to ask three people and driving back and forth in the neighborhood for about twenty minutes.

By then it was around seven at night. As Hari turned the car into the driveway of Ahmed's colony, I was struck by how dimly lit it was. I had obviously not noticed this on the night of the storm. But now I could see that the colony was lit with low-wattage bulbs, glowing a weak yellow and failing to dispel the darkness from most corners and nooks. In my neighborhood, we are used to huge vapor lamps that turn night into day. This difference made the place seem even sadder and poorer than it had on my last visit.

I recognized the spot where we had parked. I asked Hari to stop there and, picking up the box of chocolates, went to the stairs. The half-broken mailboxes were still there, one of them bearing Ahmed's name. I ascended the stairs slowly. Now that I was there, I was uncertain whether I wanted to see Ahmed again. Can one ever go back to the past anyway, I asked myself. Why disturb the past? But I was holding the box of chocolates, which gave me a sense of purpose, and I continued up the stairs.

Ahmed's flat was locked. Not just locked as it had been last time, with a key; it was bolted from the outside. There was a huge steel lock—brand new from the look of it—hanging on the outside. A part of me was relieved; the closer I had ascended to his flat, the more reluctant I had become to enter it again. A recollection of that sensation from the last time had returned to me, that feeling of entering a different medium, something slower, denser, more resistant. Thank God the place is locked, I remember thinking; now I can just leave the box for Ahmed and head home.

But leaving the expensive box outside his door would not be safe, I thought, not in a neighborhood like this. It would probably be purloined before Ahmed returned. The double lock suggested he intended to be gone for some time.

Then I thought of his neighbors, the Sens. What had Devi said? Something about how they were an ailing, lonely couple and Ahmed often looked after them, did their shopping, fetched the doctor. "They love him as a son," Devi had said. I remembered the line. Surely they would be happy to take my box and pass it on to Ahmed?

I turned to the other door on the landing and pressed the buzzer. There was no response. I waited and pressed it again. Just as I was about to turn around, I heard someone fumbling with the latch. The door opened slowly. A small, wizened old man, wearing a banian and dhoti, peered out from behind thick bifocals. "Yes?" he said suspiciously, in a querulous treble "What do you want?"

"It is about Ahmed," I explained.

The man opened the door another inch.

"Are you family?" he asked.

I explained who I was.

He turned around and said something in Bangla, which I do not understand, to someone else in the room. A woman answered him. He opened the door and gestured for me to enter. A rather fat woman, of about his age, was sitting on a sofa in the room. She made an attempt to get up, but it was mostly for show, out of politeness, and remained where she was. Mrs. Sen, I told myself.

"Come in, sit down," she said to me in a loud, deep voice. "So you heard?"

They could read the question from my expression: Heard what?

"You don't know?" the woman asked.

"I just came to pay Ahmed a visit," I replied.

"He doesn't know," the old man said.

"No, he doesn't," the woman replied.

"You see ..." Mr. Sen began.

"Let the man sit down first," Mrs. Sen interrupted him.

I sat down in a chair.

"You see ..." Mr. Sen began again.

"Let me tell him," Mrs. Sen ordered. Then she turned to me and stared. Her eyelids fluttered as if from an irritation. She licked her lips. She spoke suddenly, abruptly.

"He had been wasting away for some months, but looked strangely happy, almost as if he was bathed in an invisible light. He mostly stayed in the flat, but when he came out on occasion to sit in the sun, he would be talking and laughing to himself. As he often did, but a bit more so, more oblivious of others. Nothing obviously wrong with him though. Just two or three days before he, you know, before he, well, he had knocked an evening or two before that day. That was the last time we saw him. He had a heaped plate of *nimkis* for us. 'I was making some for a very dear friend,' he said to me, 'and I made too many.' Nothing wrong with him but there was a mesmeric look on his face, as I told Mr. Sen, who of course cannot see more than a foot in front of him. Then one morning the cleaning woman could not get in. The flat was locked from the inside. When she did not get a response in the afternoon either, some neighbors fetched the spare key he always left with us and opened the door. He was lying in bed, eyes open, with something like a grin on his face. It was unearthly," she said, and as suddenly as she had spoken, she started sniffing into a handkerchief. "Such a quiet man, so helpful …"

Mr. Sen patted her on a shoulder. There, there, he said. She shrugged off his hand.

It took me a while to figure out this had happened seven days ago. Ahmed had been buried within twenty-four hours, in keeping with Muslim traditions, Mr. Sen informed me. There had been no family members. The neighborhood had taken care of it. And now his flat was to be rented out again.

"That greedy landlord," Mrs. Sen sniffed. "He put a lock on it, as if the furniture was his, the moment they took poor Ahmed out."

"We had hoped you were family," Mr. Sen explained in his treble. "You could have taken the landlord to court."

The fragrance hit me like a blow to the face when I returned to the car and Hari opened the door for me. Hari saw me wince and asked me if I was fine. "It's nothing," I assured him, "I just remembered some work."

But what I had remembered, if I had ever forgotten it, was the time when I had failed to see or smell the *halwa*. Ahmed had been alive then, sitting in front of me, eating. The open window, the pool of water on the floor. His mother's face from the wall, with the stare that said, I know you, *but* I do not hold anything against you.

What was it, I wondered as I stooped into the car: Had I been prevented by the closeness of life from seeing and tasting the *halwa* that time, and had the distance of death enabled a connection that life no longer allowed? All along, I had seen the failure as Ahmed's: Why did he have to insert me into his madness, I had asked. But what if the failure was mine? What if it was *my* failure to see, feel, smell, touch—a lack Ahmed could not have imagined or expected after all those years we had shared?

I dropped off Hari at a bus stop, telling him I would drive home myself and giving him two days' leave. Then, I texted the missus that something urgent had come up and I needed to make a quick outstation trip. She was not surprised; it has happened in the past. Business comes first in such cases.

I thought I had to be alone in solid, rational surroundings. The container was still in the car, filling it with smells from a wondrous, forgotten, dense earth.

Which is why I checked into this hotel—what's more solid and rational than an international five-star chain? But I could not rest in my room.

I came down to the bar and found a stranger, lonely like me. We exchanged smiles and names, though perhaps he, like me, assumed a name. We bought each other drinks. Believe me, I did not look like that ancient mariner of the poem we had read in school. Glittery eyes and all. But I must have frightened him anyway. He started looking uneasy when I told him about the tiffin carrier in my car, how it had appeared out of nowhere in my office.

I asked him, what do I do with that tiffin carrier with the ghostly *halwa*? What happens when I open it for the missus—or for you—and you see nothing, you smell nothing. What happens to me then? Can I trust myself any longer? Shouldn't I fire myself in that case, dismiss myself like I sacked Ahmed, politely but definitively, for how can a person who eats and smells invisible sweetmeats run a successful business in a rational manner? I do not even dare open the tiffin carrier in front of you—or anyone else. I do not dare take the risk!

Ignore it, I had hoped he might say. But I knew I could not ignore it; the smell filled my mind even at the bar. I could not talk about it to anyone I know, for then … then that person would be like I was in Ahmed's flat that night of the deluge. That is why I had to talk to a stranger at the bar.

But he was not strange enough. He started squirming on the stool. He mumbled something about it getting late, and went away, leaving his beer half-drunk.

I do not blame him. We all hang on to thin spider threads of sanity, swinging over a chasm, and I had not even told him anything about Ahmed. How could he begin to understand? He sidled away, abandoning his Kingfisher. But I could not stop. I had to tell my story.

I went to the reception and got reams of paper from them, and two extra pens, just in case. I had an idea. I had a hope. I knew I had to find the perfect stranger to listen to my story. I returned to my room and started writing.

The thick curtains helped. The "Do Not Disturb" sign that I hung from my door handle helped. I know that there has been light for a few hours now. But the curtains have kept the room dark, and I have been sitting here, at the desk, in a small pool of light, writing, writing, writing.

My right hand is almost cramped. The story is all told, though I do not know if it is my story or Ahmed's, or whether, as I believed once, we even have separate stories. I will find a title for it, because I am the sort of man who likes to label and file. I will put all these sheets in a folder, if I can find one, and put the folder in the drawer that contains the hotel's copy of the Bible and the Bhagavad Gita. You I can talk to, for you will not even meet me. We won't know each other.

You will stay in this room after I have left, and the women have cleaned it up, smoothened all the sheets, replenished the bar, restocked the bathroom with its little bottles of shampoo and conditioner. You will open the drawer, and read my story, or maybe you will let it stay, to be read by the next guest, or perhaps one of the management staff. Whoever it may be, you will be a total stranger. That is best. Absolute strangers do not need to stop and greet. But sometimes they do. Wasn't that why the ancient mariner had to address strangers too? How can the strange be narrated except to a stranger?

Ignore my story if you want, stranger, but I cannot ignore it. And I cannot share it in my normal world either. That tiffin carrier with the fragrant *halwa* will not leave me alone; I know it will come back next Shab-e-Barat if I try to ignore it. I need to solve this; I have to find a solution to it. Perhaps you, in your remoteness, will be my solution. Maybe it is a kind of redemption to speak, freely and truly, to a total stranger? Maybe there is no other redemption? I will find out. I hope to find out.

And then I might also find out why, as I came down the stairs from Ahmed's flat that evening, what I felt was a vague guilt, like a bony hand clutching at my heart—not the rational irritation I had felt on the previous occasion, or even fear, as one should dread the irruption of the past into the present, the dead into life. Was that why I left the box of chocolates outside Ahmed's door, locked as it was, bending to place it carefully, with both hands, as if it was an offering to something unknown and unknowable?

II
OTHER STORIES

THE CORRIDOR

I grew up in such safety that, inevitably, my first real memory is of fear. They go together, safety and fear; they hold hands surreptitiously, like all those newlyweds used to in my town, pretending to be oblivious of one another.

It was a corridor and a staircase in an old whitewashed mansion, variously partitioned and rented out by a family that had graduated to running a cinema hall. The multihued theater rose next to the house and in stark contrast to it. My teacher lived in one of the partitioned units of the peeling house. She was also my private tutor.

Every evening, when my father went for the second shift at his private clinic—dispensary is what it was called—I would be dropped there. His dispensary was just two buildings farther on, in a sprawling complex of rooms, most of them locked, some used by distant relatives, usually students from the ancestral village. This had once been a street on the outskirts of the town, which had swallowed it up in due course, and the old families had built their *havelis* in it. Now my father drove to it from the new outskirts of the town, where we lived. Those were the years when you did not leave town; you just moved with it.

My father would be driving his slate-colored Fiat; he used the driver only when he was not in the car himself. He was an impatient, irascible man, but he liked driving. He was not irritable when he drove. He drove carefully, his face peaceful. Years later when he taught me to drive, he told me, "The point isn't that you should not make a mistake yourself; the point is that you should be able to avoid the consequences of other people's mistakes." Looking back, I am not sure he managed to do so anywhere in his life except in the driving, though he tried—and he tried to protect his family, desperately, from such consequences.

At six in the evening I would be dropped outside the side door, leading to a flight of stairs sandwiched between a cycle-repair shop and a clothes retailer, up through a dark corridor to the rooms rented by my teacher-tutor and her parents. The corridor was full of discarded and broken furniture, some covered with a tarpaulin. The tarpaulin moved sometimes, disturbed by a stray gust or the rats that nested in the furniture. I was frightened of climbing this stretch of stairs and walking down the corridor to my teacher's flat. That is my first real memory; everything before that might just have been stories implanted in my mind by others, by adults. But this one I remember vividly, not just with my mind but also with my body.

My teacher's name was Sushmita; she was a Bengali. We lived in Bihar, and in those days the best teachers in Bihar came from Bengal. Or, actually, their parents or grandparents came from Bengal. Now, unnoticed to us in the 1970s, they were moving away. It was a trickle; by the 1980s it would be a flood.

Bihar was no longer a safe place for them.

It was not unsafe in the ways in which developed Gujarat or Maharashtra became unsafe for Biharis from the 1980s onward; Bengalis were not chased down streets and beaten up. No one was really chased down Bihari streets and beaten up for not being Bihari. Not as far back as I can remember, not even now.

If Biharis felt an urge to bash up other people, they found fellow Biharis—Bhumiyars against Yadavs, Hindus against Muslims ... it was a long list.

Bengalis had started leaving for different reasons. But in 1970, we had not noticed that they were leaving. The Bengalis had not noticed it themselves.

Sushmita, *Miss* Sushmita, and her parents were not leaving. They had no plans to leave; they spoke disparagingly of the Bengalis who had left. Miss Sushmita must have been close to thirty by then, which was old for a single woman in Bihar, but not too old for the working middle classes in Bengal. I remember her as pretty: compact, rounded, nubile, those are words I would use now.

Then, I just saw her as a strict teacher, who, surprisingly, mothered me in weak moments. I was used to being mothered. I was an only child, and the only son in my generation on my father's side. My parents had had one other son who died in infancy. My father's only sister had three daughters. I took mothering for granted.

As I ascended the stairs to Miss Sushmita's flat, I heard sounds. That narrow dark space was full of startling sounds, largely due to the cinema hall next to it. Voices and music seeped through the walls—muffled, distorted, ghostly. There were sudden silences and explosions of noise. The tarpaulin shapes lay in ambush farther up. My father was always running late (he had a busy practice) and he only waited in the car, engine running, until I had entered the door and Miss Sushmita had appeared in the balcony above, with freshly washed hair—she had long, perfumed, jet black tresses, usually tied into a strict bun with a garland of white flower buds—and waved in response to his sharp honk. He never left before I had entered the door, though, and Miss Sushmita had appeared upstairs. He was frightened of something happening to me. His dead son haunted him. Lots of other things haunted him too, but I didn't know. He was not a man to betray his fears.

I was much less manly. I sometimes intuited that my timidity was a source of worry to my father, but he hid it well, being unbendingly loyal to blood. Even though I knew Miss Sushmita was waiting up a flight of stairs and a short dark corridor, cluttered with generations of broken furniture, haunted by the sounds of whatever film was running next door, I had to force myself up every step. I wished for a brother. I wanted to run down, but I could not. I was not a baby anymore. I was close to ten, as the heavy schoolbag on my back reminded me.

At the head of the stairs, there was a weak yellow bulb dangling naked from a wire. It fused every few weeks and then would not be replaced for days until my father, on one of his visits upstairs, noticed it and got it replaced. The bulb was in no-man's-land; both the landlord and the tenants refused to replace it, ascribing the duty to the other. But then, in any case, there would be power cuts lasting for hours. Private generators had not arrived in Phansa yet. Much of my tuition was conducted by the light of lanterns, flames flickering in the sweet stench of kerosene, soft shadows ebbing like waves on the walls. The lanterns—we called them laaltens—had a small knob that you could turn to reduce or increase the glass-encased flame, which was a source of fascination to me. I was not allowed to handle lanterns back home, so the moment Miss Sushmita left the room, on some quick errand for her parents, I would stop doing my homework and manipulate the flame, creating a theater of shadows on the walls. I was not frightened of shadows in the room.

But each step up the stairs was an effort of will. It did not change for the six years that I continued going to Miss Sushmita's for tuition, from class four to class nine. By the time I was thir-teen, I had stopped believing in God, and consequently also in ghosts. It did not make any difference; Phansa was chock-full of gods and ghosts. My lack of belief rarely survived insertion into other spaces in my hometown.

Upstairs, there was light, finally. And Miss Sushmita. Smelling of soap and some subtle fragrance, usually sandalwood. For the next three hours, she helped me do my homework and crammed me with extra information. I was not the most receptive of students. As I grew older, I merely stood confirmed in my prejudices: mathematics bored me to death, unless it was geometry, and I liked only the theoretical parts of physics. Biology and chemistry always struck me as secular versions of the Quran and Arabic lessons that had been imparted to me for a year at home by a maulvi who committed the mistake of twisting my ears once too often. My mother spotted him in the act and told my father, who promptly fired him. My father was not against a disciplinary twist of the child's ear, or even a slap or two, but he felt, very strongly, that such punishment was the parents' prerogative, and solely the parents'.

Like the Quran and Arabic, chemistry and biology seemed to consist of rote learning with very little practical significance and even less entertainment value. Compared to the threats and dire warnings of the Quran, which did serve to wake you up when the maulvi also had a hand itching to twist your ears, chemistry and biology offered little in terms of human interest. In later years, chemistry picked up a bit, when we were allowed into laboratories, but even then the more interesting chemicals were behind lock and key. Civics and geography and history were similar, though they were sometimes relieved by stories and exotic photos. What I really loved was moral science—it was a Catholic school—and English literature. They were full of stories and human dilemmas; I reveled in both. The nuns thought I was a highly moral boy; they never realized that it was the potential immoralities and actual frailties suggested by the stories that interested me. I was not always convinced by the answers, but I was intrigued by the problems.

Miss Sushmita noticed my love for stories and tried to encourage it. She was herself an avid reader, but she was also an eminently practical young woman, able to do difficult sums in her head without blinking. The books she recommended to me were far too practical and sensible for me; they gave too many answers. Undaunted, she tried for three hours every day of the week except Sundays, from six to nine in the evening, to make me overcome my weaknesses and learn my replies. I think she largely failed.

My father was supposed to collect me on his way back from work around nine. If I sat out on the veranda and leaned over just a bit, something I was fearful of doing, I could even see his car drive out of the gate to the dispensary and drive up to Miss Sushmita's building. He would occasionally come up the stairs to collect me.

We were supposed to eat at nine thirty at home. But I seldom returned before ten, sometimes as late as eleven thirty. My father tended to get delayed. By the time he arrived, I would have been—at least in the early years—fed by Miss Sushmita and sometimes put to sleep in an armchair on the veranda. My father would carry me down to the car. But, on such occasions, he would spend some time, up to half an hour if it was not past eleven, talking to Miss Sushmita. They spoke with an avidity that I would recognize only much later. They did not know that I was not fully asleep, just pretending to be so. I had long realized that the only way one discovered anything of interest from grown-ups was by pretending to be asleep or not there. Papa and Miss Sushmita never said or did anything that they would not have done if I had been awake, and yet I also felt that it would be wrong of me to wake up and deprive them of this short chat, in which both of them—serious people in different ways—laughed more than they usually did.

Going down that dark, frightening corridor and stairs, either in my father's strong arms or holding his fingers, was another matter. Ghosts do not bother you when you are with your father.

At a quarter past ten, the night is dark and deserted, apart from figures huddled at the road corners, warming themselves over a boarsi-fire, and the occasional rickshaw, empty, jolting past in a drizzle of metallic sounds. My father's Fiat is one of the few in town installed with a cassette player; he still plays music on it. It is getting less and less frequent, though I am to realize that much later. A *qawwali* by Sabri Brothers is on. The headlights cut into the cool February night.

Papa honks once before turning into the gate, and the gateman, ancient Boodhe Mian, who also doubles as the gardener, opens the gate even before the car reaches it. There is a short, curved driveway of red bricks and a portico under which he parks. The driver, in a rush to go home, hovers around us, waiting to take over the car and drive it into the garage by the side of the large, solid house, built, I have been told, under the direct supervision of my father.

My mother is waiting up, the food ready. She has not eaten. She never does. She always cooks the dinner herself, despite the cook. The cook only serves to prepare the other meals, or dinners when we have guests.

I can see the happiness on her face when she perceives that I am not too sleepy. It means she will be able to eat with me. She sees me for less than three hours a day, sometime between three thirty, when I return from school, and six, when I drive off with my father for tuition at Miss Sushmita's. The only meal she is certain of having with me on weekdays is breakfast. Often I return fully fed from Miss Sushmita's, and if I am too sleepy, I am put to bed immediately by Zaibun or Sajjo Bua, while my parents eat.

We are used to elaborate meals. Any dinner with fewer than four dishes will be criticized by my father. He grew up in a household with cousins and village relatives eating together, all lavishly served by my grandfather's two cooks. He is sometimes unhappy about the fact that he employs only one cook and two maidservants, plus Boodhe Mian, the gardener. The driver comes only for the day. There is an army of other part-time "day servants," but they do not count for Papa, who is used to servants living in special quarters attached to the house. When he built this house, he got such quarters added at the back, though the Patna architect's plan had not provided for them. But my mother, who usually accepts his wishes, refuses to hire more people. Not "full-timers," as she calls them. "We don't need more full-timers," she says, and rightly so.

To which he shakes his head and says, "There were at least ten servants living in my father's house."

"They had to feed at least twenty people at every meal too," my mother replies, sensibly. "We are only three."

Even I can see that she regrets saying this, whenever it slips out. It reminds them of their lost child, my older brother who died a few days after birth, and the miscarriage that my mother had when I was less than two years old. They never speak of these matters, almost never. I learn only later that my mother cannot have another child because of the miscarriage, which had nearly been fatal.

One night my father arrives early. Miss Sushmita is still trying to explain some algebra to me despite exaggerated symptoms of drowsiness on my part.

My father comes up. Miss Sushmita goes out to the veranda. I hear him say, "They have bombed our airfields." There is a moment of silence. Then Miss Sushmita says, "It really is war then." My father replies, "Officially." There is another moment of silence, and then he adds, "Well, it was coming. We'd better get it done with now."

I go out into the veranda. I still remember their faces. Miss Sushmita's face is what our poets love to call "moon-shaped," and my father's is rugged, much darker, but more like that of a Hollywood star than a Bombay one; there is a strong resemblance to Cary Grant. Both faces are full of concern. But there is a difference too. On my father's there is an extra shade of worry. I notice it; I do not fully comprehend it.

The evening is unusually silent. Has the theater been closed because of the news? That could hardly have happened. Maybe it was a break between shows. Maybe it is just the way I remember it. But what I recall is an intense silence, as still as a delicate plate of china on a mantelpiece.

Miss Sushmita's parents are in their room; they never come out during my tuition hours unless required to do so. But they must have overheard. The silence is broken. A radio is switched on in their room; I can hear it being fiddled to catch the news.

I go up to my father and, unusually, take his hand. I don't know why I do this. He looks startled.

Miss Sushmita offers to make tea. My father shakes his head. "There is tension in town," he says, "I think I should get back home to Zubeida." Zubeida is my mother's name.

Miss Sushmita looks surprised. It takes her a second to understand the statement; it is as if she has to translate it from a less familiar language into her mother tongue. Then she says, "You don't think there will be riots?"

My father shrugs his broad shoulders. "But we are safe here," says Miss Sushmita.

"Yes, you are," replies my father. Does he actually stress the "you"? No, I am almost certain he would not. It is my memory that stresses it today, as I write this down. It is what has happened since then that puts the accent on that word.

My mother has already heard the news. She often has the radio on when she cooks or relaxes, though never if my father is around. TV has not come to Phansa yet, and my father does not like the radio. Too much noise from the world, he growls, though Ammi once divulged to me that they used to listen together to the radio, especially the songs on Amin Sayanti's Binaca Geetmala radio show, in their early years together. Papa can still whistle entire film songs, a surprisingly artistic talent in a man of his type, though he never does so without much urging.

I know Ammi has heard the news because, unusually, she is waiting on the veranda. She runs down the five marble steps and hugs me as I get out of the car.

Boodhe Mian shuffles up after locking the gate and carries my father's medical case out of the car. He puts it in the drawing room and leaves. Boodhe Mian is an aborigine from Chota Nagpur and, by tacit and mutual understanding, seldom enters the house. He has a shed next to the cowshed at the back of the fields; he will not live in the servant quarters in our backyard. He has a fascinating weapon, shaped like a bow, but used to shoot stones or hardened baked-clay pellets. Once or twice, he has demonstrated it to me by shooting down a bird or a squirrel— something my father forbids— with incredible accuracy. He eats them. He also eats crows. As I am allowed to shoot crows (and lizards) with my air gun, I often gift him with dead crows, which he accepts with glee and then grills over an open fire, between two sets of bricks. He is an old man but walks erect and fast; he seldom says more than a word or two.

My mother asks Papa only after Boodhe Mian has left, "Is it true?" It is typical that she wants Papa to confirm news that she has heard on radio.

"Yes," says my father, "there is war." Then he adds, again, "It had been coming in any case."

I have known that too. Ever since March, when the Pakistani army went in to prevent a democratic upheaval in East Pakistan and the Mukti Bahani opposed them, war has been in the air. The more warlike of my classmates have been going about chanting nationalist slogans in the schoolyard until stopped by the nuns. Miss Sushmita and her parents—Mr. and Mrs. Basu, as I called them, both retired and surviving on savings and various government pensions—had been glued to the radio at times, following the development across the border, rooting for their fellow Bengalis, even though the Mukti Bahini was mostly Muslim, as were the opposing Pakistani forces. Almost everyone I knew was in favor of Sheikh Mujibur Rahman and his Mukti Bahini, though in my family this support was tempered by a degree of unease. I knew why it was so: my father had cousins, some of whom had grown up with him, in both East and West Pakistan; three of my mother's many sisters and brothers were in West Pakistan too, as was my grandmother's twin sister, who haunted family talk like a ghost, occasionally made real by a "long-distance trunk call" from Karachi. But I still did not know fully what difference all that made.

The dinner was laid out as usual, though it was early. My father must have called. Everything was as it would have been, but only Zaibun was there to serve dinner, which basically meant refilling my father's water glass at regular intervals and clearing up afterward. Sajjo Bua, who was actually one of my grandmother's servants, had gone back to Maalkini, as she and all the old servants called my grandmother. I called her Dadijaan.

My mother had made a special effort. Apart from the two vegetable curries and daal, there were shami kebab and murgh musallam, teh-daar roti and matar-pulao to go with them, and, finally, phirni for dessert. Dinner was the heavy meal in those days, and not just in my family.

It was heavy in all families where people had the leisure to pity those who went without food on the streets.

But despite the lavish spread, we ate in silence at the old mahogany-topped table my father had inherited from his grandfather. There were twelve chairs, five on each side. My father sat at the head, my mother and I on each side of him. Zaibun hovered around us. The cook, Wazir Mian, came in only once or twice to ascertain that all was well.

I think my father spoke only once during the meal. "It is good that you sent Sajjo Bua back to Ammijaan. I will call her." He called my grandmother Ammijaan.

To which my mother replied, "Do you really think there will be trouble?" My father did not say anything. He helped himself to another piece of chicken.

When I wake up next morning, the sun is stronger than it should be. Usually I am woken up around seven, so that I have forty-five minutes to get ready and eat my breakfast before being dropped by car at my school. My school bell rings at eight. If we are more than five minutes late, the gate closes, and we have to wait until the morning prayer and assembly are over at 8:15. Then the principal, a much-dreaded sixty-plus-year-old American nun (one of two left over from colonial times) with a stout wooden paddle that she does not hesitate to employ on our bottoms, turns up and gives us, and our parents in absentia, a thorough dressing down, in which our chronic unpunctuality is exposed as an offense against God, humanity and the nation, in that order.

But this morning it is not the seven o'clock sun that greets me. And I have not been woken up; I wake up on my own. I look at the bedside clock; it shows 7:55.

I sit up, frightened. I will be very late this morning. I shout for Zaibun, for my parents do not seem to be around. "Why didn't you wake me up?" I cry out in Urdu. It is her job to wake me, alarm clocks not being considered reliable enough. "Now Sister Lisa will *paddle* me." I use the word *paddle* in English because there is no Urdu equivalent for it, and anyway it is a kind of euphemism. It is when Sister Lisa makes you stand stiffly and hits your bottom, or, if you are older or a girl, your outstretched palm, with her softball bat.

"Sister Lisa-visa *baddle* your enemies," replies Zaibun from the lobby, where she is dusting something. "There is no school today, babu."

If this is what war entails, I remember thinking, then it is a pity we do not go to war more often.

After breakfast, my father says to me, "Let's go visit your grandmother."

It is only now that it strikes me: my father is also home. "Aren't you going to the dispensary?" I ask him.

"Not this morning," he replies. "Maybe in the evening. We will see."

My grandmother dresses in white saris with colored borders. Her house is white but bordered too.

She does not let anyone talk until she has fed them. She still has more "full-time" servants than my parents. All of them bustle around me; all of them seem just a bit terrified of my father, perhaps theatrically so. They have been with her for years. She pays them from money that she has saved up, which is not much—a matter of much consternation to my father, I discover later—and a monthly sum that my father sends her. When she runs short, she sells off a bit of the land that she has inherited from her husband. The land has been divided up between her, her daughter and her son, that is, my father, in keeping with Islamic laws. This means that it has been divided into four equal parts, with the women getting one part each and the son inheriting two parts. The house she lives in should have been divided up as well, but her two children will not think of it; it was built by their father.

Dadijaan is a small, compact, imperious woman. She sits in her armchair and expects me to come and kiss her on the cheek, after which she kisses me on my forehead and mutters a blessing. She continues sitting in her armchair as Sajjo Bua, in her fifties the youngest of her old retainers, and a couple of decrepit crones lay out a second breakfast for us. We protest that we have already eaten, but she ignores our protests. "Children can always eat again," she says to me.

It is only as we eat our second breakfast—Dadijaan joins

us at the table but hardly eats anything—that my father gets to bring up the matter that has brought him here.

He talks between incursions by Sajjo Bua and the decrepit crones to serve us, mostly me.

"You should move in with us, Ammijaan," he says, with the directness that he is infamous for.

She ignores the remark and urges me to have another jalebi. This brings one of the crones bustling in to plop two steaming kachoris on my plate. After she returns to the kitchen, where they are probably eavesdropping on everything in any case, my father repeats what he has said.

This time Dadijaan answers. "What will I do at your place, son?"

"What you do here, Ammijaan."

But she just smiles in answer to that and shouts an order to the decrepit crones.

"At least move in with us until this war is over," Papa presses the issue. "Nothing will happen in these parts. It is the Civil Lines."

"Who knows? If something happens, it will be too late to act. Mobs materialize without prior notice."

"Nothing will happen." She closes the discussion and switches it with another remark. "Aapa called last night."

My father looks even more worried. Aapa is what she calls her twin sister, older by a few minutes, in Karachi.

"She and her family are fine," Dadijaan adds.

"She should not have called," my father says, petulantly. "Not now."

"Of course, she had to call. She had heard the news too, and she is my own sister."

"Don't shout it from the rooftops, will you?" says my father, irritably.

"It is not as if other Muslim families do not have relatives in Pakistan."

"Other Muslim families live in *mohallas* that cows fear to enter!" my father retorts. "Anyway, they are not as visible as we are. You should move in with us, Ammijaan."

"You have not taken a single jalebi, Hussain," says my grandmother in reply. "Here, have one."

I know that whenever she addresses my father by his first name, she is either happy or angry.

SCAM

A little Turd sits outside the metro exit closest to Jantar Mantar and offers to polish your shoes when you leave the cool, clean interior of the underground for the smog and heat of the pukka-baked roads. You say no, having little time for Turds of that sort and because your boy-servant has already polished your shoes twice this morning, once of his own volition and once because you were not satisfied. So, yes, you say no, and plunk, the little Turd has deposited a real piece of turd on your shoes. Oh, you do not see him do it, but where else does real turd come from if not from little Turds like him? See, see, saar, says the Turd, speaking Ingliss to you because he can see that you are the type, not phoren but polished. See, see, saar, he says, Ssuu durrty.

The little Turd has made a mistake. Just because you are polished does not mean that you only speak Ingliss. You slap him on the head, twice. It is a language he understands. You thrust your shoe out to him and say in Hindi-Ingliss-Punjabi: *Saaf karo, abhi saaf karo shoes, harami,* and you add a few choice gaalis in Punjabi that need not be put down on paper. If you had not added those gaalis, the little Turd might have raised a racket. But he is convinced he has made a mistake. He was fooled by your patina, like those Spanish adventurers were once fooled by the shine of the copper on the Indians in America: What

glittered on you was not gold. The little Turd realizes his mistake.
He is a quick learner. You have convinced him in two expressive
local languages: Punjabi and Slapperi. He wipes your shoe with
a rueful pout. Then, as you turn to leave, he cannot resist the
question. He is still intrigued. He needs to place you. Perhaps
he maintains a record of his mistakes. He is a professional, just
as much as you or anyone else in Delhi these days. So he asks
you with a comic salaam, still in Ingliss, Vaat you do, saab, vaat
job-vob, saar?

You have won this battle. You are in an expansive, forgiving
mood. You decide to answer him and mention your profession.

Repoder? Jurnaalis? he says.

Then he shakes his head, as if that word explains his mistake.
Jurnaalis, he repeats. Jurnaalis. Repoder.

The street outside Jantar Mantar is a favorite haunt of journalists.
Next to the nineteenth-century observatory are broad pavements,
and these broad pavements often host impromptu protest groups.
Sometimes for months. There is one occupied by victims of the
Bhopal gas leak. They have been sitting there, on and off, for at
least a few years, down to five or six people now, mostly ignored
by journalists. A much larger group, bathed in flashlights, belongs
to the Narmada Bachao Andolan. They are an intermittent fixture
on this road, and because their champions include celebrities like
Arundhati Roy, they attract media flashlights once in a while.

Actually, they are the reason why that little Turd doing
his Su-paalis-and-turd-on-shoe scam made such an error of
judgement when staff reporter Syed Malik of the *Times of India*
exited from the metro. Reporter Malik has long harbored a crush
on Arundhati Roy. Hence, he had dressed up with extra care
this summer morning and left his Bullet motorcycle behind to

avoid the blackening traffic fumes, before doing his round of the Narmada Bachao Andolan protest meet. Not that it is going to be noticed. The famous Roy is there, but too uninterested in her fame to give interviews, let alone be whisked away for a fawning chat in one of those three-, four-, five- and probably-more-star hotels around the corner.

So, after jotting down the day's press declaration in his spiral notebook, and pocketing the day's press release, Repoder Malik heads for one of the four-star restaurants on his own. The Sangharsh Morcha had announced a press meet there, and now that Syed is here he might as well look in, collect the releases and, hopefully, guzzle down a cold beer or two. On the way, he notices that a new tent has come up at the corner of Jantar Mantar; it bears the obligatory banner, stating "Justice Delayed Is Justice Denied" in English. There is no one under the tent—a rickety affair, broad enough to harbor four or five people at the most—so Repoder Malik cannot inquire about the nature of the justice that has been delayed or denied, though it is doubtful that he would have stopped to do so anyway.

Past the revolving glass doors of the restaurant, in the air-conditioned, potted interior, Syed spots the table reserved for the press meet by the Sangharsh Morcha. Not much of the press has met. Apart from Syed, there are only two other reporters, one of whom is actually the editor of his own newspaper and, it is rumored, subsists on the beer and snacks offered at such meets. Handouts are handed out, appropriate noises are made over soda and lemonade—it appears that the Sangharsh Morcha has a Gandhian aversion to alcohol, which might also explain the low turnout of reporters. Just when Syed is about to sneak away from a rather drab press meet, the room is visibly brightened by the entry of two women.

Two very different women. Syed knows one of them: Preeti, who works for one, or probably more, of those internationally visible NGOs. The other is a sturdy blonde woman wearing a kurta and jeans. Preeti is wearing kurta and jeans too, but while the blonde looks tired and sweaty, Preeti, like all women of her refined class (at least to Syed's working-middle-class eyes), never looks ruffled or unkempt. Syed has seen women like Preeti step out of 45-degree heat in July without a bead of sweat on their foreheads, no sign of a damp spot under their armpits. He suspects that their air-conditioned cars offer part of the answer to the riddle of their unruffled coolness, but there are moments when he feels that they are another breed, a superior subspecies that has evolved beyond bodily fluids and signs of discomfort.

Preeti spots Syed and, ignoring the others, launches into the kind of direct speech that, Syed suspects, is also part of the evolutionary progress of her subspecies. For God's sake, Syed, she says, what are you reporter-veporters doing here in this fake palace? There are two dharnas just outside, near Jantar Mantar.

Been there, Preeti, replies Syed.

Not the Narmada one—Preeti is too radical to espouse specific causes—there is another one. From near some Tikri village in Bihar, where there has been a caste atrocity that has not been reported by you guys.

If it has not been reported, it has not happened.

Oh yeah? Ask the woman sitting there, and her cute little son. They have experienced it. Father killed, uncles chased away …

Just two? A woman and a child?

Both Preeti and her foreign friend nod in affirmation.

A scam then, pronounces Syed. Look, Preeti, these days you cannot have a caste atrocity without a couple of politicians turning up to squeeze the last drop of political mileage out of it. If it's just a couple of people, it is a scam. Another way of begging …

Oh, you are so cynical, says the foreign woman, in a vaguely European accent.

Not cynical, just a regular reporter, a staff reporter, contributes Preeti, and then she introduces the two to one another. The foreign woman is a visiting journalist from Denmark called Tina. But it is spelled with an "e," she explains: Tine.

Why don't you check it out?

Check what out?

Your scam.

Waste of time.

Or afraid of being proved wrong?

I am not wrong.

Check it out then. They are just outside anyway.

What if I am right?

I will buy you dinner.

Where?

Chor Bizarre.

Deal?

Deal.

Good. Preeti, you are the witness. Let's go.

The Press Club on Raisina Road, not that far from Jantar Mantar, has been nicknamed the Depressed Club. Its whitewashed colonial facade has worn thin, its floor stained by tired feet, bleak notices and cuttings on the bulletin boards in the drafty corridor, lawn outside showing only a hint of grass, tables piled with dirty plates, broken chairs, a slight smell of urine from the toilet next to the main entrance. There, that evening, seated at a corner table, wreathed in miasma, which consists largely but not only of cigarette smoke, we can find Repoder Malik, Preeti and Tine. Plates of kebab and beer have been ordered—gin and lime for Preeti—and conversation is going strong. It is still hovering around the scam protest, which, on inspection, had turned out to be that rickety tent with the banner in English: "Justice Delayed Is Justice Denied."

I told you it was a scam, said Syed.

How do you know?

I recognized the boy with the woman. He runs a shoe polish scam there. Tosses rubbish on your shoes so you have to pay him to polish them up.

So?

So!

So, it proves that he does something for a living. They said they have been here for months, petitioning every person they possibly could. They showed you the petitions and letters that they have actually paid people to write for them.

Another way to beg.

Oh Preeti, are your journalists always so cynical?

Only the men, Tine. Only the men.

Oh c'mon, Preeti. You know I am right. Tine doesn't know the place, but you know how these things happen.

I am not sure I do, Syed.

What do you mean?

Look, that woman had a plausible story. Small village in Bihar. Land dispute. Husband killed, murdered one night on the way back from work. Police not interested in clearing the matter. Dismissing it as the kind of thing that happens to people who belong to the so-called de-notified tribes. Uncles frightened into moving away. Land forcibly occupied. The woman tries to get justice, finally takes whatever she has and comes to Delhi with all her papers. Sounds plausible to me. Given a plucky tribal woman, which is what she seems to be.

She is not a village woman from Bihar, and that boy is too slick. He has grown up here on the streets.

You would be surprised how quickly kids pick up habits and words.

Still, I bet you my bottom dollar—a scam.

Why don't you go to Bihar and check it out? asks Tine suddenly.

Check it out? The woman's village does not even have a name. Near Tikri village she says. Even if I could locate Tikri village.

Take them with you, says Preeti. We will come along. I will raise the money for it.

I'll have to take leave, Preeti.

Take leave, Syed.

Take leave, Syed, will you please? Tine adds, looking soulfully at Syed with her speckled greenish-blue eyes.

What a waste. OK, if you ladies insist. Let me see …

∽

Time does not fly around Jantar Mantar. That is the magic of such places. The buildings change their billboards; the streets change their beggars, protesters, pedestrians, cars. But all change is for the same. Time simply repeats itself, again and again.

Jantar-mantar, say children—abracadabra. Whoosh! Something happens. Plastic flowers turn into a dove; a rabbit is pulled out of the hat. Jantar-mantar, murmur old women in villages, and they talk in whispers because they are speaking of devious doings, black magic, sorcery. Jantar-mantar, say foreign-educated doctors in the cities, and they are referring to the hocus-pocus of quacks, the *vaids* and hakims who still cater to the rural poor and either heal them or kill them.

But Jantar Mantar in Delhi is a sprawling observatory built in the nineteenth century. It is used to observe nothing. It is useless. Around it rise useful buildings: offices, hotels. Buildings that change and are always the same. Around it walk useful people: reporters, politicians, businessmen, doctors, bureaucrats. People who change and are always the same.

So what surprise is there if, a month from the time we last saw him agreeing to go to Bihar, we see Repoder Malik walking out of the same metro exit where he had encountered the Turd, the boy whom—along with his mother—Syed and Preeti and Tine had escorted back to Bihar just a few weeks ago? Repoder Malik has changed and perhaps he is still the same.

In any case, he is looking around. He has been doing this almost every day since all three returned from Bihar: he looks around for the Turd, the little boy, for he knows that the Turd must have returned to Delhi. After all, scams have their fixed scenarios, tricksters their territory.

Repoder Malik walks slowly, darting quick glances to the left and the right, thinking of that lightning trip to Bihar. He is not sure what happened there, but he will not concede this uncertainty to himself.

The woman and the boy had refused to go back to Bihar; Preeti and Tine had to convince them with assurances of safety and gifts of money. And it had been like that all the way to Gaya, by train, and then to the village of Tikri by taxi; the woman and the boy had wheedled a minor fortune out of the two women. Syed had expected that; it confirmed his suspicions. But he had not anticipated the certainty with which the woman led them to Tikri, and then two kilometers out to a small village and a plot of land she claimed was the disputed property. That is when it all happened, and Syed is not very certain even now about what it was.

It was late, the summer evening still steamy, the wind having dropped. Tine was pink, a few beads of sweat had appeared on Preeti's neck. Both were conservatively clad—a reflection of their notions of rural Bihar—in cotton *shalwar kameezes*.

The plot they stood on was rocky; it did not look worth fighting over to Syed. The woman and her son, the Turd, were pointing out things like the palm trees that demarcated one end of the field, the huts—thatched, hunched—of their village in a far corner, and the small hillock that marked the other end of the field. A fly kept buzzing around Preeti, evading her attempts to fend it away with her *anchal*, which she wore draped loosely around her shoulders. Tine had long discarded her *anchal*, displaying a rather low-cut *kameez* that, Syed felt, was less conservative than most shirts and T-shirts.

As the woman rambled on—the usual lament, how the land was taken away from her, how her husband was murdered, how the police did not listen to her—suddenly, on the hillock, there stood a group of men. They appeared as if by magic— jantar mantar Syed almost thought—burly, impassive men against the reddening sky, leaning on their staffs. They could have been any group of villagers on their way back from work, attracted by the sight of a taxi and three obviously urban types, one of them a *firang*.

But that is not what the woman and her son, the Turd, thought. Or pretended. Syed is not sure. For suddenly there was a cry of fear from the boy, and the woman started cursing and weeping. The boy said, Run, ma, run, they said they would kill us if we came back, run. Then both were running—in the opposite direction, toward the palm trees and the brambles and jungle behind the bleak, tall palms. Syed shouted, but they did not stop. Preeti and Tine had not even had the time to react. When Syed looked up at the hillock, the men who had been standing there were gone too.

They waited an hour, until it got dark, and the taxi driver insisted on going back, with or without them.

They came back the next day. They spoke to the local police, who denied that there was any land dispute or that any murder had taken place. What woman and son, the thana inspector asked. Syed's press card turned the police obliging and polite. The inspector took the three outsiders to the nameless village—fetid with garbage next to mud huts with holes in their thatched roofs—and shouted for some old man to come out. Come out, hey you Dhanarwa! When the man, stubbled, limping, coughing, came out of the low hut, the inspector said to Syed, Sir, describe the woman and her son to the man. He is the headman here. He knows everyone.

Syed did as he was asked to do, with Preeti adding a word or two of detail.

Description done, the inspector addressed the old man in a gruff tone. So, he said, do you know this woman and the boy?

The old man shook his head silently. A crow cawed and perched on the sagging roof of a hut behind them; with its dagger-like beak, it started to dismember a small rodent held in its talons.

Speak up. Has someone cut your tongue off? Speak up. Not to me, you dolt. Tell sir and the madams here, the inspector barked.

No, huzoor, said the old man.

You do not know the woman? barked the inspector.

No, huzoor.

Or the boy?

No, huzoor.

The inspector turned to Syed, Preeti and Tine, all three now sweating profusely in the hardening sunlight of the late morning. See sir, he said, see madam, what did I tell you? 420. The woman was a 420. A chaalu fraud. You should lodge a case with us. We will catch them for you.

On the way back next day, as the train shuddered on the old tracks, Syed had his doubts. He was familiar with such interrogations by police officers. The way they asked questions often determined the answers. And though he laughed away Tine's offer to buy him dinner in Chor Bizarre on their return to Delhi—I lost the bet, she said—Syed still could not settle the matter in his mind.

However, Preeti and Tine had been converted: they spent much of their waking hours on the train trip back to Delhi calculating the money they had paid out to the woman and her boy, the Turd, on the way. By the time the train reached Aligarh, they had agreed on the exact sum of 5,941 rupees.

But doubt nibbled at Syed. All the way to Delhi. And that is why now, even weeks later, when Preeti and Tine have already turned the experience into slightly different anecdotes for friends, Repoder Syed Malik walks past the Jantar Mantar area, on the lookout for that little Turd. Under the tall gleaming buildings he walks, on the broad sidewalks with protest banners, past this useless observatory, always darting glances to the left and right. On he walks in this place that changes and is always the same, looking, looking, looking.

THE UBIQUITY OF RIOTS

1.

"It is not a riot, is it?" asks Ammi, as always trusting my father more than the radio. Papa has not left for his dispensary, which he usually does around eight in the morning. "Well, that may come too," he replies, drily, "what with this war going on." Then he notices me hanging around in the room. They stop talking. My parents never discuss Hindu-Muslim matters in front of me.

School is suspended. It is the day after news reports of "communal tensions in town." Stock phrase, sometimes followed by the stock word "riot." Even I know what it means. The Hindu day servants, who went home early yesterday when the rumors incubated, have not returned. This too is to be expected.

Later, my father goes to the dispensary, but only around noon. This is late. His "compounder," Khan Saheb, calls to say that there are patients waiting for him, and everything seems to be "theek-he-thaak" in town.

My father is not afraid of going to work. He appears to believe that "communal tensions" have nothing to do with him, as if he is neither Muslim nor Hindu. This is strange, for, unlike one or two people that we know, he is not a communist. He pities the poor but believes in the sanctity of private property. He prays whenever he can, though he never goes to the mosque on Fridays. He has strong faith in the Quran as the undiluted, revealed word of his God. And while he acts as if he occupies a charmed space where he cannot by harmed by rioting Hindus or rioting Muslims, he is also very afraid of leaving us alone.

Our house—and that of Dadijaan, my grandmother— is in the Civil Lines; they are the only two houses that belong to Muslims in the neighborhood. Around us are the houses of motley middle-class families, one Sikh and the others Hindu. Behind us lies a colony of less affluent Yadavs, struggling up the Hindu hierarchy in recent years, who have the reputation of existing on the fringes of the law. By contrast, my father's clinic—"dispensary" is what it continues to be called—inherited from his father, who had inherited it from his father, who were both successful general practitioners, is on the margins of a Muslim *mohalla*. It is to this place that he drives off in his Fiat. The driver, Mohun, has not turned up. My mother wants Papa to take Boodhe Mian with him, but he rejects the suggestion, brusquely. It is as if Ammi has said something insulting.

"Theek-*he*-thaak?" Ammi mutters to a maid, as they stand under the portico watching the car leave. Sparrows and mynahs are loud on the lawn. There is no sound of traffic from the street. "Why didn't Khan Saheb say a clear theek-thaak?"

2.

With my father gone to work, I have the day to myself. Most of the large house is unoccupied, but I prefer to play in our compound, the front of which has been sculpted into a garden, and the back contains a field used to plant seasonal crops, a cowshed and groves of mangoes, guavas and other trees. My mother is busy running her household, complaining about the servants who have not turned up to the servants who are there. Her complaints, unnoticed by her, for she does not have that kind of mind, are turned into something else by the live-in servants, all Muslim, who agree, vehemently, about the "untrustworthiness" of the absent lot.

Running the household is not a simple matter of feeding my father and me. Even the servants ("staff" is considered a big city affectation), who outnumber us, do not explain the full scope of her concerns. The burden of the past rests on her. It is often recounted—in language hazy with nostalgia—that my grand-father was joined by at least a half dozen guests for each meal, including breakfast. "Everyone from that English lady doctor to the Congress mayor would come to eat on such short notice that I always had to employ two cooks," says Dadijaan, and she is the only person who recalls it with impatience, not nostalgia. My father has not continued that tradition, partly from choice, as he is less sociable, and partly due to changing times. But he still returns for his lunch around three, usually collecting me from school, with a guest or two. It can be a junior doctor he has taken a liking to, some visiting relative who catches him in a good mood or, on occasion, pharmaceutical representatives—and once the manager and star clown of a traveling circus who had fallen ill and been treated by him. If the person is a woman, stranger or not, or if it is a man related to the family or one of my father's doctor friends, she or he eats inside with us. Otherwise, he is served on the veranda, with Papa joining him after the main dishes, for dessert.

Such eventualities combine with sundry other chores to keep Ammi occupied throughout the day. She lets me play all over the compound, occasionally sending out a servant or walking up herself to check. This cannot happen if Papa is around; he is worried about me getting bitten by snakes, or falling into the old well next to the cowshed, or being gored by the two cows we still maintain, despite the fact that ancient Boodhe Mian is invariably around and keeping an eye on matters.

My mother understands me better; she knows I am a timid boy who will neither poke my hands into a hole nor approach the cows alone. Though I am bigger than most of the other boys, I never pick fights in school or climb trees beyond the safer, thicker branches. The only bit of wildness I indulge in is my insistence, despite subtle discouragement from my father, to go hunting with my air gun and, occasionally, the slings that I have been taught to make by Boodhe Mian. From the few stories I have been told about him, I know even then that my father had been different. He had gotten into scrapes, and once—Dadijaan had narrated, in a rare reminiscent mood—when he was only eleven or twelve, Papa had driven off a hyena that had grabbed a younger cousin during one of their trips to the ancestral village, simply by launching himself unthinkingly at the beast. But hyenas only exist in zoos now, as far as I can tell. And I love hunting, though more in my mind than in person: that immediate communion with another being, those vast regions of aloneness it opens up.

3.

I sneak out with my air gun. Papa has expressly instructed my mother not to let me walk around with it. Today. Why not, I had asked. My father had frowned. Not today, he had stressed, addressing my mother more than me. He is not a man used to offering explanations. But, given the shortage of day servants, my mother is too busy to notice me pull the air gun out of the box-room where it is stored and leave by one of the back doors.

I like to imagine myself alone in that large compound, lost in a jungle, tracking animals and evading cannibals. I still read

Tarzan, Lord of the Apes, and *Phantom: The Ghost Who Walks.*
The attempts by my tutor, Miss Sushmita, to move me on, rather
precociously, to Dickens, Premchand and Tagore have been
partial failures; these texts I've read as mere chores, though I
have finished most of Louis L'Amour and series like the *Three
Investigators* and the *Famous Four.*

It is a warm afternoon for December. There is no wind; I
cannot fly a kite. All the servants are busy and unusually irritable. I have no sibling. The air gun is the only option.

I am trying to get close enough to a crow—the only bird
I am permitted to shoot—but crows are wary creatures, with a
fairly good radar system; if you stalk a crow on one tree, crows
on a tree much farther off spot you and caw a warning. That
is when I see it. A parrot, but not of the usual sort. This one
has a fringe of incandescent colors running around its neck.
It is hanging from one of the top branches of the huge gular
tree that overshadows the cowshed, pecking upside down at a
gular fruit. It is too far away for me to be able to hit it. I prowl
closer. The space around the gular is used to tie and groom
the cows and is bare of bushes or trees. I expect the parrot
to spot me and fly off with a squawk. But it doesn't. I reach
within shooting range, though the parrot is still high above
me—the gular, along with the jackfruit tree, is the largest in
the compound. It knows I am there but stays hanging from the
branch, twisting its head around to look. The parrot's bright
green shows through the duller green of the gular leaves. The
day hangs heavy like wet clothes on a line. But that far up, there
is some breeze, and the small leaves seem to shimmer around
the parrot. I do not imagine I can hit it; air gun pellets are
easily thwarted by leaves and twigs. I take aim, still expecting
it to fly away.

The little breeze that there was must have been behind me. My pellet carries to the parrot. No twig diverts it. The magnificent bird squawks and falls, fluttering from one branch to another and finally to the ground, from which it tries to fly again—I can see one of its wings is not working. It hops, falls and then propels itself into some bushes growing by the back wall.

I am so shocked that I just stand there. Then I look around to ensure that my accuracy has not been observed. Not only am I not supposed to shoot any bird other than crows, parrots and such exotic species are specifically under my father's aegis. Having ascertained that I have not been observed, I go back to the house, tuck away the air gun and pretend to read a book.

4.

My heart is making a noise that I am afraid must be audible all over the house. I feel I have done something wrong, played a dirty trick of some sort. There is a deep sadness in me about that wounded bird, desperate in the bush. I want to help it, mend it, but I do not know what to do. I know that my powers to bestow death do not come with the ability to restore life.

I tell myself that the stray cats frequenting our compound will get it. There are monitor lizards, one about four feet long. Dhanwa snakes—essentially small pythons—have been spotted. They are not killed, as they are not poisonous. There is even a family of mongoose somewhere in the increasingly tangled reaches of the compound. Not to mention the swift shadows of hawks. I think of all the ways this parrot can be put out of its misery and be of use to some other animal or bird. I tell myself that this is the way of nature. I am a proper little philosopher in my room, with a book shielding me from scrutiny.

But I do not fully convince myself. Not then, not later.

5.

My mother enters the room at about three. "Papa called," she says. "He will be here with your Miss Sushmita and her parents. They are staying with us for a few days."

Miss Sushmita is my class teacher, one of the "civilians" employed by the nuns who run my school. She is also my private tutor: I go to her place for tuition every evening, except on Sundays.

"Mr. and Mrs. Basu too?" I ask. I know Miss Sushmita's parents only as Mr. and Mrs. Basu.

My mother confirms it.

"But why, Ammi?"

I sound petulant. I do not feel comfortable with Mr. and Mrs. Basu and though I like Miss Sushmita, I resent the idea of having her in our house. A class teacher, even one who is also your private tutor, is not supposed to live in the same house as one's parents, not even for "a few days."

"They have to stay with us."

That is all Ammi offers as an explanation. In her own manner—softer, slightly distracted—my mother is as little given to offering explanations as my father.

6.

Let me confess this now: My parents were unwitting victims of what I later came to think of as the Prince Siddhartha

Syndrome. Remember Siddhartha-who-became-the-Buddha?

Siddhartha was brought up by his parents in total ignorance of all the troubles and sufferings of the world. My parents did something similar. Problems were rarely discussed within earshot; they never indulged in any intimacy in front of me that well-behaved siblings would not permit themselves; I had to wash myself, and gargle with Dettol and water every time I went to the cinema. It was a long list.

But they forgot one thing. Prince Siddhartha must have slept in his own room in another flank of the palace. I did not.

Despite all the bedrooms in the house, I still slept, in a separate bed, in my parents' master bedroom until the age of twelve. They assumed that when I was supposed to be sleeping under my sheets and the mosquito net, I was actually asleep. That was seldom the case. I would lie there, eyes shut, sometimes even half-asleep, waiting for them to start speaking to one another as they changed in the storage room, what we called the box room, or the bathroom and then lay in bed. Mostly, they uttered a phrase or two between pauses. But sometimes they argued; sometimes they discussed problems. It was all forbidden territory to me, had I been awake. That is why, I guess, I had learned to pretend to be asleep. The forbidden is always irresistible. I remember thinking quite early in my life that if God, or Allah, was as smart as they said he was, he would not have forbidden Adam and Eve that apple or jackfruit or whatever it was.

With or without the Serpent, Adam and Eve could hardly have resisted forbidden fruit.

7.

Miss Sushmita and the Basus arrive with my father and are given a couple of rooms upstairs. Papa does not go to work that evening. I know why. The "tension" has increased. There is "curfew" in parts of the town. I do not fully understand what a curfew means, but I assume that it is a bit like when the math teacher has us all standing on one leg as punishment for a misdemeanor, and we are not allowed to move or whisper. I imagine the streets of Phansa filled with grown-ups standing on one leg, unable to whisper, and even though I know the scenario is not probable, I understand that Miss Sushmita and the Basus would not like to be curfewed. What I do not understand is why they have to come over to us. They could have just stayed in their flat. It is obvious that people are curfewed only if they go out into the streets.

My mother is fatigued that night. My father seldom has people staying overnight—and she has made a special effort for dinner. My parents have also looked unusually strained ever since news of the war broke out. I know that some of it is due to the fact that we have relatives in both the Pakistans, of whom the closest is Dadijaan's twin sister and her family in West Pakistan, though Papa is even more concerned about a school friend, Sikandar, who had settled down in East Pakistan. Still, that does not seem to explain why they look so strained: How can a war being fought almost a thousand kilometers away to the east and more than a thousand kilometers away to the west affect us here in Phansa?

There is a dressing table next to their large double bed. My mother sits there, removing her make-up, undoing her hairdo and taking off her earrings. She had dressed formally for the evening and the dinner, while the younger Miss Sushmita had appeared with even less makeup than usual and no flowers in her hair. That must have been when I notice, for the first time, that this is what happens every time they meet: My mother makes more of an effort and dresses as if she is going to a party, and Miss Sushmita rubs off her makeup and dresses as plainly as possible. I also notice that while my mother, never very talkative, speaks as little or as much as she usually does to my father, Miss Sushmita, who loves talking to my father on other occasions, says much less.

Outside, the wind has built up, and I can hear it in the large mango tree at the corner of the house. It is a langra malda, "the king of mangoes, which is the emperor of fruits," as my father would say, invariably, every summer. The tree, I have been told, was planted by my grandfather to mark the birth of my father.

Papa is in the bathroom; he always takes some time in there, as he shaves in the evenings, not the mornings, before going to bed. He leaves the bathroom door slightly ajar. They are talking softly across the room, assuming that I am fast asleep.

They are discussing some blasts in town in the Muslim *mohalla* on whose fringes my father has his dispensary and where the Basus rent their flat. It catches my attention; this is news that has been kept from me all day.

"Some idiots," says my father. "They set off a few crackers to celebrate news of some rumored Pakistani advance up north. Fools. Donkeys."

Idiots, donkeys and fools in the same breath. I wake up fully but stay sensibly under the razai. Papa never uses harsher words: He has only three other words that are worse: "flirt," "communist" and "intullcatool," which is his purposefully mispronounced "intellectual."

My father continues from the bathroom, "Of course, then some Hindus threw stones at them, and they threw stones back, and soon there were mobs on both sides, clamoring to do a mini-version of the war next to my dispensary."

"I hope you didn't go out," my mother says. She knows my father feels that not just the dispensary but the entire area around it needs to be treated with the respect that his father and grandfather, who had practiced there, inspire in him.

"I would have gone out and thrown a few bricks at both the sides, but the police were prompt for a change. They turned up in a jeep and fired a few rounds—thankfully in the air—which sent all those warlike braves running into their houses. And now we will probably have a curfew for two days. What a waste of time!"

My mother is silent for a moment, as she removes her long earrings. Then she says, almost under her breath, "Well, we shouldn't complain; we have guests as a result."

For a moment, it looks like Papa, still in the bathroom, has not heard her. Most people would not have. But Papa has exceptionally sharp ears, honed by the stethoscope perhaps, though my mother had once joked that it is genetic: "For your Dadijaan evidently hears half of what we say from her house." (But I know it is just the servants in both the houses gossiping.)

After a longer silence, I hear my father respond, "What could I have done? They were frightened, and they live in a Muslim *mohalla*."

"We live in a Hindu *mohalla*. It is not as if we are moving anywhere safe," my mother counters, unusually. She does not argue with my father; it is not in her nature and my father does not take contradictions lightly. He either retorts harshly or, what is worse, goes into a long, injured sulk that makes everyone feel guilty.

"We don't need to," my father replies from the bathroom. I can hear his voice filling with irritation, and I am afraid he will say something cutting to my mother. I hate such occasions.

"We have been in Phansa for three generations." There is a
pause as he runs the tap to wash the shaving foam off his razor.
Then he adds, "The Basus came here only some years ago ..."

My mother is in an uncharacteristically argumentative mood
that night. I hear her mutter, "Well, I married into Phansa only
some years ago."

I pray my father has not heard her. But he does. There is a
snort of exasperation from the bathroom. Just as I am preparing
myself for a hurtful retort that will set my mother's and father's
faces against each other for the rest of the night and well into
tomorrow, as if on cue, the phone rings.

8.

It is unusually late at night for the phone to ring. My father
steps out of the bathroom, some shaving foam still on his face.
My mother is startled too. She looks up at him expectantly and
moves to the lobby to pick up the phone only when he nods.

I hear my mother speak into the phone; her voice slips from
a terse hello to more relaxed tones. She re-enters the bedroom.
By then, my father has washed his face and is clad in his night
dress of lungi and banyan.

"It is Benarasi-uncle," she says to him.

"This late?" he replies, "Is someone ill?"

"No, he just wants to speak to you."

Benarasi-uncle is past seventy, closer to eighty; he was a
friend of my grandfather's. His family name is Agrawal, but the
family is from Benaras, and that is how he is known to us. My
grandfather, while he was alive, was called Doctor-uncle in the
Agrawal family. After my grandfather's death, my father—called
simply Dr. Mallik, the uncle being dropped because of his lack of

seniority—has taken over the role of family doctor in the Agrawal family. It is not a professional role; no money is paid or demanded, instead there is a regular tradition of reciprocal dinners every few months. Only the Agrawal men eat meat, so only the men come to our house for dinner. When we go to their house—for rigorously vegetarian Marwari cuisine, which is a culinary highlight for us—we take sweets, bought from a Brahmin restaurant, for the women in the family. In the summers, we send them a large wicker basket of our mangoes, layered on fresh straw.

Papa speaks for some time on the phone. When he comes back, no trace of his irritation at my mother's remarks remains; he is smiling.

"What did I tell you?" he says to Ammi, "Benarasi-uncle called about the situation in town. He wants us to move over to his place. I told him we have no reason to feel threatened."

My mother smiles and shakes her head. "His place is in the heart of the chowk. Not even one Muslim family there," she adds, musingly.

"So what?" exclaims my father in a debonair voice, parting the mosquito net to get into bed.

9.

Of course, there is no school the next day. Curfew is lifted all over town late in the morning, but the nuns, always a bit wary of religious people of other faiths, decide to play it safe and cancel two further days of class. I see it as a bounty: a holiday! It makes it bearable to be taught at home, for a couple of hours, by Miss Sushmita. Even there, my mother intervenes, and dissuades Miss Sushmita from teaching me any longer, as she does not want the Basus to feel that they have to justify their stay.

On the second day of my holiday, after Papa drives off to his dispensary, the Basus retire upstairs to their room. They have offered to go back too, but my mother has asked them to stay for one more night and dinner. One of my father's many cousins—all of whom seem to have moved to Pakistan or the Middle East and are now heading westward ho!—is going to visit us for a couple of days, and my mother feels uncomfortable with most of my father's family. This cousin lives in the USA. He is visiting our ancestral village—he goes there every year, on his annual visits to India, while my father was last in the village years ago—and now, with the curfew over, he is going to visit us too. I think my mother retains the Basus largely as social distractions and local support. It is not the cousin who worries her, but his retinue: He always travels with a flock of distant relatives from the village, who attach themselves to him the moment he arrives in Patna.

Papa is driven off in the Fiat, a bit later than usual. The driver is back. Miss Sushmita stays downstairs with my mother, helping out with the domestic chores. Both my parents have requested that she not teach me today, and, finally understanding their insistence, she has acceded. With Papa gone, the women relax. Apart from the fact that they do not resemble each other, they could be sisters, bustling about the house, attending to domestic matters or listening to news or music on the radio.

I go out to the backyard and am in the process of stringing up a kite—the breeze is back too—when I spot the parrot again. It has fluttered into the back courtyard. What impulse has brought it toward us, toward human habitation and away from the temporary safety of the bushes by the back walls? I can tell it is the parrot I had shot yesterday: one of its wings drags, and it has that brilliant ring of color around its neck.

It has snuggled against the trunk of a guava tree, and could have almost passed for a clutch of fallen leaves. But it moves feebly when I approach it. I rush back into the house to fetch my mother. She is sitting at the dining table, Miss Sushmita opposite her, with a bowl of rice between them. The Philips radio is playing some old songs. They are sieving the rice for impurities and giggling at something. They do not understand me at first; they think I want to drag them out to show them a parrot on the guava tree, and they are obviously having too good a time to want to indulge in ornithology.

"I think, I think it is hurt," I announce. No George Washington by any means, I know enough to keep my fibs to the bare minimum and be economical with the truth too.

"Get Boodhe Mian," says my mother, but then Miss Sushmita, more indulgent as the guest, suggests, "Let's go and take a look." The women pick up their shawls, and we troop through the pantry and the kitchen to the back veranda.

"Oh, poor thing," exclaims Miss Sushmita, adjusting her shawl against the breeze, "It is hurt."

"A cat must have got it," I add, quickly.

Boodhe Mian is called, and he catches the bird in his large, gnarled hands; it makes almost no effort to evade him.

"What do we do with it?" my mother wonders.

The parrot is covered with a wicker basket. Boodhe Mian is dispatched to the local market to get a cage, while pieces of fruits and a bowl of water are prepared. We are interrupted by squawks from inside the basket. But they are not squawks. They are words. The parrot is repeating, in its high-pitched voice, "Siya Ram, Siya Ram, Siya Ram." It belonged to someone, a maid notes, it must have escaped from a cage. "It is an unbelieving *kafir*," adds the maid, looking pointedly at one of the Hindu day workers who has returned and is now sweeping the yard. "So, cut its throat, na," the day worker retorts. My mother and Miss Sushmita pretend not to comprehend their dialect-inflected bickering.

By the time the parrot, not chanting anymore, is put in a large cage, along with the water and pieces of fruit, we hear honking at the gate. Papa's cousin, whom I know basically as Umrika-walley Uncle but address generically as "chacha," has arrived.

10.

Umrika-walley Uncle has recently moved to USA, I think he was in Houston in those days, after accumulating a small fortune working as a banker in Saudi Arabia. He belongs to a number of uncles and aunts—all my father's cousins—who had grown up with my father, as their own father had decided, early in his career, to quit working as a lawyer and live off the family lands in the village. The family lands provided him with a comfortable income, but not enough to send his large brood of children, mostly sons, to good schools and colleges. That job had been entrusted to his successful older brother, my grandfather, who had only a daughter and a son in any case and was more than willing to adopt his brother's children when, roughly at the age of six, they were shooed out of the ancestral village and deposited in our town to live with my grandfather. I knew it was something my grandmother had resented but was not able to stop. All the boys and the two girls had proved to be bright students and had gone on to become doctors, engineers and, in this case, a banker. The girls had been married off, because their father had not only quit law, he had also discovered religion around the same time. It was said by my father's cousins that their progenitor had quit law because "it involved lying and he refused to lie." But once when I mentioned this to my grandmother, she snorted and said that, well, it also involved listening to others, and he preferred to talk all the time, may Allah have mercy on his soul.

In any case, the cousins—as their father had left them nothing apart from his share of the ancestral lands—had all slowly moved to the Middle East to make a tax-free fortune and grow identical beards, and were now, as inevitably, drifting westward. It took me years to make sense of this drift because all of them were inordinately proud of being part of Western science and technology, as if moving to America had put them on the same level as Einstein, and extremely disdainful of Western lifestyles and cultures. In my family, we had nothing like it—neither awe at the technology nor disdain for the cultures, except in a polite way, when my father unthinkingly agreed with his cousins in fleeting conversation.

The honking breaks into our ministrations to the wounded parrot, which is studiously ignoring us except when, once, Miss Sushmita moves her hands too close to it and it tries to take a bit off it. It had not tried to bite Boodhe Mian probably because his cracked, gnarled hands are impervious to almost everything. Boodhe Mian shuffles off to the gate. Both women utter exclamations of surprise, addressed to different gods, and hurry away to clear the dining table.

Umrika-walley Uncle—whose arrival has changed his designation to "chacha" in my vocabulary—pulls into the driveway in a canvas-covered Mahindra jeep. He sits next to the driver, beard luxuriant in the breeze; at the back of the jeep jolt sundry, vague relatives from the ancestral village. Chacha is clad in kurta pajamas, with a plain shawl wrapped around him; the relatives are dressed in fancy bell-bottoms. We are half-expecting this particular lot; they are his usual retinue. They come with him every time—they are three brothers, each resembling the other so closely that I can barely tell them apart—and they always dress identically. This time, however, I can see that one of them has grown a small Frenchie beard, nothing as luxuriant as Chacha's though.

They spill out of the jeep and would have pinched my cheek and made a lot of familiar jokes to me, which would have left me blushing and confused, but they catch sight of Miss Sushmita standing behind my mother and are subdued. I thank my mother, silently, for her foresight. Chacha is more natural; he always is, and I quite like him despite his habit of giving me a friendly lecture on Islam and the Quran every time he visits us.

Ammi phones Papa, who replies that he has only a few patients left and should be back in an hour. This, we all know, could mean two or three hours. Coffee—not tea, which would be served within the family and to local guests—is brought out with snacks and offered to the guests on the front veranda. Miss Sushmita sits down with my mother, much to the discomfort of the village relatives.

Ammi asks a servant to take the luggage up to the "guest rooms" and there is a hurried consultation among the guests, after which Chacha apologizes to my mother and says that they were actually planning to stay with my aunt—my father's sister—as they had stayed with us last time. While he conveys this to my mother, the village relations cannot resist stealing a few hostile glances at Miss Sushmita.

My mother is sincere in her regrets. She insists that all of them have to come back for dinner tonight—which they accept—and that it would have been no trouble at all to have them stay here, for there were rooms enough in the house, and in any case they were family. My mother is seldom this verbose with anyone except me or Papa, or her own sisters, or the older servants. It is the first time, perhaps, that the suspicion dawns on me that my mother is by no means as "innocent" as my father considers her, or as "simple" as my father's family implies that she is.

Less than two hours later, as soon as my father has arrived and greeted them, the horde piles back into the jeep, in the precise order in which it had exited, and drives off to my aunt's place. They will be back for dinner in a few hours, at eight or so. We never eat before nine.

Really a pity you could not stay with us, my mother says as the Mahindra jeep drives off. She sounds—and probably is—genuinely sorry.

"I wish he would not bring along his gang of aluminum *chamchas* with him," is the only thing my father mutters.

Obviously, aluminum *chamchas*—literally spoons, figuratively sycophants—are cheaper than stainless steel ones.

11.

The trick to making proper Murgh Musallam and the trick (pickled mustard sauce) to making Sorshe Diye Macher Jhol; Ammi and Miss Sushmita had exchanged such tips all evening, as they took over the cooking totally, much to the consternation of the cook, who would otherwise have been asked to make at least a dish or two.

Both Murgh Musallam and Macher Jhol are ready and being kept warm by the cook when our guests turn up at nine, not eight, following my father's car as they had gone to the dispensary at eight instead of coming to us and facing a man-less— I and servants obviously do not count—universe. It is a small cavalcade, as a thin man on a black Yezdi motorcycle follows the jeep. He sports a black leather jacket, a rare possession in Phansa in those days. I know him as Med Rep Shaqil, which is the way my father refers to him; he is a medical representative, vaguely related to my father through his intricate village connections, which have proliferated like weeds in the four generations that we have lived outside the village. He is one of those medical representatives and junior doctors who turn up every winter evening at my father's dispensary, where they have rigged up, at Papa's expense, an outdoor, spot-lit badminton court. On occasion, one or two of them are invited over for lunch the next day, but almost never for dinner.

The elder Basus had decided to avoid the gathering; they have pleaded age and, eating hurriedly at eight, had retired well before the cavalcade arrived. Miss Sushmita has stayed up, partly because she has been exchanging culinary tips with my mother, and partly because she has surreptitiously supervised my home-work between trips to the kitchen. She is very plainly dressed, as always having divested herself of makeup or flowers in the presence of my mother. Ammi has made a bit more effort, but far less than she would have done in order to go to a party in town or to the cinema.

Dinner is served almost immediately. It proceeds sedately, with the village relations not addressing Miss Sushmita at all, and Umrika-walley Uncle addressing only one or two formal remarks to her. They do not have to bother, as Med Rep Shaqil, who evidently knows Miss Sushmita from before, is monop-olizing much of her attention. It cannot have escaped Miss

Sushmita's attention that all the guests, except Med Rep Shaqil, are somewhat hostile to her presence in the house, and I sense my mother notices it too. Of course, my father does not, which is not surprising—he is not sensitive to social nuances—but which is fortunate, as he would have taken umbrage on Miss Sushmita's behalf.

12.

The only time the hostility becomes visible is when the Macher Jhol is brought in. It is introduced by Ammi as having been made by Miss Sushmita, at which my father helps himself to a double portion, remarking that the one thing we Biharis cannot cook, and Bengalis can *blindfolded*, is fish. At this, one of the village relatives—the one with the Frenchie—sniffs and says that actually he thinks Bengali fish dishes are … are … "I lack the word for it," he falters, dramatically, "being a crude rustic."

"Smelly?" an identical brother suggests, not looking up from his plate.

The second of awkwardness that settles on the table at these remarks is dissipated by Med Rep Shaqil, earning him a grateful glance from Miss Sushmita. "So says the famous rustic who has been living in the state capital most of his life and is going to work in Dubai now!" he quips laughingly. They are vaguely related, as is almost everyone in the clan. Frenchie-beard grimaces at that, but he has no option but to treat it as a good-natured joke, for Chacha, obviously not wanting to spoil the atmosphere, laughs uproariously. Maybe Chacha also appreciates the reference to Dubai, because he has arranged the job through his contacts. Frenchie-beard and his look-alikes observe Chacha's cue; over the next few years, they will even grow their beards to resemble his, as all of them follow Frenchie-beard to Dubai for stints of tax-free work and return to buy properties in the village and Patna.

13.

The dinner is over around ten and the jeep leaves soon afterward. The brothers, swathed in blankets on top of their woolens, huddle together at the back, for the December night has grown chilly. Med Rep Shaqil is the last one to go, and that too very reluctantly when Papa, infamous for such directness, remarks to him that it is late and he ought to be getting home now. As there is no school tomorrow—the last day of my holiday bounty—I am expecting to be allowed to stay up. I seldom return from my tuition before ten on regular schooldays in any case, but now I am bundled off, as Papa, Ammi and Miss Sushmita lounge in the drawing room, having a last round of lemon tea. Papa unusually puts on one of his old Nat King Cole records. He has stopped buying music, but he still retains a pile of 45s and LPs from his college days and the early years of his marriage. My introduction to music, until I finish high school, comes largely through these records, and I can still recall some of the covers: Belafonte, Nat King Cole, Doris Day, Talat Aziz, Begum Akhtar, Mohammed Rafi, Asha Bhosle… There is one Beatles record but no Bob Dylan. The Indian collection, I later realize, is more up-to-date than the Western one.

I want to join them too. I get out of the mosquito net ostensibly to inquire after the parrot, which has finally nibbled at the fruits, I am told. I take advantage of the inquiry to linger in the drawing room. I have seldom seen all three of these adults looking happier. I am being sent back to bed again when the air-raid siren goes off. We have been instructed to close the windows, draw the curtains and switch off all the electric lights whenever the siren sounds. Now we do so. Miss Sushmita stays where she is, surprised by the urgency with which we go about switching off lights and drawing the curtains under my father's instruction. We even switch off the record player. We return to the drawing room, now lit by a single candle, and my father asks Miss Sushmita if she is certain that the lights are off in their rooms upstairs.

She is bemused. "It's just an exercise; the Pakistani air force cannot reach us, and why would they even care to bomb this pathetic little town," she replies, laughing. "We don't switch anything off in our flat when these stupid sirens go off."

My father looks irritated, but he always speaks gently to Miss Sushmita.

"We do," he says. "Can you please check?"

"But why? It's not as if anyone cares!"

My father is uncomfortable, so my mother has to provide the answer. "You don't have to be careful. We have to be careful," she notes, her face studiously neutral in the weak yellow candle flame.

It is then that realization dawns on Miss Sushmita.

"Hé Ram," she exclaims, and runs upstairs to make sure that the lights are switched off.

SHADOW OF A STORY

There was a time when I worshipped stories.

In this, I was typical of a certain class of people from my generation. My education in the humanities predisposed me toward it, as did my situation in small-town India, where so many stories circulate and are trusted. When I wrote my Ph.D. on Salman Rushdie and Amitav Ghosh at Magadh University, published three years later, in 2006, by Cambridge Scholastic Press, stories were the linchpin that held together my argument. Rushdie and Ghosh are very different writers, as everyone knows, but they are both obdurate champions of stories. Arabian nights in shining armor! I looked at how these two major writers interrogated history through stories. It was already a common perspective to adopt in the 1990s, I know that now, but I had grown up in a small town, Phansa, and was doing my Ph.D. in another, Gaya, and I felt, while writing my Ph.D., that I was at the cutting edge of thought. And maybe I was. It was thought that cut both ways.

But that is what I say now. Nearly two decades after I completed my doctorate, having left Phansa for Gaya, and Gaya for Patna, where I had a contract position for a few years, I finally obtained tenure at a private university in Surat, which is where I write this essay. I have come to look at stories with greater suspicion. If you look at my Cambridge Scholastic Press book, you will find a chapter—it verges on euphoria—on Rushdie's *Haroun and the Sea of Stories*. Sometime back, I returned to the novel as part of a master's course offered at my Surat institution, and though I loved much of it with my old enthusiasm, I was also irritated by its celebration of stories.

"Believe in your own eyes and you'll get into a lot of trouble, hot water, mess," says Iff, the genie, in that novella. It forms the core of Rushdie's celebration of the imagination. But I was rereading *Haroun and the Sea of Stories* after the pandemic, during which even some of my colleagues had believed that consuming and bathing in cow dung was a cure or a protection. I was rereading it with the remembrance of Donald Trump, and his cries of "fake news," and his supporters' remorseless tendency to believe in his conspiracy theories. I could no longer ignore the fact that the capacity to imagine what cannot be seen—and to will it into some sort of existence—seems to exist on all sides. Religions, for instance, depend heavily on belief in what cannot be seen: All Ayatollah Khattamshuds are loath to have their theological P2C2Es explained away. Why had I not noticed this, or made anything of it, in my thesis?

But the realization had come to me over the past few years; a distinct unease with stories had started to limn my earlier, and continuing, belief in stories. For instance, when, while recovering from a largely asymptomatic bout of Covid in late 2021, I finally found time to read Ghosh's *Gun Island*. The novel had come out in 2019, but I had been saving it up for a calmer period; I am a great admirer of Ghosh's oeuvre, especially his early works, discussed in detail in my thesis. *Gun Island* started beautifully, with Ghosh's trademark combination of creativity and scholarship, but somewhere around page 34, I stumbled across a conversation that made me put the novel away for the time being. It was between the narrator, who is a Bengali scholar, and another character, a famous Italian scholar, Cinta.

The narrator is taking Cinta around Calcutta, and they run into a tent featuring a *jatra* performance based on legends of the snake-goddess Manasa. Cinta wants to attend the performance, and the narrator disdains it as something that "goes on for hours with absurdly costumed figures screeching in falsetto voices." Cinta, who attends the performance while the narrator goes for a walk, is delighted by it. The narrator tries to attribute her delight to Cinta's possibly exotic view of India, but Cinta points out the total involvement of the audience in the stories and notes how religion is also part of supposedly secular Western cultures. It is all about celebrating stories again, as if the belief that stories evoke in many was simply a life-affirming matter.

Two decades ago, while writing my Ph.D., this would have been manna from the postcolonial heavens for me. I would have lapped it up. I still saw the truth in Cinta's observations, but the passage irritated me, and I put aside the novel until I was in a better mood to read it. I thought about why I was irritated, and what came to mind were recent media photos of pyres burning, bodies floating down the Ganges during the pandemic. I also recalled my frustration with my servant who, in April 2021, simply had to attend the overcrowded Kumbh Mela, for, as he told me, "This is a special year, as foretold by our sages." There were stories everywhere, and not all of them had the same effect. The same story could mean so many things, as Macbeth discovered far too late. I knew that now. I tried to discuss it with some of my colleagues, but they scoffed me for being influenced by "Western thinking," in terms that uncannily resembled Cinta's dismissal of the narrator's objection in Ghosh's novel. But I was not like the narrator. I had never even been abroad, unlike many of my colleagues who are better placed politically to avail themselves of academic jaunts funded by government bodies. I wanted to say to them: but stories are also terrible things, like God, who, after all, is the greatest story of all! There is nothing reassuring about stories! Even their beauty can be deadly! They cast strange shadows!

It was then that the story came back to me. How had I forgotten it? Well, almost forgotten it. I had thrust it into the depths of my subconscious, where it had glimmered occasionally, like a trace of bones in the desert, but then been promptly smothered under more sand. Surely, it must have been because I did not want to remember it, because it ran against some of my deepest convictions—convictions that, to be fair, I shared with my generation, and with such great writers as Ghosh and Rushdie?

Because when it had happened, it had left me shaken, sleepless for nights.

It had happened soon after I finished my Ph.D. I was back home in our ancestral village, to which my parents had just retired, after nearly four decades in Phansa—my father had been a grade two officer in PWD. We are traditionally a landholding family—I guess, technically, you would call us "landlords," but that would be misleading, as we have enough land to live off and cultivate with the help of hired hands, but not more than that. There were never elephants or horses in my family's past. But my parents were happy to be back in the village, tending the fields directly and not via middlemen and on the occasional visit, as in all those years when my father was "in service." It helped that my father had more status in our village than he had in Phansa, and my mother's family had belonged to the village too, though they had sold off their lands and migrated years ago. I was the youngest, and with nothing to do, unmarried, it made sense to live with my parents, help out a bit on the farmstead and apply for jobs.

It made sense, but it was also difficult. I had visited the village two or three times every year, mostly for weddings or festivals with my siblings or parents, but I had grown up in Phansa and gone to university in Gaya. I was a townsperson. After the first few days, my parents could see that I was restless, walking the same three paths and participating in the same two conversations, usually about crops or indigestion. Jobs were not coming my way—I had not even been called for an interview yet. I could have gone off to my older brothers now settled in Phansa and Gaya, but then I would have had to share a room with one of their children and listen to their well-meaning but deeply irritating lectures on my future prospects. Here at least I had my own room. And I had my father's motorcycle, an ancient Bullet that he had brought back with him from Phansa. He never used it now, preferring to go to the neighboring mart in a village eleven kilometers to the north, on the highway, on his Mahindra and Mahindra tractor. I could take the Bullet and drive around—a motorcycle being the best way to negotiate rural paths. I just had to be careful to return by night—Maoists are active in these regions, especially in the forests and tribal villages to the south, though I did not see why they would bother with me; we are not really upper caste or rich. And the other drawback was the occasional effort by my mother to marry me off, using the stick of unemployment and the carrot of a dowry. You can start your own business then, she would note. I had nothing against dowry, but there are reasons, reasons I have not told my family, why I could not marry a woman, why I am still unmarried, and happy with that.

So I would chug back on the Bullet in the evenings, wash the dust off myself at the well in the courtyard, go into the kitchen for a bite and listen to my mother try to foist a girl on me. But my mother, I knew from experience, was far less of a haranguer than my brothers or their wives. Sooner or later, some other woman would pop in, and mother would be distracted by the village gossip. It was better this way. My father mostly let me be, unless he needed help in the fields, which, of course, I provided.

That is how my days were passing. I read the newspapers and, once a week, accessed the solitary computer cafe at the neighboring mart, looking for positions, sending off applications, also for a postdoc or two, and checking for the replies, which, if they arrived, were inevitably in the negative. During the busy seasons, I helped my father. The rest of the time, I prepared my thesis for publication—there had been a couple of rejections there too, for I had aimed big to begin with—or I took the Bullet out for a spin.

It was on a day toward the end of the kharif season, when there is still water in the furrows and runnels, but not on the roads and pathways. The land looks kinder. It is green. Not just the paddy, which is yet to be harvested, but also the roadsides, the hills, the forested regions. This is not a region where the wilderness is green all through the year. Even when you bike on unpaved roads into the hills and forested areas to the south, what greets your eye is not the canopy of a forest but a ravaged land, far more brown and red with the soil underneath than green with leaves. Even the trees are mostly stunted and twisted, hardy survivors in a land drained of water, with gnarled branches, leaves wrinkled like old paper, foliage powdered with dust. All this changes with the first monsoon outpour, when suddenly there are explosions of chlorophyll, as if nature was lobbing hand grenades of greenery at you in a guerrilla skirmish.

Suddenly, within a day or two, there is too much water; there is too much greenery. But by the end of the kharif season, all this has settled down. The rainfall has stopped, or diminished to occasional drizzles. The green has receded but not disappeared. There is a ceasefire between civilization and nature. Soon the fields will dry, and crops be harvested, and civilization will take over. The green will disappear; the brown and red will show themselves again. Civilization will march on, also into the hills and forests where you do not see many settlements, sheering them of greenery, draining the underground water as it gets sucked up by tube wells in villages, dammed and channeled into towns. Dust will descend on the leaves and shrubs as if they were the furniture of an abandoned house covered with thin sheets until the owner returned. And then, summer would arise, with mangoes true, but also with drought, and blistering heat, and hot winds of dust blowing across the region, winds that the elders claimed were like and not like the loo winds of yore.

This was the truce in-between: the monsoon of nature's short rebellion and the summer of a more obdurate reality. It was the best of times to sit astride my father's black Bullet and strike out on the roads, the paths, even the footpaths of the region, wind in your hair, the helmet put away. Often, I would take a book along, and pack some samosas or pakoras. I always had a plastic bottle of water. I would mostly head into the hills and forests to the south, and it was on such a trip that I saw it.

I was about seven kilometers out of the village. This is where the level fields ended and the forest and hills started. You could still encounter some plots, but much of it was difficult to cultivate and, technically, part of a forest reserve. The tribals living inside and around it mostly used it for foraging, though, obviously there was a lot of poaching and illegal felling of trees, blamed on villagers and Naxalites, but almost invariably the work of organized mafias from neighboring towns like Gaya and Phansa.

The last bit of paved road had ended a kilometer back, and I was now on a dust lane. Soon I left it for a narrower path, carved out by the feet of humans and the hooves of cattle, leading up the hills. Only a motorcycle can negotiate such paths. It is, however, a bumpy ride, and you seldom go faster than ten kilometers an hour. It is better not to, as sometimes the path curves around the hills with a fall of twenty or thirty feet on one side, a height that can kill you if you slip down it on a motorcycle. My intention was to reach a vantage point higher up on the hill and sit down to read. Soon it became risky to continue on the motorcycle, so I stopped, took out my small *jholla* with the book and refreshments, chained the Bullet to a tree—though it was unnecessary—and continued on foot. Twenty minutes later, I was seated on a slab, near the summit of the hill, biting into a samosa.

To the north, after an expanse of hilly terrain, there spread the desiccated plots of land that, I knew, stretched all the way to my village, which lay just below the horizon. Another village, a neighboring one, was visible to the east. Essentially, all the land up to this hill belonged to the richer farmers, like my father, of these two villages. To the south, the land was far more forested and hilly, and the few terraced plots that I saw on the hillsides and in the valleys were cultivated by the tribals from nameless hamlets scattered all over the place. Most of the men worked in fields belonging to villages like mine, or in towns nearby. It was the women, children and old men who cultivated these paltry, stricken-looking terraced plots.

The northern side of the hill just next to mine in the south was actually a sheer fall, as much of it had been blasted away for stone. This must have been before the area was declared a reserve, but I was not sure; some of the debris looked recent. There is much illegal mining in these regions, mostly hit-and-run quarrying where stones are blasted on one day and loaded onto trucks and carted away within another day or two. The authorities arrive, of course, but always too late. Reports are filed away. It is a well-organized process.

It was while I was peering at the blasted hillside, trying to discern, for nothing is more curious than an idle mind, how much of it had been dynamited recently, when I saw it. At first, I thought it was just some rags left behind by the tribal workers who are hired, at an absurd pittance, to break and load the stones. It was lying partly obscured by some rocks, right at the foot of the drop. But I felt that it was moving in a way that could not be attributed to the light breeze. So I cupped my hands around my mouth and hallooed. My halloo bounced off the hillsides and reverberated into silence. There was no response. Just your idle imagination, I told myself, and turned away, returning to my book and boulder, but a faint doubt kept nagging me. I could not concentrate on my reading. After a while, I put the book back in my *jholla* and took a small goat track down the hill on that side. I was still some distance from the rags when I knew I had not been wrong. It was not just rags. It was the body of a girl, six or seven years old. She was all decked out, clothed like a bride, and there were flowers and other marks of a ceremony around her. It was obvious she had been dead for some time. Surprisingly, the body had not been torn apart by predators, but it was stiff, and there was the stink of putrefaction all around it. Still, to be certain, I approached it and shouted. Then I noticed the slit in the girl's neck, which was almost hanging by a strip of skin. She had been killed, ritually from the look of it. At least two days ago. What I could not figure out was why I had felt the rags were moving and why the body had not been eaten by vultures, feral dogs or foxes.

After I had ridden back to the village and then reported the body to the local thana—my father, who knew the sub-inspector, and called him SI-sahib, had come along—it was inevitable that I got involved in the investigations. To begin with, I had to lead the SI and his men to the spot. We went in two jeeps, my father having stayed behind after making sure the SI knew who I was, for otherwise, as he told me later: they need to close a case, you know, and they take the first person they can.

We reached the spot by another route, which enabled the jeeps to get within a kilometer of it, and then we walked. The inspector and his men went fast, as evening was descending. They had shanghaied a couple of tribals from a nearby hamlet, who were expected to carry the body back to the jeeps. At the spot itself, they suddenly relaxed, taking a few photos of the small girl—the body stiff but still surprisingly intact—smoking cigarettes, poking around a few bushes and then ordering the tribals to put the body in a plastic bag and lug it back to the jeeps. Do you know the girl, the SI asked the tribals, but the men just stared, sullenly, and then shook their heads. They never know anything, observed the SI to me, with a smirk. When the tribals, with obvious reluctance, put the body in the plastic bag, the head fell off and rolled away. It was collected, put back in the bag and lugged to the jeeps, after which we set off. Of course, I was in the jeep with the SI and not in the other jeep, which contained the body in the plastic bag, securely tied up but still emitting a stink that made the two policemen in that jeep wrap their faces up in *gamchas*.

The SI, however, was in an expansive mood.

My third case, he told me.

Of murder? I asked.

No, no, he replied, who counts murders?—Of child sacrifice!

So it still happens, I observed, immediately regretting my words because they exposed me as an urban ignoramus.

Ha ha ha, laughed the SI. Happens? I would say so. More often than the records show.

Then he narrowed his eyes at me. Also in towns, he added. They are just better at hiding it away. All those brick walls and concrete pavements, you know. But these tribals, they are dolts. Totally lacking in the upper chamber.

Then he laughed again, slapping his thigh as if he had cracked a brilliant joke.

It surprised me how little happened after that. The girl was soon identified. She belonged to a hamlet farther south, but sometimes she helped out, with her parents and older siblings, in the harvesting and sowing at our village. On such occasions, the girl and her parents were often employed in the fields of a family we knew, though not too well. The family had tradition-ally been Sahukars, or moneylenders, in our village, but had now expanded into various petty enterprises, including stone quarrying. The Sahukar family was rich, much richer than my parents, but they were generally pitied because they had only one son, who was said to be cursed. It was known that they had taken him to doctors in town, once even to Patna; the mother had him treated by all kinds of sages and saints, who had tried remedies that would be difficult to apply in public—the father often caned him in frustration—but none of it had worked. I had seen him once or twice on the streets. He was what would be called the village idiot: a very fat boy of maybe six or seven, with a perennially open mouth, drooling, head tilted to one side. He hardly spoke more than a word or two. Had he been from a poor family, he would have been the butt of ridicule and harsh practical jokes. But given who he was, and perhaps the fact that the village knew or suspected all the treatments attempted on him, he was pitied and ignored.

There was of course a controversy, about which I heard from my mother. When the dead girl's tribal family was informed of her death, they accused the Sahukar family of being involved in it. *Jaadu-tona*, said my mother a few weeks later, sieving some newly threshed rice in our courtyard with four other women. Black magic.

These tribals, said one of her companions, they only believe in black magic.

I knew that she was a deeply religious woman; the walls of her house were covered with idols, portraits of gods and charms.

Who knows? Another of the women interposed. These things do happen. Some of these tribals know tantra…

What was this black magic supposed to be about? I asked my mother.

The usual stuff, my mother replied, concentrating on the grains. They said the Sahukar family did it to pass on their son's curse to the girl. They employed a baba from…

She named a village farther off.

These things do happen, said the woman again.

The woman with the icons on her walls was more skeptical.

176

She spat in the dust under her charpoy and said: Well, the boy is no better for it then. I saw him just this morning playing outside their house, with no more sense than a one-year-old.

What happened next is the most blurred part of this story. When I try to recollect it, it resembles what we call *godhuli*— the hour of cow dust—when the herds return to the village around sunset, and the diminishing sunlight combines with the dust raised by their hooves to shroud the world so that everything assumes a hazy edge. And, actually, it was at the hour of *godhuli* in early summer when the cry went up.

If you have not lived in a village, you will not understand this. Villages are places of innumerable bickering and feuds. People are mostly polite to your face, though there are always a few known for their "sharp tongues," but all inevitably gossip behind your back, mostly repeating with relish, even when they do not believe it, the worst that has been said about you. And yet, if something bad happens to you, they rally around you—sometimes in ways that people in towns, with their frayed communities, cannot imagine.

Which is why, when the cry went up that evening soon after Holi, with the colors of the celebration still on some walls, most young men of the village rushed to the Sahukar house. It was, like my parents' house, an inherited one, made in the old pattern of a courtyard, with a door in a high wall on one side and rooms lining the other three sides, all opening onto the closed courtyard. There was already a crowd—my parents had not come—when I and others from our side of the village reached the house. The SI's jeep drove up right then, and he asked me to come with him. I want a reliable witness, not these unreliable villagers, he said to me.

Hurrying to the place, I had already heard a bit of what it was all about. According to the rumor that had reached us, there had been sounds of screaming and howling from inside the Sahukar house. Horrible sounds, like people being flayed alive. When their neighbors had rushed up, they had been unable to enter, as the door leading to the courtyard was barred from the inside. They had shouted and banged, but there had been no response. The house had fallen silent. They had run around the house, but all the windows were shuttered and barred. With some other households, they might have climbed the walls and jumped inside, but the Sahukar was known to guard his place—it was said that he kept his cash buried in one of the rooms—with a gun. So instead they had run back to the door to the courtyard. This time they had been met with the sound of children playing. This was strange, as there was only the son there—Munna, as he was called. But who knows, maybe they had visitors from elsewhere, though it is rare that anyone enters a house in a village without others noticing it. Munna, they had shouted, fetch your parents. The sound of children playing had ceased after they called out a few times, and then a child's voice had called back: Go away, you all. Let us play.

It sounded like the voice of Munna, but the villagers were surprised; Munna rarely spoke more than a word or two at a time. His vocabulary did not extend beyond a dozen basic words. This was where the matter stood when the SI, with me in tow, and his men, parted the crowd and reached the door to the courtyard. This was a massive thing, more like a gate, studded with metal knobs and rings. The SI gave an empowering twist to his mustache—he had an impressive one—and commanded the crowd to stop talking. In the sudden silence, all of us could hear the sound of children playing gleefully. The SI harrumphed and cleared his voice. Munna, he shouted, Munna, open the door!

The sound of playing did not cease.

Munna, shouted the SI again, Munna, where are your parents?

This time the voice of Munna, but raised in a good mimicry of his father's irascible tones, came back: Go away, you idiot. I am playing with my friend.

There was the peal of another child's laughter behind that retort. Then some complicit giggling, obviously at an adult being called an idiot.

The crowd that was mostly silent until now gasped back into voice. Everyone started talking at the same time. Essentially, they were saying what the SI muttered to himself as he gestured to his men to break down the door: When did the fat retard begin to talk this legibly?

I later wondered why the SI did not command one of his men to scale the wall, and I could find only two answers. Either he was an officer too used to drama to embrace a simpler solution, or, more disturbingly, he wanted more than one person to witness what was inside, for he expected the sight to be more than what a single mind could bear.

It took the men about ten minutes to pull one of the door panels partly off its hinges; the door was massive and strong, but the wall was old and crumbling. The SI waved them behind and gestured to me to enter with him. Witness, he repeated to me, to ensure that I knew my job.

Inside, the courtyard was shrouded in that un-light that comes after dusk. Motes of dust were suspended in the air, stirred up by passing cattle and still settling over the village; shadows were creeping out from the corners. You could see, but the edges were not clear and the shapes shifted. As I bowed and stepped in through the narrow opening—just behind the SI, his two men standing behind us, blocking the crowd from pouring through the gap—I distinctly saw the fat boy playing with some toys in the middle of the courtyard. Next to him was a girl about his age, her back to us. There was something strange about the girl. Her head seemed to loll on her shoulders. The boy ignored us, but the girl stood up and turned around, slowly, stiffly. It was then that it seemed to me that her head fell off and rolled onto the ground of the courtyard.

The SI stopped so abruptly that I bumped into him. I unthinkingly shoved him aside, as his broad back now blocked my view of the boy and the girl, and he cursed. But when I looked again, there was just the fat boy playing with his toys, shrouded in half-light, and no sign of a girl.

Where is the girl? I asked the SI.

He stood there, frozen, staring at the boy.

Where is the girl? I repeated in a harsh whisper.

He turned and looked at me. It was a hard, fierce stare. What girl? he said. It was then that I knew he had seen her too.

They never did find any trace of the boy's parents, but the boy, ah, the boy, the village marveled in the days he was there before his uncle came from town to sell the lands (no one wanted to buy the house) and take him away; the boy had learned to speak in perfect, clear sentences. He still spoke like he was four years old, but he did not drool. His head did not loll. And he did not seem to miss his parents. If you asked him what happened to them, he only said, the girl made them go away.

Where, you asked him. Into that wall, he said, pointing.

But though the police broke down the wall the boy pointed at, and prodded into quite a few others with iron rods, they recovered nothing.

ELOPEMENT

Holi always marks a change of season. There is the hint of claws in the sun and of a furnace in the wind, sometimes exactly on the first day of Holi. Some Muslims shake their heads and envy the Hindus their calibrated solar calendar, which keeps Hindu festivals tuned to the season, while Islamic festivals migrate, with the nomadic moon of their calendar, from one season to another. That year was no exception.

The exception was Miss Sushmita and her friendship with Med Rep Shaqil. That is how we knew him, as he was a medical representative, often dropping in at my father's "dispensary". I started encountering Shaqil during my tutorial evenings, when he would sometimes stop in for a cup of chai, providing me with half an hour of relief from Miss Sushmita's intensive tutelage. Mostly, though, I encountered him going out when I went in, thus removing some of the terrors of that dark staircase and corridor to the Basus' flat. The Bangladesh war was two years behind me by then. I was older, but the fears had not disappeared entirely.

Med Rep Shaqil seemed to time it quite precisely on such occasions, so that I knew he would be coming down the stairs as I went up. We would cross with a *salaam-alai-kum* or a less formal hello; he would reach the bottom of the stairs as I reached the top, and I would see him stop and, backlit by the ajar door, begin to roll a cigarette. He did this inevitably, never stepping out until he had rolled one and lit it. So that by the time he was out, my father would have already driven away and turned into the gate of his dispensary.

Once in a while, though, Med Rep Shaqil would roar up, Miss Sushmita on the pillion, for the evening badminton rounds at Papa's dispensary. On such occasions, he was dressed very smartly, and, as the year wore on, Miss Sushmita started putting on more makeup too, sometimes even a garland of flowers in her jooda-hairdo. They would be inevitably returning from a film show, and the slight frown that I noticed on Papa's face when the films were discussed I attributed to my father's dislike of the local cinema halls, which, he claimed in his doctor's voice, were infested with "bedbugs and bad characters."

Papa had once been an avid filmgoer; he could still whistle, impeccably, entire songs from films, mostly in fading Kodachrome and Eastmancolor, which I considered dated. He was whistling less often; I had memories of him being requested to whistle a song at parties when I was younger. He used to oblige in the past, but now he claimed not to remember the tunes. He did remember them though; I heard him whistling while driving at times and, on rare occasions, in the bathroom as he changed for bed.

Med Rep Shaqil, who was at least ten years younger, was a film aficionado and a Rajesh Khanna fan. Rajesh Khanna was the big star in those days. Most fashionable young men dressed, walked, talked and combed their hair like him. Med Rep Shaqil did so too. Papa held a dim view of Rajesh Khanna, holding him personally responsible for encouraging insipid young men to make passes at women. He preferred, in that order, Dilip Kumar,

Dev Anand, Humphrey Bogart, Richard Burton and Shammi Kapoor, though he had stopped watching repeats of even these stars with the years, allowing me, grudgingly, to be taken to the "cinema hall" by my aunt's family. Two or three times a year, he would agree, because of Ammi's importuning, to take us to a theater, always one of the two owned by people he knew (and treated), where we would be specially ushered in, with an entire box reserved for us. We never went when the theater was posting placards that declared "houseful." It was always during the last two or three shows. I enjoyed these occasions—as I would be plied with free Coca Cola by the cinema owner—though I still dreaded the stretch from parking the car to reaching the box, because that was the stretch in which a lewd gesture or a wolf whistle by a young man could galvanize Papa into sudden violence. He would, regardless of how outnumbered he was, accost the man and ask him to apologize to the woman. It could be any woman; almost always it was no one we knew, and in one case it was "just a tribal," as a bystander skeptically murmured. If the man refused to apologize, Papa would respond with a flurry of doublehanded slaps. In those days, slaps were bestowed by the upper classes (and castes) on poorer people with more liberality than money, it sometimes seemed to me, but my father mostly got it wrong; he usually slapped a well-dressed man. I dreaded these occasions—terrified for my father and embarrassed by him—though eventually the bystanders, neutral until then, would support him. Only once did he notice my terror and told me, as we walked away, "Hit a person only if it is a wrong that cannot go unchallenged. And then land the blow before he can hit you."

It was advice that was wasted on me. I did not even get into fights in school.

I could not imagine Med Rep Shaqil as stepping up to a man and slapping him because he had pinched Miss Sushmita's bottom, which made it difficult for me to imagine both of them going to the cinema together. There was a kind of softness to Med Rep Shaqil that had to do with the Rajesh Khanna persona, the slightly effeminate, highly mannered characters that were played by the superstar and rigorously copied by young men. Amitabh Bachchan had yet to arrive, and the "hero" of a film could still be a failed artist or poet; in a few years, all such characters would disappear and be replaced by heroes who were, inevitably, either policemen or hoodlums.

But Med Rep Shaqil could not be a failed poet; there was a briskness and certainty about him that all medical representatives—fast-moving, fast-talking, fashionable young men who considered themselves to be junior doctors—displayed. My father seemed to be the tougher, less forgiving, more intolerant person next to Med Rep Shaqil, and actually next to most other people. Those two-handed slaps were not the only thing he was quick at: his likes and dislikes were instantaneous, and usually unchanging. How could he be so certain of what was wrong and what was right, I wondered? I had never thought of my father along those lines until then. I think that was the year when I started becoming another person, for better and for worse, and not just my father's son.

One evening, as I climbed the stairway to the Basus, the sound of some film from the adjoining theater filling the dark space with hollow echoes, Med Rep Shaqil descended at a brisker pace than usual, neither noticing me nor responding to my greeting. Soon afterward, Miss Sushmita went rushing past and joined Shaqil at the bottom of the staircase, where he was rolling a cigarette. They were still speaking when I turned into the corridor upstairs. Miss Sushmita came up after five minutes, exchanged a sharp retort or two with her mother—in Bangla, which I did not understand—and put me through my scholarly paces with even greater efficiency and briskness than was her wont.

The dress rehearsal for the "half-yearly exams" took place a few weeks before the summer vacation. By then, the sun was hot enough for school hours to have changed; school began an hour and half early and ended two hours early so that we could get home before one in the afternoon, when the heat became dangerous. Stories of heatstrokes started trickling in. Birds hopped around with their beaks open. We put bowls of water out under a couple of trees in the garden.

The school playground stayed mostly empty during the lunch break now, which had in any case become a brunch break. All but the wildest "market" and "*mohalla*" boys—who were seasonally "failed" and pruned from school by the nuns whenever possible—preferred to play in the shade of trees and in the pavilions and verandas. We were even allowed to stay in our classrooms during the breaks, which was not the case over the rest of the year.

Sometimes a student or a teacher did not come, and we assumed that the person had suffered a heatstroke. These were not fatal in our circles, given the care that we took, though we heard of farmers and laborers dying of the heat and the sun. We might even find a dead bird on the ground. But we—students, teachers, parents—invariably recovered from what would be described as a "mild heatstroke" after a day or two, during which we stayed in bed and drank lots of water with glucose.

As such, I did not make much of it when Miss Sushmita did not come to school one day, and when, that evening, my father left me behind while going to work. An evening without tuition was not unwelcome to me.

The next day I was sitting on a bench in the schoolyard, under the shade of a tree, talking to my best friend, Gyan, when another classmate—a boy from mid-town who seemed to know all the news partly because his house was the neighborhood's RSS office—came up to us. His name was Narender.

"Have you heard?" Narender said to us. "Miss Sushmita has eloped!" He pronounced "eloped" in capital letters.

I did not have a clear notion what "eloped" meant, but I gathered from his tone that it was something extremely bad.

"And guess what?" Narender added. "She has eloped with a mullah."

"Mullah" I understood better. Narender and a couple of other boys in class used "mullah" to refer derogatorily to Muslims.

"That is all they do," Narender spat on the ground. "They make babies with their women and run away with our women!"

He was obviously repeating a line uttered by some adult; it had that air of authority.

Gyan looked uncomfortable. "Sameer is Muslim," he whispered to Narender, nodding slightly toward me.

Narender was taken aback. "No, he isn't," he replied. Then he turned to me, "You are not Muslim, are you, Sameer?"

"I am," I confirmed.

Narender looked doubtful. "You do not behave like Muslims, you do not look like one, you do not even live in a *mohalla*."

"But he is," Gyan insisted. "I have been to his place for Eid."

"Oh, well, there can be some good Muslims too," said Narender. "I am sure he would not run away with Miss

Sushmita." He laughed and went back to his group of boys.

I wasn't sure I would not have run away with Miss Sushmita. Over the past few months, I had become aware of her proximity, and had to make an effort not to shy away when she leaned over my shoulder to correct something, her perfumed hair falling on me, her breasts almost brushing the top of my head. But I had not thought one could run away with her. I still did not fully understand what it meant to run away with a woman. My life had been a secluded one, carefully tended and pruned, like the roses in my parents' garden.

The next three or four days, Narender was the source of our news about Miss Sushmita. If my parents discussed her, they took care to do so out of my earshot. The nuns and other teachers at the school pretended that she was ill. Only Narender, with his "sources in town," had the news; we heard, variously, that Miss Sushmita had run away with "Mullah Shaqil," that they had been trailed by both the families and, it appeared to me, a few dozen vigilantes from both the communities, finally been located in a hotel in Patna, and separated. Looking back, I am not sure whether any of this was true, but that did not matter then.

Now, Narender said sagely, the question was whether they had married or not, and whether the ceremony—court, Hindu or Muslim—was valid or not. He also added that this kind of thing only happened with "Bengali girls" who, as was widely known in our Bihar, had "loose characters" because of the communist education they received in Bengal. A proper Hindu girl from here would not have eloped with a mullah, he said with conviction, and in any case, she would have been cut to pieces by now or burnt alive if she had. But Bengali girls! What can one say of them! He shook his head in disgust, spat in the dust, after looking around to make sure the nuns, who forbade spitting, were not watching, and returned to his group—leaving Gyan looking deeply irritated but at a loss for words.

I learned a bit more about it, quite inadvertently, later that week. Mrs. Basu, with Mr. Basu in tow, descended from a rickshaw around five in the afternoon, which was about as early as one could go out in the summer heat without running the risk of a heatstroke. The rickshaw was kept waiting. Our lawn had just been sprinkled with water, partly to irrigate it and partly to cool it down, so that wicker chairs and a table could be put out for the evening tea. I loved this moment; the grass gave out a pleasant fresh smell, as that of early monsoon. Birds, which had largely disappeared for the afternoon, were out again: the usual mynahs and sparrows, a bunch of seven sisters and a wild wood dove, which had flown in from the adjacent barren hills looking for water. Squirrels scampered up and down the litchi trees, chasing one another.

As the lawn was still wet, the Basus were ushered onto the veranda, also hosed with water some moments ago and swept dry, where Papa and Ammi joined them, after asking a servant to take me away. I was sent away but, as was the wont with servants, not paid much attention afterward, so that I could sneak back to the door and overhear the conversation on the veranda. It was not the first time I had done so. Looking back, I realize that my parents had a kind of religious trust in my obedience; it never struck them that I would seek to overhear conversations forbidden to me.

Mrs. Basu was doing all the talking. This was not unusual. Mr. Basu had a reedy voice, which was not a bad indication of his physical dimensions, while Mrs. Basu's voice, like her, tended to fill much space.

It had taken me a few minutes to slip away from the servants, as I had to be unobtrusive in my desire to evade their chaperonage and, hence, had to wait for them to get distracted by chores or gossip. It was a well-tried strategy; I had honed it over years. If I showed any sign of wanting to slip back to my parents once I had been sent away, the servants would take turns keeping an eye on me. If, however, I looked content to be on my own, they would—as soon as a chicken had to be plucked, some onions chopped or a floor cleaned—stop paying attention to me. Once that happened, I could do what I wished, as long as I did not make my unchaperoned state visible to my parents.

The conversation on the veranda had proceeded briskly in my absence, and when I ensconced myself behind the door, Mrs. Basu was launching into a litany of the woes that she, as a woman, had suffered, largely thanks to her husband and her daughter. Miss Sushmita's elopement was obviously the nadir of this deep well of suffering.

"Such a girl, such a girl she used to be," Mrs. Basu was saying, "always running off, tumbling down the stairs, scraping her knees, talking nineteen to the dozen. And him" (I assumed the reference was to Mr. Basu) "being what he is, it was all up to me to bring her up. And I did a good job. I did a good job. She grew up to be a lovely woman, who knew how to behave … If it had not been for that, that, that medical representative …"

"Shaqil," filled in Mr. Basu, helpfully.

"I know his name," retorted Mrs. Basu. "Shaqil insinuated his way into our household. He did this, he did that. He turned up now, he turned up then. We suspected nothing. We are Bengalis; we allow our women the freedom to go out, to meet men … But this, I had never expected this!"

"I had not expected it either," said my father. "I was most sorry to hear of it."

"To elope! As if life was a bad film. And with a Muslim boy, who then goes back to his family!" Mrs. Basu choked, either due to her emotions or because she realized that the last statement was a bit out of place in a Muslim household.

I held my breath. The word had come up—finally. Elope. I would perhaps now understand the mystery of its effect. The literal meaning, "to run away with someone," which I had looked up, did not explain to me why the word was always spoken at a different pitch than the rest of the sentence. So, run away? It was bad, no doubt. But I had, occasionally, contemplated running away—on being denied some request or liberty—and once had done so, all the way to the Gandhi Maidan almost two kilometers away, but then had thought better of it and returned. If Med Rep Shaqil and Miss Sushmita had run away, surely they would return too—perhaps after a longer while, as they probably had more money in their pockets than the single rupee I had in mine when I ran away, and which was exhausted at the phochka-wallah's cart just five hundred meters from our house. If my mother was like Mrs. Basu, I might have run away for longer too, I mused.

Mrs. Basu was speaking again. "What face do we have left to show in this town, tell me, Doctor sahib. What will I do with Sushmita now? Who will marry her? We cannot even continue to live here if nothing is done about it! They say they had just gone for a trip, but who cares what they say? What matters is what the town says. You … you are respected here … you, you will have to do something, Doctor Mallick," she said. She always addressed my father formally as "Doctor Mallick."

There was a moment of silence.

"What can he do?" I heard my mother say.

"Med Rep Shaqil is from your community; he always said he was related to you," Mrs. Basu responded. "If he had not been related to you, I would not have trusted him and allowed him to see ..."

"He is related to us, only in the way in which every member of the Mallick clan is in some way or the other related," replied my mother. "We do not know his family ..."

"It does not matter," interposed my father. "It is my responsibility."

"It is not," replied my mother. I had never heard her contradict my father in public.

My father ignored her; he was good at doing that to family members when he had made up his mind. He addressed the Basus.

"I will take care of this," he said to them. "You have my word. You are people of a good family; you deserve to be treated better than this in my town."

My mother left the gathering, and I had to retreat from my hiding place. When she passed by me, I could see that she looked angry. "His town," she muttered. I knew she had grown up in another town, a neighboring one.

That night my parents went to bed without a single word to one another.

A couple of weeks passed. In the absence of Miss Sushmita's tutoring, I did worse than usual in the half-yearly exams. But my parents were preoccupied, and it went almost unnoticed. My father did not purse his lips and give me a scolding; my mother did not look tearful and guilty, as if she had failed in her duty as a parent.

The summer vacations started. Our routines changed. I was left behind when Papa went to work. He returned by noon, for the afternoon siesta days had also started. My favorite memories from childhood are outdoor ones in the winter and indoor ones in the summer, the winter days when, during vacations, I could range across the compound or run about the roof flying my kites, and the summer afternoons when, khus-khus mats on the doors, we stayed in, sharing a lunch of largely fruits (melons, litchis, two or three kinds of mangoes) from one to four. So generic are the two that I cannot distinguish individual days; all winter days seem one, as do all of my summer afternoons.

But one afternoon that summer stands out from my memories of mangoes at lunch, reading on a mattress on the floor and the fragrance of khus. It was the afternoon when Med Rep Shaqil and his mother came to see my parents. I knew that my father had told people in the clan and the "medical community" that he wanted to see Med Rep Shaqil. In those days, the town was small enough for such a wish from a person like my father to be taken seriously in both circles. That Med Rep Shaqil turned up with his mother, not his father, who was reputed to be a cantankerous and religious person, was significant. It was, looking back, a calculated move on his part—or on the part of his parents who, it appeared, still ran his life. I understood this years later.

Two things struck me about the event. They came in a car— a dilapidated Ambassador—around two in the afternoon, which was a very unusual time to call on anyone in the season. The roads were deserted then; people stayed indoors. Even laborers took a couple of hours off around then and retired to the shade of some tree or building. The other thing was the purdah that Mama Shaqil wore. Visitors to our house rarely wore a burka. And I would have imagined a differently attired mother for a smart Rajesh Khanna-type like Med Rep Shaqil.

Inside, after they had been seated in the drawing room, which was on one side of the corridor where I lay on my mattress, forgotten and pretending to read my comic books, Mama Shaqil took off her purdah. Both in voice and volume, she did not differ much from Mrs. Basu. The two could have been sisters. And Med Rep Shaqil, who had always impressed me as a flamboyant young man during the badminton games and while zipping round on his Yezdi in town, suddenly assumed the silent, slightly distracted, half-apologetic look of Mr. Basu.

There was the usual round of greetings, followed by the offer of lemonade by my father, switched swiftly to Rooh Afza by my mother, who was better at distinguishing between guests who would drink lemonade and those who would prefer Rooh Afza. The offer was accepted and the iced drink served by a servant, woken out of afternoon torpor and then firmly asked to go back to sleep in her room. It was only then that the conversation moved to the main issue.

My father, in his direct way, was the one who brought it up. He addressed Med Rep Shaqil. "I have been disappointed in you, Shaqil," he told the young man. "This is not something I thought anyone in our clan would do."

As Med Rep Shaqil stuttered, his mother took over.

"Doctor sahib," she said, in a loud voice that I did not have to strain to overhear. "It takes two hands to clap." By now, I had angled myself in such a way that I could see Mama Shaqil and Med Rep Shaqil, but my parents could not see me. Mama Shaqil had hennaed hair; she took out a small metal box and extracted what looked like a clove from it, which she carefully inserted into her mouth and commenced chewing. Med Rep was looking fixedly at the floor.

"I do not understand you," my father spoke back irritably.

"Look at the boy," replied Mama Shaqil, speaking slowly. "Look at the poor boy."

I looked at the poor boy, who squirmed but continued to stare at the floor.

"Look at the poor, innocent boy," Mama Shaqil continued. "He has grown up here in a small town; he has grown up in a family like yours. What does he know about the wiles of big-city Bengali women?"

My father snorted, but my mother intercepted his response.

"Let us not talk about what happened," Ammi said. "Let us discuss what needs to be done."

"Your poor boy," my father said loudly, "needs to assume responsibility for his act."

"What responsibility, Doctor sahib? What act?" queried Mama Shaqil, in a voice honeyed with incomprehension and innocence.

"You cannot e-e-elope (it took my father some effort to utter a word he detested) with a woman and then discard her like … like …" He could not complete the sentence. I think my mother might have put a restraining hand on him.

"But, Doctor sahib, you have heard wrong," replied Mama Shaqil. "There was no elopement-welopement. You know both of them took leave; you can ask the nuns at the school about this. They just went to Patna for a vacation. I know he shouldn't have done so—I beat him with my slippers when he came back—but he is an innocent small-town boy. What does he know about the wiles of Bengali women?"

"That is not what other people say," my father said in a controlled voice.

"What people, Doctor sahib? Bring them to me. I will rake

their faces with my nails. Jealous wretches they are, if they be-smirch the name of my poor boy."

"It is usually the woman who has more to lose in such cases, and you know that; you are a woman yourself. The Basus …" began my father.

"But Doctor sahib, why should you take the word of strangers against that of your own blood, your own clan?" Mama Shaqil extracted another clove and inserted it into her maw. "Your own faith?" she said, driving in the final nail.

"That's all rubbish!" Papa barked. I knew that voice. It usually built up to a storm. "Let us talk about what should be done!"

"What can be done, Doctor sahib? About what?"

"I am not talking to you, Madam," said my father. "You are my elder and I do not want to be rude to someone from my parents' generation. You, Shaqil, what do you say about all this?"

"What can he say …"

"I am not addressing you, Madam. Shaqil, speak up, man, what do you say about this? Have you lost your voice? Are you under no obligation to a woman you ran away with for a va-cation or whatever and, according to what the town says, even married in a temple?"

"Married in a temple! Doctor sahib! Have you ever heard of a Muslim marrying in a temple?" Mama Shaqil laughed theatrically.

"Please, Madam. Let your son answer. I want to hear him speak. I know he can speak; I have heard him speak before."

Shaqil mumbled something.

"What was that?" Papa almost shouted. "Speak up, Shaqil. Don't mumble like a woman. Speak like a man."

"I did not run away with her," Shaqil mumbled, not looking up. "I owe her nothing."

My father must have stood up. Suddenly he was there, towering in front of Shaqil, glaring at him. I withdrew my head a bit, though they were too caught up in the drama to notice me in the lobby. "If you were my son," he thundered, "I would whip you until your flesh fell off you in strips!"

Mama Shaqil looked frightened. Papa's reputation—as a short-tempered man, not averse to using his hands—was widely known. "Doctor sahib," she said, in a voice that, for the first time, sounded pleading and uncertain, "we came to you because we are the same blood."

My mother drew Papa back. They disappeared from my view.

"I should extract every drop of my blood and wash it down the drain if that is the case!" my father said as he withdrew.

The withdrawal had emboldened Mama Shaqil. "Doctor sahib," she exclaimed, "we respect you. You have no reason to insult us."

It was my mother who spoke.

"I am a woman. I have a son," she said. "We all know that names and words and descriptions do not matter in such cases. Your son spent some days with a woman. There are reasons to believe that she will suffer the consequences of such, such liberties, such rumors. I think, as a woman, that a man has to shoulder his responsibility in such matters ..."

I had never heard Ammi speak such a long and personal sentence to strangers. Usually, she kept her words and opinions for family members—close ones—and seldom spoke more than a formal phrase or two to strangers.

"But Bahurani," Mama Shaqil insisted, as Med Rep Shaqil squirmed once again, "Nothing happened."

"We know what happened," my father shot back, his voice

hoarse, as if he was gagging himself. "There is no smoke without a fire."

Mama Shaqil ignored the retort. She turned to Med Rep Shaqil and gave him a light slap on his head. "Tell me, idiot," she demanded. "Did you as much as touch the girl?" She slapped him on the head again, harder this time. He shook his head.

Mama Shaqil was well in control again. It was as if she had rehearsed this bit. She extracted and inserted her third clove.

"Who knows about Bengali women, Doctor sahib?" she said. "They do not go out with just one man."

"I know about this woman, madam," my father's voice rose again. "I vouch for her. I know about her and her family. They are good people. And, if they ask me, I will go to the police with them."

Mama Shaqil gave a short laugh. "No, you won't, Doctor sahib," she replied. "There is nothing to go to the police about. And no one except you would go to the police; no one will come with you on either side, except maybe that woman. And you know what people would say—I dare not say this to you, for we are small people—you know what people are already saying in the clan and the *mohalla*? They are saying that Doctor sahib is so upset because he has a personal axe to grind."

"What do you mean?" my father shouted this time, loudly enough to have a servant come scurrying a couple of minutes later, bleary-eyed, asking whether we had called. "What do you mean?" he roared.

"We have a small mouth and dare not utter such big things, Doctor sahib, but it is our respect for you and your family that makes me so bold. You know people say that it is not as if Doctor sahib did not visit this family almost every evening after work."

"So? So what?"

"So they say—may their tongues rot—perhaps Doctor sahib is trying to tie his turban on my poor son's head."

There was sudden silence in the room.

Then I heard my father address my mother in a voice I had never heard before. "See them out, please," he said. "If I stay here, I will, for the first time in my life, slap a woman." He came out of the room and went into the bedroom so briskly that I did not have time to shield my curiosity behind a comic book. But he was too upset to notice me.

Mama Shaqil was apologizing profusely in the drawing room. I heard phrases like, "May Allah never forgive me if I intended any harm in my heart," "Doctor sahib has always been like a big brother to Shaqil," "It is not what we say but what people say," etc. The servant had come in. Mama Shaqil started donning her burka, making small talk. It was only when she was fully shrouded in black that Ammi, unceasingly polite and self-effacing, did something uncharacteristic. She did not escort the mother and son to the portico. Instead, she said to the servant, "See these people out to their car."

My tutoring lessons with Miss Sushmita continued, though my father seldom came upstairs to collect me. Mostly, he had the driver drop me with the Basus. The Basus visited us for Eid and we went over for Durga Puja, as we always had, but these were formal family occasions. My father never really chatted with Miss Sushmita anymore, and Miss Sushmita never came over to our place alone for a dinner, as she had sometimes in the past. She stopped putting flowers in her hair. She lost some weight and looked unusually pale for a few weeks. She stopped smiling at school. The nuns no longer involved her in extracurricular activities.

The Basus lived on in town for about a year, just to prove to people that Miss Sushmita was not pregnant, Narender explained later. Then they left for Calcutta. It was still Calcutta in those days. Good riddance, said Narender, spitting into the dust surreptitiously.

Less than a year later, Med Rep Shaqil was married off to a woman from his ancestral village. It was difficult for me to imagine the flamboyant Med Rep Shaqil—hair set firmly in place, comb in pocket—married to a girl from a village. We received an elaborate invitation card, even the envelope bearing embossed lines from the Quran, which my parents did not open. They put it on a side table in the lobby. We called it the junk table, as it mostly harbored broken odds and ends, blown fuses and bulbs, old magazines, chipped china, all of it cleared away by my mother about twice a year. It was the first unopened card put on that table, but over the years, they accumulated. Cards that arrived and were not opened. Ammi's biannual clearing of the junk table also became less frequent.

Years later, when I rushed back from my businesses in Ahmedabad to bury my father, I cleared the table for her, and counted twenty-six unopened invitations on it, some from five or six years ago.

NAMASTE TRUMP

Chottu is worried. "What is it, Babu?" he asks me, after placing the post-breakfast cup of chai on my desk, to my left, as I always insist. "This gas that is going to kill everyone, they say?"

I look up from my laptop and gaze at him in incomprehension. He stands next to my desk, empty tray in hand, looking as goofy as ever, wearing those baggy trousers that he prefers. Chottu is small—hence, I suppose, his name—and it is impossible to determine his age. His face is round and unwrinkled, and he is about the height of a twelve-year-old boy. But he is not twelve years old. In fact, he probably came to us when he was twelve or thirteen, and that was—how much?—seven, eight years ago. There is something wrong with his head—he has trouble doing even simple sums; he goes about singing the same two or three film lyrics to himself in a monotone—and it has somehow stunted his body too. I suppose if Chottu showed any sign of real intelligence, one would consider him to be permanently bewildered at the world, but the word that describes him best is "goofy." I find it easier to accept too, his genetic goofiness, for I am not a person who takes to those who are bewildered by life. I have never understood the need for such bewilderment in anyone who can think and act.

"What gas?" I ask him.

He smiles his goofy gap-toothed smile. He had two of his

teeth knocked out when he stepped across the road without looking both ways some years ago. My wife had sent him out on an errand. It was sheer luck he did not lose anything else. Just those two teeth, and a broken leg, which mended but left him with a slight limp. I remember running downstairs at the commotion. He was there, spread-eagled on the curb, mouth bloody, and he gave me this same goofy smile when I ran up to him. He always smiles. Even when he is being scolded.

"This gas that they say the Chinese gave the Pakistanis to spread in India. It makes you cough, sneeze and die."

Then it dawns on me.

"You mean the virus?" I say.

He nods vigorously. If my wife had been around, she would have said something sarcastic about Chottu to me—in English—and asked him to stop thinking and get back to work—in Hindi. She has grown to dislike him over the years. He is too big to keep in a flat with young girls, she says, alluding to our two teenage daughters. I think her dislike has more to do with Chottu's missing teeth and limp—both of them indirectly caused by her. But my wife is not there, having left for her weekly yoga session, so I turn around my laptop and show Chottu what I am working on. It is a poster for the Namaste Trump event. My ad company is one of the three commissioned to make posters for it, an order that has come to me through my MLA friend. It is not a huge order, but it will lead to bigger ones. That is why I am looking after the project personally.

"Look at this," I say to Chottu, showing him the poster. "Who is this?"

"Ahhh," exclaims Chottu, his moon face lighting up. "That is Modiji." An image of Modiji is printed on one side of the poster, his palms folded in a namaste.

Chottu is a great admirer of our prime minister. Everyone in my family is, all my neighbors are, and Chottu has only us as his political mentors. He has lived with us for so long. When he first came to us, most of his salary would be sent back to his family in some village in Bihar, but two years ago he asked us to give him the full salary. What about your family in the village, my wife had inquired. We knew he was the second oldest of about a dozen siblings. "It is my earnings," he had replied, almost sullenly, eyes fixed to the floor around his feet. "I have told them I cannot send them money anymore." What will you do with the money, my wife had asked him. After all, you get food and shelter with us. He had blushed. Chottu is surprisingly fair, fairer than anyone in my family, apart from my wife. Why, I had joked, why, I think Chottu is saving up to get married! Chottu had looked surprised, and then, in a voice full of admiration and bewilderment, he had gasped, "How did you know, Babu?" My wife and I had burst out laughing. But we had accepted his request; his wages had been handed over to him, and no one had come to protest from his village.

"Yes, that is Modiji," I reply. "But who is the other person?"

"He is a Firangi, Babu."

"You don't know who he is?"

"All Firangis look alike, Babu, like our own Pappuji," he says with a cheeky smile, repeating something he has heard me say.

"Not this Firangi," I tell him. "This Firangi is a great leader, a great man."

"As great as Modiji?"

"Almost," I reply, laughing. "His name is Trump, and he is the Modiji of America."

"Ahh, I have heard his name. The dhobi was saying Modiji is good friends with this man."

"He is," I agree. "And you know why I am making this

poster on my computer?"

Chottu shakes his head.

"Because Trump is going to visit us."

Chottu looks alarmed. "Visit us?" he squeaks. "Visit us here?" And he looks around, as if to register all the things that need to be cleaned or tidied up in the flat.

"Not visit us in this flat, you dolt," I laugh. "Visit Modiji and our India. He is coming here in a few days. And do you think he will come here if there was a gas killing all of us? Would he?"

Chottu shakes his head.

"So, off with you. Do the breakfast dishes and stop wasting time on gossip by servants from other flats."

Chottu grins, gives me that exaggerated salaam-salute he reserves for such orders, and scampers away on his uneven legs.

The early weeks of the pandemic are not a problem for me. I often work from home, and my ad company is fully digitized. I suspect the only reason we still prefer having an office is to get away from our children and spouses! Even back home, it is not an issue; my children switch to Zoom classes, and my wife reschedules a few arrangements. Chottu has always lived with us, sleeping on a roll-up mattress in a corner of the sitting room. This is convenient. While some of our neighbors have to do without servants, who live in shanties elsewhere and have to be laid off for safety's sake, we go on as usual. Chottu brings me my morning tea; he prepares the breakfast and meals; he does the daily shopping, the dusting and cleaning. This is fine to begin with, but, as the pandemic unfolds, it also becomes a problem. It leaves us vulnerable.

This becomes clear to us on the day the entire nation comes out on balconies to clap hands and bang plates, as requested by

Modiji, in order to thank our caregivers. Some go down into the parks and driveways, but my family and I are careful; we stay on our balcony, having hung some purifying Ayurvedic sachets from the railings. We bang the metal plates we have, and my wife fetches the conch shell from the puja room and blows on it. Downstairs—we are on the second floor—there are people with more elaborate instruments. Drums, bells, whistles, sheets of metal. There have been messages on WhatsApp about how certain high-pitched metallic sounds ward off the virus, and many people are doing their utmost to create a noise. In my family, we are not convinced by such messages, but we are also not the kind to scoff at any effort to save the nation. We are not libtards. We look on, making our own bit of noise. Suddenly, who do I see in the crowd below? Who but Chottu! He is dragging an empty metal container while a couple of other servants from the flats in the complex—not all house servants have been dismissed yet—are banging on it with rods. They must have gotten the container from the nearby dump. They have obviously washed it clean for the occasion. They have even decorated it with party ribbons. I point Chottu out to my wife. He has been instructed not to mingle with others needlessly. My wife tries to call him up, but the noise downstairs is far too loud, and just then some kids start bursting crackers.

The noise is still lingering outside, and Chottu has not returned when we close the balcony door and re-enter the sitting room. The children drift off to their rooms to continue swapping the photos and messages that they have been posting to friends on their iPhones. I look at my wife. There is no way I can avoid this issue anymore.

"What did I tell you?" she says.

My wife has been upset for a few days about Chottu. She has

complained that he mixes too much with people in the complex, goes down to gossip as he had before the pandemic and does not even take proper care in the kitchen; she always has to remind him to wash his hands whenever he returns from a chore, and to wash the fruits with soap, not just with water.

"What did I tell you?" she says to me. "He is a risk. Nothing will happen to him, I am sure; these people have excellent immunity. But we …"

Just then Chottu returns to the flat and heads for the guest washroom. I shout his name, but he gives me his dumb grin and says, "Coming, Babu. Just washing my hands first."

I get up and follow him into the washroom. I am angry. "Haven't I told you not to take any risk, you dolt?" I say to him from the door, as he nonchalantly washes his hands.

"But I am not taking any risks, Babu," he replies, pointing to two sachets hanging from a thread around his neck. "I put on two of the sachets that Guruji gave us when I go out. Not one, Babu, two." He beams at me with the cleverness of his strategy.

That night, in bed, my wife and I hold a whispered consultation. My wife's dislike of Chottu has grown during the pandemic, and she has been suggesting getting rid of him. I am the one who is resisting it, partly from inertia and partly because Chottu always takes special care of my needs. I just have to look around for my slippers and he will run to fetch them. If I so much as say that it would be nice to have a cup of tea, he brews one, no matter how busy he is with other chores. I simply have to mention a dish I have not eaten for a long time, and, unobtrusively, that dish is served for dinner the next night or the night after that. To be honest, Chottu takes better care of my needs than my wife—or, for that matter, even my mother, while that good old soul was alive—ever could.

"Are you sure?" I say, when my wife says, once again, that we should send Chottu "home."

"Send him away," she replies. "We do not owe him anything."

"It is just that …"

"He is not a boy," she observes. "He is a grown-up man. If he was not retarded, he would be shaving by now."

That, of course, is true. But I still hesitate, wanting to have at least a good reason to send Chottu away.

Then Modiji comes on television, announces a lockdown and tells everyone to go home. National curfew, he says. It catches us by surprise. The Namaste Trump event of just a month ago had been such a success that we were expecting the country to ride out the pandemic without a full lockdown. We were taking all precautions, of course: washing hands, avoiding crowds, purifying the air in the flat with the Ayurvedic sachets—turmeric, neem leaves, dried lemon, secret herbs from the Himalayas—that my wife's guru gave us to us to hang from doors and windows. Those are the ones Chottu wears around his neck.

We are all in the sitting room, watching Modiji's address on TV. Chottu is there too, sitting in a far corner, as we have started insisting on him keeping his distance. He is not cooking for us either, just doing the washing and cleaning up now.

"You will have to go home, Chottu," I tell him, after Modiji goes off the screen. Maybe I begin by just intending to pull his leg; I don't know. But somehow, as the conversation proceeds, my joke becomes reality.

"Go home, Babu? Whose home?"

"You heard what Modiji said," I add. "Everyone is to go home."

"But I don't have a home, Babu," he replies. "I live here."

"No, Chottu," I explain to him, with greater resolve now. "That will be against the law. This is not your home. You need to go back to your village."

My wife looks at me, and I can see she is backing me up. My children—who are probably not even paying attention, focused as they always are on their iPhones—drift off to their rooms.

"But that is so many hours away by bus," Chottu replies.

"We will give you extra money," I answer him. "But you cannot stay here. You do not want to disobey Modiji, do you?"

"You do not want Modiji to get angry at us?" my wife adds.

Chottu shakes his head and slaps himself on the forehead in his customary gesture of contrition. He always does that when he feels that he has made a stupid mistake.

It is around a month after Chottu has left us, with his clothes in an old VIP suitcase—my wife and the girls, whose schools are closed, are managing the kitchen quite well without him—when one of my neighbors stops me on the stairs. I am going out for a walk in our park, and he is coming back from a rare shopping trip. Our masks are parked on our chins, ready to be pulled up if required.

"Mishraji," he says to me, pushing his mask further down to allow his chin more freedom to wag. "I have been meaning to ask you. Your chokra, he isn't with you any longer, is he?"

"You mean Chottu?"

"Yes, that's the one."

"No," I reply. "He returned home to his village a long time back."

"Strange," he says. "I am certain I saw him living in one on the canisters in the dump behind us. You know, my uncle has a flat in the other row, and you can look over the dump from the back windows. There are a group of vagrants living there, sleeping rough, and I thought I saw Chottu with them. I could recognize him, his baggy pants and limp."

"No, it could not have been him," I insist. "He went home weeks ago. We paid him an extra month's salary too."

"That's good, because my uncle and his family are worried of possible contamination. Their windows overlook the dump. They have complained to the police a couple of times now. But you know how slow the police are ..."

"Incredibly slow," I agree.

"That is why we need Modiji. A leader who can get things done. A strong leader."

The phone call from the police chowki comes exactly five days after that conversation. It comes on our landline. My youngest daughter picks it up and brings the cordless phone to me. It is some sub-inspector, she mutters, plonking it down on the sofa next to me.

The sub-inspector launches into a veritable diatribe as soon as I identify myself. He has a rough, booming voice. I imagine someone large and heavily mustachioed at the other end. All I gather from what he says is that he has arrested my "servant" for occupying a public space, and I was going to be charged with criminal negligence for not keeping him indoors. He goes on a rant about irresponsibility and anti-nationals. What servant, I demand. He does not have the name or does not wish to give it to me. He orders me to come down to the police station right now—come and see me within an hour, or we will *chalan* you, he growls into the phone, and disconnects.

I was not born yesterday; I know what his game is. I call my friend, the MLA who had obtained the Namaste Trump contract for us, and he asks me to give the details to his private secretary. Don't worry, Mishra Sa'ab, the private secretary tells me. I will take care of the matter.

The sub-inspector calls back within an hour. His tone is very different. He is brimming with details, explanations and courtesies. He explains that the police had raided the dump behind our apartment complex after receiving numerous complaints from its residents.

It is our duty to follow up on complaints, Sirji, he says to me. We are stretched. You have no idea how difficult it is to enforce the curfew. If only everyone was like you, Sirji, educated and disciplined. But, oof, these people, what to say! Too few policemen, too much work. But when we get a complaint from respectable people like you, Sirji, we always act. Immediately. I went there personally, with three constables. There were four, five vagrants there. They ran away once they saw the jeep. We chased and caught one of them. He was limping and couldn't run much. We were just, what do you say, Sirji, teaching him a lesson, our usual treatment for such lawbreakers, when he shouted out your name. He said he worked in your flat and his name was Chottu.

I explain to the sub-inspector that Chottu had worked in my flat but had gone back home on the day of the curfew. I had no idea he had come back. He never came to us.

Oh no, Sirji, he has not come back. He has been living in the containers all these weeks, him and a few others.

I wouldn't know about that, Inspector, I say firmly. I did not see Chottu or hear from him after he left.

What do we do with him now, Sirji?

I think about it. I do not want them to give Chottu what they call a treatment once again. I know all about that, and I am not a mean-hearted man.

Can't you get him admitted to one of these migrant labor camps that are being set up?

Yes, Sirji. Of course, Sirji. I will take care of it, Sirji. Sorry to bother you, Sirji. Please give my regards to the MLA Sa'ab, Sirji. You have jotted down my mobile number, haven't you, Sirji? SI Om Prakash, that's my good name, Sirji. Anytime you want anything, just call, Sirji. Om Prakash, SI, at your service, Sirji. Anytime.

I am certain I will not hear of Chottu again, at least not before the pandemic is over. I am wrong.

There is no doubt that the pandemic worsens over the next few days. Some people I know catch the virus, but they recover. Then one of my employees—a man in his late fifties with a heart condition—dies of it.

The terror of the virus finally settles on my family and the neighborhood. Streets stay silent all through the night. There are no vendors in sight during daytime. The anti-Modi social media go on and on about migrant laborers trekking for hundreds of kilometers to get home and dying on the way, sometimes in traffic accidents. But what traffic accidents, I post on Twitter, where is the traffic? It is all lies. How can people die in traffic accidents when there is a curfew? And yet, the virus is real. We know it. No sensible person dares go out needlessly.

One afternoon, the phone rings again. It is the landline, and I hesitate to pick it up, as anyone who is someone calls me on one of my two iPhones. But maybe it is the ennui of the afternoon, the lethargy of the lockdown; I finally reach for it.

The female voice identifies itself as someone or the other from the Covid Centre. I know what it is. It has been set up a couple of kilometers away from here, and mostly caters to Covid patients who cannot afford anything better.

"Come and collect your dead body," says the monotone on the phone.

"What dead body?" I sputter into the receiver. "I don't know any dead body."

"Patient 81-C, Bed 54, Name of Chottu." The voice, obviously emanating from a human larynx but somehow surcharged with a mechanical syntax, continued, "Your address and this number are on record at registration. Police to be notified if body unclaimed."

I bang down the receiver and rummage through my diary for SI Om Prakash's number. Bloody fool, I mutter under my breath. I catch him on the fifth try and I shout at him. What did you think you were doing? How dare you enter my address as Chottu's address? What impudence! How dare you?

SI Om Prakash is contrite. He spends a long time explaining, because I do not really let him do so for the first few minutes. But then, after I calm down, he explains that the rules demand a "last known address" before admitting anyone to a migrant labor center, and he had entered my address, little dreaming that Chottu would catch the disease and die of it. The address must have traveled with Chottu when he was moved from the migrant center to the Covid center.

Simple oversight, Sirji. Don't worry, Sirji. I will collect the body, personally, Sirji, and I will have it cremated properly. It is my job, Sirji. Don't call anyone, Sirji. It is as good as taken care of by yours truly.

And the man is as good as his word. He calls that very evening to tell me that Chottu has been cremated. All according to the Shastras, Sirji, properly done.

I feel sad, no doubt, remembering Chottu's goofy smile, but I also feel relieved. I am not his keeper, after all. I consider telling my wife that Chottu is dead and has been duly cremated, but then I do not do so. What is the point? She is frightened enough about the virus. Why mention another death from Covid?

It is a misty morning the next day. The mist is unseasonal. I get up earlier than I usually do. My wife is still lying in bed, snoring a bit, and the children, late risers given half a chance, are in their rooms. I go out to the balcony but can only make out the silhouettes of other buildings and trees, gauzed with mist. No one is out. Even crows are not cawing. An eerie silence envelops the neighborhood.

I re-enter the sitting room and am about to switch on the TV when there is a knock on the front door. I am not certain it is a knock. It is such a hesitant sound. But I listen, and it recurs, more like someone scratching rather than knocking.

Who could be knocking this early in the morning?

I go up to the door and peer through the peephole. The corridor outside is still lit up with the mercury tubes that burn in the building all night. I see a boy with his back to me. The light from the mercury tubes is falling like a thin white shroud on him. His back looks vaguely familiar. Then the boy turns. I gasp. I know the face. It is different now, thinner, stained with what looks like charcoal on one side. But I know the face. It is Chottu. And, as if to remove all doubt, the face then smiles at the peephole: it is Chottu's goofy smile, daft and childlike. For some reason, he is dripping wet.

I recoil into the sitting room. What is Chottu doing out there? Has it all been a mistake? Had someone assumed Chottu's identity? Was someone playing a trick on me?

The scratch-knock is repeated, but I have no intention of

letting Chottu into the flat. That man-boy could be carrying a hundred diseases! Why is he so wet? There is only one thing to do. I call SI Om Prakash. This time I get him on the first try. He sounds half-asleep, but he tries to hide the irritation in his voice.

"What did you mean by saying that you cremated Chottu last night?" I demand.

"I did, Sirji. I supervised it from a distance."

I describe Chottu to him. Yes, he says, that was the boy. A man, I retort, he is a man, he just looks like a boy. Yessirji, says the sub-inspector, Yessirji, that was him.

"Then what is he doing outside my flat right now?" I demand of the sub-inspector.

"Your flat, Sirji?"

"Right outside my door!"

"It cannot be, Sirji. We cremated him." Then he hesitates. "The boy had been dead for hours, Sirji. He was stiff like cardboard. For some reason he did not burn. You know how short of wood the cremation grounds are these days. But we cremated him with what we could procure, and I even bought the ghee myself. We cremated him as a Hindu, because it was your order, Sirji. Except that his body did not burn, and so, as other people were doing too, we floated it in the river. There is nothing wrong with that, Sirji. Our Shastras say that once the body has been touched by fire, it can be given to water, if required. The soul will still be released for rebirth …"

"You fool!" I shout at him. "You half-burnt a live person and then threw him into the river!"

"No, Sirji, it cannot be," the inspector is adamant. "If there is anything I can recognize it is a dead body. That boy had been dead for hours. He was like, like … plyboard."

"Then why is he standing there outside my flat, dripping wet?"

"Dripping wet, Sirji? It is not possible, Sirji. Give me ten minutes. I am coming to your place. Do not open the door until I get there. This is a conspiracy, Sirji. Let me catch the bastards who are creating this drama."

My wife had come out into the sitting room, rubbing her eyes, while I was shouting into my phone. The children, of course, were still sleeping. Even an earthquake cannot wake them up.

"What are you so upset about?" my wife asks me.

So shaken am I that I reply without thinking, "Chottu is back."

"Chottu?" exclaims my wife. She moves toward the door as if to open it, but I stop her. I tell her not to open the door. "He looks ill. Who knows where all he has been?"

She hesitates and then tiptoes up to the peephole and looks out. She gasps and tiptoes back to me.

"There is something wrong with him," she whispers. "His clothes are burnt. And why is he dripping wet? It has not rained for days. It almost looks like there is water pouring out of him."

"It is Chottu, isn't it?" I ask her.

"Oh yes," she replies. "It is Chottu. No doubt about it. The same smile. Teeth missing. It is Chottu, for sure. What do we do with him?"

"Don't worry," I reassure her. "I will have him taken away to some care home. You go back to bed. It is too early."

"I can stay with you."

"What for? Just go back to bed, I will join you in ten minutes. I have asked an inspector to come and take him away."

"Give Chottu some money too," says my wife as she returns to the bedroom.

SI Om Prakash calls from outside my door. "I am here, Sirji. You can open up," he says.

I open the door. The sub-inspector is standing there with a constable. It strikes me that this is the first time I am meeting him, and SI Om Prakash, unlike his voice, is a small man, thin, pot-bellied, with a clerical mustache. The constable behind him looks more like a police officer. Then I notice that the floor is wet, as if it was recently flooded.

"Where is the boy who has been bothering you, Sirji?"

I look around, bewildered. Though the landing is wet, there is no one there.

"He was here just five minutes ago," I say.

Then I look up, and there, right where the staircase turns onto the landing above us, there he is, somewhere within a heap of ragged clothes, half-burnt, with water dripping from them. He is lying crumpled on the stairs, his back to us.

"There he is," I shout, pointing.

SI Om Prakash follows my finger.

"Where, Sirji?"

"There, there, on the stairs," I shout, my fingers quivering. "There, as big as a blazing fire."

The pile of rags on the stairs shakes and stands up slowly, its back still to us.

"There is nothing there, Sirji," the SI is saying.

But I can see the half-burnt rags that are giving off steam or smoke and have water seeping out of them, I can see the body clad in those rags turn …

"Nothing on the stairs," the big constable echoes his boss.

… and I can see it is Chottu, face blackened and singed, most of his hair burned off, but the smile recognizable as ever, because when he sees me he gives me that familiar goofy, gap-toothed smile as water burbles out of his mouth and runs in rivulets down his chin and over his chest onto the stairs.

OLDEN FRIENDS ARE GOLDEN

Giridhar sat in a wicker chair on the balcony of his palatial new house in a suburb of Bhopal, and browsed through the seven daily newspapers, three in Hindi, to which he subscribed. It was seven thirty in the morning. He had been up from five thirty, as was his routine: first his puja, then yoga and a stint on his exercise bike before taking a shower in cold water, for that was good for his circulation. Now he had exactly half an hour on his own before the business of the day began: seeing people. Giridhar was a municipal councillor, hoping to get a ticket from the Congress Party to become a Member of the Legislative Assembly. He had retired early as a police officer to enter this field.

His wife walked in with a tray. On it were a cup of tea and a plate with two arrowroot biscuits. She put it on the wicker table and went back into the house to instruct the cook. Breakfast had to be served exactly at eight. One of the three smartphones on the table buzzed. Giridhar looked at it with annoyance; this was his private moment. Then he saw it was a message from the WhatsApp group he shared with his old school friends from Phansa, a small town in another state. He picked up the phone.

Lakshmi had finished supervising her husband's office-going rituals. His office was in another part of the house. What he did there was partly a mystery to Lakshmi. One part of it. The part that had to do with making money. The money that had enabled them to move out of Phansa and buy this sprawling farmhouse outside Lucknow. The other part she knew and understood. Her husband wrote historical novels. He published them under his own imprint because established publishers were so biased. But since 2014, her husband had started receiving prizes and attention. The prizes were awarded by organizations with names like the Hindu Renewal League or Sanatana Dharma Sahitya or the Yogi Trading Association—not the Booker Committee or even the Sahitya Akademi—but Lakshmi was not familiar with the distinction between such organizations. The prizes showered on her husband seemed impressive to her, and the functions involved ministers, dozens of impassive-looking people, sometimes even TV and film stars. Just last year, when they had finally visited the USA, her husband had been felicitated as a "best-selling author" at literary events organized by the Indian High Commission. Lakshmi was happy with her life—she designed dresses in her spare time—and proud of her husband. She devoted full attention to him when he was around. But the moment he left—a servant behind him carrying a pile of books—she picked up her iPhone. That is when she saw the WhatsApp message.

Santosh saw the message at eight in the morning, on the company bus that he took to work. Even though he had a car, this was Delhi. He did not want to drive needlessly and could not afford a driver. Or, actually, he could afford a driver, if only drivers were not such cheats, because the last one had not only asked for repeated raises but had also siphoned off and sold petrol from the tank of his Hyundai i20. There was no point. The corporation he worked for ran company buses, and it took just thirty to forty minutes, an hour if the traffic was bad, so Santosh mostly left his car behind. It also enabled him to catch up on office gossip in the air-conditioned bus and check his iPhone, for, unlike the other men he knew, Santosh was a progressive person and actually helped prepare breakfast and his three children for school, after which both he and his wife left for work. His wife taught in a kindergarten in the neighborhood.

Manish had a flight to Kolkata. He was at the Patna airport, which was far too small for the city. To think that when he was growing up in nearby Phansa, he had considered this a metropolis! Years of innocence. The Air India flight was forty-five minutes late. But now it had been announced and they were being called to board. He was not worried about being late. Manish was high enough in the multilayered Life Insurance Corporation for people to wait for his arrival. As he walked to the gate, he felt his phone vibrating in his jacket pocket. He already had it on silent mode. Manish took it out and switched it off without looking at the messages. It was his policy never to check anything on his mobile while boarding a plane. The last time he had done so, about a decade ago in 2008, there had been news of a share market collapse that had cost him more than four lakhs before his plane had finally landed and he could sell off his shares. It had been the worst flight of his life. He would switch on his phone only when he landed. What happens, happens.

Sunita almost missed the message. She had left in a rush for her work at a private Bangalore college—having finally managed to get tenure at the age of forty-nine, just six years ago—and by the time she took her lunch break in the college cafeteria, so many messages had piled up that she could not even look at all of them. But then a colleague in the cafeteria remarked, "Olden friends are golden." It reminded her that she had not checked her old school WhatsApp group for a day or two now. She could see twenty-one unread messages highlighted there. The number jumped out at her. Some were from yesterday, but most were from the morning. They were all in response to a message by Narender that had been posted early in the morning, at 7:32 exactly. Narender was the only person from the group who was still in Phansa, the town where they had all grown up and whose best English-medium school they had attended. Six boys and girls (out of a graduating class of twenty-three) had stayed on in town. They did not connect to the WhatsApp group; one boy had died of alcoholism, though no one talked about it, and two were struggling financially; another boy, always a loner, was said to be depressed; and the two girls who had been married early into families in the town claimed they were not on WhatsApp. Narender ran a successful clothes-retailing business in Phansa and was the only one in the group. He was their source of news from their old hometown.

Sameer had two iPhones: one for work/family and one for fun. He never looked at the latter until his lunch break well after two, depending on when he'd finished examining all the files and orders piled up on his desk, as well as the previous day's productivity charts for the eleven employees in his export–import business in Ahmedabad. The old-school WhatsApp group was obviously on his "fun" iPhone, and he saw the message only when he switched it on at 3:07. It had been a busy day. The last message was from Arjun. This was rare. Arjun was the only one from the batch to become a doctor; he had moved to the USA and seldom participated in the group chats that erupted abruptly every few days. Sameer read the conversation carefully. He frowned. He read it again. He wondered if he should reply. It was a difficult choice. He felt he should say something. But he hesitated.

Narender

I thought I should inform you that Aurangzeb's brother has left for Pakistan. Local police investigating his family here. National security issue. His parents interrogated. I was told this morning. It all took place last night. You know Aurangzeb had been arrested before he left for London ten years ago... Very worrying developments. For all of us.

7:32

Giridhar

Calm down, dost. I have been in the police. Aurangzeb was arrested for some street protest, nothing devastating. People leaving for Pakistan is not a national security issue. No one's parent interrogated for that let me assure you. Been there done that

7:35

Narender

Giridhar Babu you might know but I do not know anyone who has left for Pakistan. I am quoting reliable sources. Believe not believe

7:36

Giridhar

What? Dost dost na raha? Of course believe you Guru, but sources please? ☺

7:37

Narender

Reliable. Cannot reveal name for obvious reasons

7:40

Lakshmi

Oh God! We do not need this. I did not even know Aurangzeb was in this group. He was trouble even in school. It was lucky he was not rusticated. Who put him on? Who else has been sneaked into this group? This is beyond belief! This is a private group.

8.03

Giridhar

Guru Narender, do not give me all that classified stuff... I have been an officer. ☺

8:34

Narender

Giridhar Babu, not everyone flies as high as you or your precious Lutyen Congress does. I have been told by sources that anyone corresponding with Aurangzeb or his family will be under surveillance. Lakshmi ji, I think Sudeep put Aurangzeb on.

8:41

Lakshmi

Sudeep!!!? He left us in class seven! Why is HE in the group? I have seen no posting from him or Aurangzeb anyway. Why are they here if they do not post? What is the point? Why are there so many people here who do not post? MANISH, did you make Sudeep the coordinator? I thought you were the coordinator? Who did this? Oh my God, my husband will be so upset. He knows all these government high-ups... We had dinner with a state minister just last Saturday.

8:42

Narender

I agree this is looking bad, friends.

8:46

Sudeep
Lakshmi ji, your husband was in touch with
Aurangzeb just a year ago, when he wanted some
books to be shipped over from London. I know.
Aurangzeb told me, he went to a library for the
first time since college to order photocopies of the
three books... So, if you excuse my Sanskrit: wtf?

10:48

Lakshmi
I am not talking to you, Sudeep ji. I hardly remember
you from school. You left for another school, when, in
class seven? This is a group for people who graduated
together, as far as I am concerned. I am asking Manish.
MANISH, where are you? I am going to call you on the
phone now. This needs to be sorted out. You stay out
of this, Sudeep ji.

10:53

Narender
Sudeep Babu, this is serious. I will be leaving the
group if Aurangzeb continues to be part of it. I have
no desire to associate with people being investigated
by the authorities. His brother was interviewed by
security at the airport I have it from reliable sources.
I think some of us will have to leave as we do not live
in liberal metropolitan circles you know

10:57

Giridhar
Take is easy, Guru. It means
nothing. Who are your sources?

11:06

Sunita
Oh no, I just saw this. I am shocked. Aurangzeb
has been in London for years. Didn't he gradu-
ate from Aligarh Muslim University?

12:16

Narender
Yes. His brother was a
student leader there too.
12:18

Lakshmi
I finally got in touch with Manish. He was on a flight. He
is going to delete Aurangzeb as soon as he gets home.
We cannot have the police looking into our group.
Not that we have anything to hide, but we want to be
free to talk about our lives and common experiences.
We do not want to be watched. You should not have
connected him, Sudeep ji. It was very immature of you.
You knew his background. It is not as if he is like
Sameer: he was always a trouble-maker.
12:47

Sudeep left.

Sunita
I do not understand what is up. Why did Sudeep leave?
12:53

Santosh
Just saw this. R we sure about all this? I mean
Aurangzeb was a bit wild, and so was his bro,
I guess, but I recall him drinking beer with us.
Not really the Pakis type, if u ask me...
1:21

Giridhar
Guru Santosh, who can doubt
Narender Guru's sources? ;-)
1:25

Narender
Thank you Giridhar Boss. That is good coming from you and your party...;-)
1:56

Manish
Doing it in five minutes, if no objections. Sorry for the hassle, friends. Let's all just stay calm. OK?
2:01

Aurangzeb removed

Santosh
I still think we shouldve given Aurangzeb time to respond. Maybe he wouldve clarified? Just saying. ☺
2:03

Sunita
Well, he did get time from 7:30 this morning. I do not like this, but why didn't he clarify? It is unfair to do this to your school friends. We all have our own lives, our own troubles. I know my college-board... They do not want people with controversies teaching in college. Jobs do not sit on branches for some of us...
2:08

Giridhar
Perhaps because England is about four five hours behind us, Sunita ji? Not that I have been there... ☺
2:13

Lakshmi
We have to be careful who we allow into this group. It has to be close friends. People we know. People we can trust. These are dangerous times. Did you read about the ISI agents arrested just two weeks ago?
2:13

Santosh
Oh well, whats done is done.
Narender, now don't u leave 2!!!
2:13

Arjun
What's up? Where is
Narender going????
3:07

Manish
Yes, Narender, stay on, yaar.
Let's not break old ties.
3:15

Arjun
Sorry friends. Just got up. Have read it now. Sad.
Sad. Never thought... But Narender, don't leave...
3:18

Narender
No reason for anyone to leave now.
Yes, Arjun Boss, very sad.
4:06

Giridhar
Attaboy! Ye yaari hum nahin
todeingey...
4:15

Lakshmi
Sudeep should have thought about this. Just put
us in a spot, without thinking. Selfish of him. So
relieved things are getting back to normal.
4:17

Sunita
Great you are staying Narender. You are our man in Phansa. And olden friends are golden.
4:19

Lakshmi
I just had this idea, friends. Why don't we make a shared online album of photos from our high school years? I have quite a few. Should I do it, and then give access to you all to post photos? Nothing like school days...
4:21

Giridhar
Good idea, Lakshmi ji.
4:27

Sunita
Why didn't we think of this earlier? Great idea! Wow, Lakshmi you are the creative one here!
4:27

New shared album created

Sameer sits down to dinner with his two children. His wife is still in the kitchen making roti. He has been thinking about this all day, ever since he first read the messages during his late lunch break. He has seen it unfold on WhatsApp. He has hesitated half a day. But looking at his children, he feels he has to respond. Not to write anything seems worse than writing something! He takes out his "fun" phone and keys in his message quickly, before his wife comes out with the food and tells him not to work, at least not at dinnertime...

Sameer

Hey, friends! What's up? Having dinner here. It has been a very busy day at work. That GST bureaucratic shit means even more work for us businessmen. I have not been able to follow anything online for days. Giridhar Bhai, you want to change professions? I am told you only sit in your office for three hours every morning! Gotta run now, guys, steaming roti on the way ...

9:39

THE THING WITH FEATHERS

At first it was unintentional, just a slip of the tongue. Rakesh Sir was on his way home from work, which usually entailed stepping across the rubble of the back wall of the private college where he taught, cutting down an alley littered with refuse, balancing along the cemented banks of a nullah with black bubbling water and emerging on to the bazaar road through a gap in a fence. It saved him a kilometer.

There he stopped for a cup of tea at a kiosk that still gave its patrons the option of sipping chai in earthen cups. Rakesh Sir liked his chai in an earthen cup. He had half an hour to sip his tea—sometimes he ordered a samosa along with the tea, savoring the smell of the cup, which always reminded him of the first monsoon rain—before he walked briskly to his house in the suburbs, where students would be waiting for their private tutorials. After that, until ten thirty, sometimes eleven, at night, Rakesh Sir gave tuition to students, even eating his dinner— ordered from a nearby restaurant and fetched by a randomly picked student—at one of the rectangular plastic-sheeted tables around which he dispensed useful information. This half hour at the tea kiosk was his single solitary moment of the day, apart from the morning, when he brushed his teeth, before going out for breakfast and then directly on to his college. Not that Rakesh Sir had ever desired anything more than this half hour. He was so used to his routine that he could not imagine anything else.

This had been his life for thirty-one years. In those days, his mother was alive, and sharing the two-bedroom house that Rakesh Sir still occupied. The house had been built by his father and was meant to be of two stories. But just the ground floor was complete when Rakesh Sir's father died. Rakesh Sir was completing his BA then, and his three much younger brothers and sisters, who were still in secondary school. It fell upon Rakesh Sir to assume the mantle of the breadwinner of the family, which he did quietly and effectively, first by tutoring school students, then getting a job at the private college. He continued to study, and completed an MA, after which the college confirmed his tenure, though he had to abandon his plan of going to Patna or even Delhi for a Ph.D. He had become too popular. He had earned a reputation for training students not for the top competitive exams, like the ones for entry into the civil services, which he had failed to crack himself, but for everything under that. In a place like Phansa, where success in the civil services was more a dream than an ambition, this ability was highly valued. Rakesh Sir did things properly, always within limits; it was this systematic manner of pursuing a reasonable education or a practical career that he imparted to his students. The flashier ones never came to him. They mostly went to bigger cities in any case.

Sometime in those thirty-one years, Rakesh Sir not only educated his younger brothers into successful careers as engineers in bigger cities, married off his sister to a doctor in Ranchi, cremated his mother, but he also forgot to get married himself, or to complete the second floor of the house he had inherited, where rusted iron girders still stuck out of the roof. Now he lived on as he had, even though he had no economic constraint to make him continue providing instruction; it simply did not strike him as something that needed to be changed. It also gave him a reason not to leave the town or visit his siblings in their bigger cities too often.

Rakesh Sir's usual routine at the tea kiosk was to greet the owner, whom everyone knew as Sharmaji, then put his cash on the scratched counter, sticky and covered with flies, after which Sharmaji's chokra would ladle out a cup and hand it to him. Lurking in the shadows of the kiosk, Sharmaji was a vague bewhiskered figure, dressed in vests and lungi in the summer and wrapped in coarse brown shawls in the winter, one shawl over another as the cold deepened, and if Rakesh Sir had met him outside the kiosk, he might not have been able to recognize him.

That evening, Rakesh Sir followed his time-honored routine, but his greeting came out slightly wrong. Instead of "How are you?"—which is what he had said almost every weekday for thirty-one years, receiving a grunted *"Bhagwan ki daya hai"* in reply, and sometimes not even that—Rakesh Sir found himself saying to the brown-sheeted indistinct figure in the kiosk (it was November), "Who are you?"

Not *"Aap kaise hain?"* but *"Aap kaun hain?"*

Even as Rakesh Sir was going to rephrase his polite inquiry, the man in the kiosk did something uncharacteristic. He looked scared, pulling the edges of the shawl closer around his face, as if trying to hide, and stammered some kind of answer, which, from the little Rakesh Sir got of it, was about how he, the man in the kiosk, had been visiting and had found Sharmaji ill in bed, and how ... But that is when something even stranger happened: the chokra in the kiosk climbed over the counter and tried to run away. He was immediately grabbed by other customers and the mob, for this was a bazaar road in Phansa, and roads like that breed mobs as easily as a human being bleeds from a cut. At this, the chokra started weeping and crying and shouting that mai-baap he was innocent, he had been forced to do it mai-baap, and then the man in the kiosk made a run for it, but obviously had no chance given the relationship of that road to mobs.

It was only next morning that the matter became clear to Rakesh Sir. It was in all the newspapers, and it was on the lips of all his students and colleagues. One newspaper even identified Rakesh Sir, almost, as "a teacher at the local Shri Veer Singh Memorial College, who first exposed the imposture." It appeared that Sharmaji was not Sharmaji, that actually Sharmaji had not been Sharmaji for some days. Instead, Sharmaji had been murdered by a cousin from his ancestral village—there had been some property dispute—who had then assumed his identity in order to negotiate the sale of the kiosk and the two-room house, from under whose brick-and-gravel floor the plastic-sheeted, partly decomposed body of Sharmaji was recovered.

His colleagues looked upon Rakesh Sir with new respect, not untinged with alarm, and quite a few of his students told him that the newspapers should have mentioned his name, for out of the hundreds who had frequented the kiosk he was the only person to see through the imposter. But Rakesh Sir did not pay them much attention. His mind was fixated not on the details of the murder, for he had read about enough murders and homicides in the newspapers, but the difference that one slipped word from his lips had made. For someone who had ordered and lived his life with the least slippage of action, thought or word, this was a revelation.

That is the reason why, when one of his siblings called him the next evening—they called about once a month—the conversation took an unusual turn and ended awkwardly. There had been a pattern to these phone conversations. His siblings inquired about his health and work; Rakesh Sir asked how their jobs (in the sister's case, her husband's job) and children were faring. The responses were predictable. The calls culminated with the siblings inviting him over to their place, though the last time he had visited any of them was at least five years ago. On his few visits, years ago, he had realized that his stay was difficult for everyone, for he was restless without his routine, and they were busy people, deeply inserted into the far more hectic social networks of the extended families into which they had married. And yet, all the calls ended with the same invitation.

You should visit us sometime, Bhaiya, the sibling would say.

When? Rakesh Sir would reply, half-jokingly.

Then the conversation would end with some suggested dates—winter vacation, I think the kids do not have plans; maybe Diwali, but I need to check with my spouse—all of which, Rakesh Sir knew, were just a postponement of the answer.

So this time when the sibling said, "You should visit us sometime," Bhaiya, Rakesh Sir, only half-aware of the word slipping from his lips, replied, "Why?"

The slippages multiplied. Rakesh Sir did not make much of it. They were such slight matters; he was not always fully aware that he had said "who" instead of "what," "what" instead of "when," or stressed a vowel differently, or added an extra consonant to a word. For instance, instead of telling people that his sister had married a doctor in Ranchi, he told them that she had married a doctor in Karachi. Or he switched codes: instead of saying "namaste" or "pranam" to his Hindu acquaintances, he started saying "salaam-alai-kum" to them, and absentmindedly greeting all Muslims with "namaste" or "pranam." And he referred to his sister's mother-in-law, who ran her only son's household with an iron hand, in the masculine gender, and once or twice he even referred to himself in the feminine gender.

Then it got more elaborate. Very soon, when colleagues asked him for an opinion, he would say something that was always slightly awry. When he was in the college's common room, the place filled with the smell of words that had gone off, a strong verbal smell that his colleagues found far more offensive than the usual smell in that room: of food that had actually gone off. When students asked him a question, he gave answers that even the students knew would not get them high grades. For instance, as everyone knew, the correct answer to "What is *King Lear* about?" is "old age, power and ingratitude." But Rakesh Sir told his students that it is Shakespeare's attempt to say that there is no God in an age when such a statement, in any other shape, would have cost the great writer his immortal head.

A little over a year after the occasion when Rakesh Sir had become, almost, a neighborhood hero for his perspicuity in recognizing the imposter who had murdered Sharmaji, he was someone people abruptly crossed the street in order to avoid. Keeping in mind the congestion of the streets of Phansa, this was neither an easy nor a safe course of action, and yet people were desperate enough to avoid being accosted by Rakesh Sir. He had been forced to go on early retirement by the college management, and his tuition had shrunk to three or four students, mostly children from poor families, who still sent them to him largely because he forgot to ask them for his fees. Money was not an issue for Rakesh Sir: the house was free, and he had enough in his providential fund, as well as fixed deposits into which he had put all his earnings once his siblings were educated and married off. And these were kids so used to being asked hard questions and given wrong answers—it had to do with the poverty of their parents—that they did not mind Rakesh Sir when he went off at a tangent, which he increasingly did.

Had Rakesh Sir been living ten years in the future, he might have released his words on Twitter or Facebook, and no one would have noticed, but this was the 1990s, and those online options were not available to him. Perhaps that is why, when people, family, friends and strangers started avoiding him as if he were a rabid dog, Rakesh Sir took to frequenting corner meetings, political rallies, residential committees, impromptu gatherings, milaad or puja functions, all neighborhood weddings, always answering questions that were not even addressed to him. For instance, when the local MLA thundered rhetorically at a gathering in his old college, "Who in the world does not want progress and development?", Rakesh Sir jumped up and, with a surprised look on his face, shouted "I, Sir. I."

It was soon obvious to everyone that this could not be permitted to go on. Why, you would be talking to two friends at the *nukkad*, discussing something obvious, like, if you were Hindu, that Muslims had too many children, or if you were Muslim, that Hindus could not be trusted, and just at the point when the matter had been unanimously summed up, and you lit a cigarette or bidi to inhale the smoke of peace, for all was again well with the world, out would jump Rakesh Sir, who had been lurking behind a lamppost, and contradict you. Anyone else would have been beaten up a dozen times every week, but Rakesh Sir had taught most of the people in the area, or their cousins, or their children, or their spouses, and beating him up was not an option. True, there was hardly anyone in the neighborhood who did not want Rakesh Sir to be thrashed, but no one was willing to take the initiative. It was also doubtful, as the more perceptive intuited, that a thrashing would shut up Rakesh Sir. And who, these days, was willing to go beyond a thrashing, taking the matter to its logical conclusion, as would have been done in the past—and might still be done if the right khap-panchayat took it up in some villages? But, alas, this was a town.

Attempts were made to uproot Rakesh Sir. Some brave parents and a couple of senior ex-colleagues descended on him, singly or in twos, but they were roundly routed by his wrong responses. His brothers were urged to demand their share of the house, which might have forced Rakesh Sir to pitch his tent elsewhere, but after a couple of telephonic conversations with Rakesh Sir, his brothers balanced the value of the property, which was not much, against their peace of mind, and found the scales tipping heavily toward the latter. In any case, the house was not going anywhere, for Rakesh Sir had no other heirs, and it was best that Rakesh Sir did not come to them before—in due course, may he live long—death came to him.

Matters came to a head during the municipal elections, when Rakesh Sir attended every single meeting in his municipal district, and the neighboring one, and asked so many inappropriate questions and offered so many unexpected responses, regardless of leader or party, that the voting percentage fell from an all-time high of 27 percent in the previous election to an all-time low of 12 percent this time. After the expected candidates won nonetheless, both of the municipal councillors got together—across party differences—and decided that something had to be done.

It was an impressive meeting. Apart from the two municipal councillors, the brother of the local MLA, the civil surgeon, a couple of mullahs and all the neighborhood pundits, the officer in charge of the thana, as well as numerous respectable citizens—including a number of Rakesh Sir's ex-colleagues and at least one cousin—participated in it. Various remedies were suggested. Rakesh Sir, for instance, could be reported under the national security act, and, given his penchant to give wrong answers all the time, he would surely incriminate himself during any interrogation and be put away, without the possibility of a trial, for a few years. This, however, was opposed by both the secular councillor, for he would not misuse the act, oh no, not him, even though his party had framed it, and the communal councillor, for Rakesh Sir was a Hindu and had voted for him in the past. The possibility of the house catching fire was dismissed by Rakesh Sir's neighbors and the thana-in-charge, for the post-conflagration paperwork would be incredibly complicated, do you have any idea? Other suggestions were also rejected.

Finally, the civil surgeon, who was known to take the bull by the horns, interrupted the debate. Why are we even talking about all this? he said. Why don't we just go, all of us, to Rakesh Sir and give him an ultimatum? We tell him he has to pack and leave the house, or …

Or what, someone asked.

Or we will tar and feather him and parade him naked in the streets, the civil surgeon answered, in a flash of brilliance.

This struck everyone as a good solution. It did not really involve violence, I mean, not real violence, you see, no? And how could Rakesh Sir refuse to vacate, for to be tarred, feathered and paraded nude in the neighborhood would reduce him to a laughingstock for the rest of his life!

Accordingly, the committee marched, gathering adherents along the way, stopping at a kiosk for some *paan* or cigarettes, to Rakesh Sir's incomplete one-story house, with iron girders sticking out of it, called him out, and gave him the ultimatum. They had expected Rakesh Sir to get angry or be horrified, but his response surprised them.

He stood in his veranda, which was full of folded chairs and tables that he had used to teach his students—in the summer evenings, he would teach his students there—and heard them out calmly. Then he said, thoughtfully, "Tarred and feathered?"

Yes, shouted the crowd.

Rakesh Sir thought a bit more.

"Naked?" he asked.

Yes, thundered the crowd, louder than before.

Then Rakesh Sir frowned, like he used to when solving an intricate problem for his students, and said, "Come back tomorrow morning at ten."

With that, he abruptly entered his house and closed the door.

It was twenty past ten. The sun was out in full splendor, for it was May. Never had the neighborhood seen such a gathering. News had gone around, and people had come from far colonies to watch. It would have been the envy of any political leader. Trees groaned under the weight of climbers. All the nearby balconies were full, and some people had charged a hundred rupees a person for access to their balconies. There were vendors calling out their wares. Women had even dressed up for the occasion. It was like a festival.

People waited. Crows cawed. The heat built up. Someone kicked a street dog, which ran away, yelping. By eleven, the sun would be too strong. It was almost ten thirty now. The committee, which had crowded onto the stairs of Rakesh Sir's incomplete house, was getting restless. Some of them shouted, Rakesh Sir, Rakesh Sir, where are you? Come out now!

There was no response. The thana-in-charge walked up and banged with a large, hairy fist on the warped wood of the door. Then he stepped back. Maybe he was afraid to face us and left during the night, he said to the other committee members. Coward, muttered the civil surgeon, disappointed.

Just then the door was flung open from the inside. At first, there was nothing. Then an apparition stepped out that made even some of the men shriek. It was dark, with tufts, like fur, stuck all over it.

The committee tumbled off the stairs of the house. The crowd gasped and fell back. It was Rakesh Sir, tarred and feathered, stark naked. Simply, as if he was going out to shop, nodding to people he knew, Rakesh Sir walked down the stairs and onto the street. He dripped tar and feathers. The crowd parted before him.

Rakesh Sir was like Moses dividing the sea. But the sea did not just divide; it dissipated. Even before Rakesh Sir, walking slowly and normally, had crossed the fronts of three houses on the street, the crowd had disappeared. So had the committee. If people still looked, they did so from behind pulled shutters or the foliage of trees. No one laughed.

Rakesh Sir walked on, tarred and feathered, stark naked.

LAST INSTALLMENT

Exactly 6,892 kilometers to the east of the *parcelhus* in which
I sit and write, in a North Indian village that is beyond the
comprehension of my Danish neighbors, who, like me, even an
immigrant (white-collared) like me, own neatly hedged houses
stocked with their pasts, with albums, dresses, books, furniture,
middling artwork and framed photos on their walls, inherited
silver, entire cabinets, wardrobes and trunks full of the past;
exactly 6,892 kilometers from here,

1.

a muscular young man of twenty-three finishes his hundredth
push-up, though push-up is not the right word, push-ups are
done on a vertical axis, where you push your chest down to
the ground without touching it, vertically, and then up again,
vertically, but what this young man is doing involves a curving,
dipping forward-backward motion too, and if you ask him to
name the exercise, he would not say "push-up"; he would say
"dand" or "dandwat."

Every morning, just before or after dawn, Ashraf, for that is
the young man's name, does two hundred dands, which he had
started doing when he was nine, though he had only managed
twenty or so at that age and had built them up slowly, and there
was even a time he had gone to the neighboring akhara for

wrestling, winning far more often than he lost, true, but all that stopped last year when his father, Abba to him, fell ill, so that now he works on the land, staying close to his Abba, who will otherwise, despite the instructions of the doctor, whom he has not seen for six months because there is no point, and anyway there is no money, where's the money, Beta, we have not even managed the last few loan installments, but still Abba would, for that is the kind of stubborn old man he is, start lifting loads or digging channels far beyond his capacity, and so Ashraf stays close to his father all the time.

This morning, though, Ashraf knows there is no work, the crop has been harvested and sold, the fields are bare and stubbled, his father is still asleep and will be sleeping into late morning, exhausted by the task of stacking the harvested grain into tractors until eight in the night, he and his Abba and two of the contractor's men, and then later this noon the contractor who had bought the crop will come with the cash, and the two of them, father and son, will go to the neighboring town in an auto-rickshaw that runs from this village to town every two hours, more or less, the trip taking forty-five minutes one way, they will go to the bank they have mortgaged the land to and maybe explain why they have not been able to pay regularly, and why this time too they are offering a bit less than what is due to cover the back arrears, for they need a few thousand to survive the next few months, not to mention to procure the seeds, fertilizers, and other things necessary for the next planting season, though at least they do not need to worry about the bullocks anymore, for they had sold the pair in order to manage during the pandemic, and now they rent bullocks from wealthier neighbors, having sold even the goat and retaining only a few hens for eggs.

Ashraf walks in his underpants to the small ready-made toilet cabinet that was installed outside the house a few years ago by officials, where there is just enough space for him to squat and for a curved plastic badhna with water next to him, and then, coming out, he washes his hands in the water left in the badhna, using a small hard piece of blue detergent, refills the badhna from a covered bucket by the tap, which is obviously not running this early, then uses two or three mugs of water from the covered bucket to take a quick bath in the open, still wearing his underpants, always being careful with water, as they have no well on their land, and water is precious, and then he wipes himself with a piece of cloth, which used to be a lungi but has now become a towel, such distinctions ceasing to matter when his mother passed away three years some months ago, suddenly, just before the virus, probably of a brain hemorrhage, the hospital informed them, though she was already unconscious by the time they reached the hospital in town and died within an hour of arriving there, which a nurse said was a mercy, both to the old woman and to her survivors, for if she had lingered she would have been a vegetable, and it would have cost them a fortune, he could see they did not own a fortune, so it was a mercy, all said and done, that she died within six hours of first complaining of unease and a splitting headache, Allah is merciful, said the nurse, who was a Hindu, not a Muslim, but could see from Abba's beard that Ashraf, with a thin mustache but no beard, and his father were Muslim, and so the nurse used the word Allah, not God or Bhagwan or Devi or something else, and then he told them that the medicines they had just bought could be returned to the apothecary, and he would go with them if the shopkeeper refused, it was the least he could do, for they seem to be decent people, the old woman looks so peaceful too, and Abba could not say anything in response, but Ashraf thought that maybe the nurse was right because his mother had always said that she did not know, who does, when the Maker would call her back, but she prayed that whenever He did it would be quickly, that she would go quickly and not linger and be a burden on others, at which Ashraf had sometimes scolded her, jokingly, telling her she was such a bundle of bones, too light to be a burden on anyone, and in any case she needed to wait until he got married, and that would distract her, and she would start telling Ashraf about some distant cousin's daughter in a village further off who would be just perfect for him, such a pretty and obedient girl and only sixteen, not too old, just the right age to marry, though of course both mother and son knew that weddings took time and money, and until the mortgage was paid off they had neither time nor money for a wedding or the bride gift, and surely it just needed a couple of good monsoons, so what was the rush, he was only eighteen, he was only nineteen, he was going to turn twenty, wasn't he?

Because Ashraf is going to the next village, which, as the name Islampur proclaims, is a Muslim one, not mixed like this village, he puts on his only pair of jeans, avoiding the lungi that can mark him out as a Muslim on the way, for such are the times and it is better to be careful, and then, carefully so as not to wake up his Abba, in the early light of the dawn creeping into the semi-pukka three-room house, he opens the wooden cupboard and takes out the fifty rupees that were handed to him by Abba last night, with the words go and have a good breakfast tomorrow, I will be sleeping late and then we will go to the bank when you return, and when Ashraf had tried to give the money back, his father had said, do not, Beta, do not give it back to me, for I want you to eat well next morning, and it would please your mother, for you must remember that she always gave you money after the harvesting was over, and asked you to buy something you wanted with it, but I cannot give you more, this is all the cash left in the house, it won't get you a new shirt or lungi, but it will get you a hearty breakfast, something you want to eat, go to Islampur, they have a couple of good hotels there, and eat well for your mother's sake, for we will be getting paid tomorrow noon, and Allah knows I do not need these fifty rupees anymore, so hush you, just take it and gladden a father's heart.

Now Ashraf folds the fifty rupee note into his shirt pocket, it is his best shirt, bought in town less than three years ago, from money he had earned doing some daily work in town during the off-season, a shirt he wore only on occasion, and he puts on his only pair of jeans, a tight pair he is quite proud of, though Abba had frowned at them when he had brought them home, also from town, all the rest of his clothes, two lungis, another trouser, one T-shirt and one kurta, were much older, though he also has a good pair of pajama-kurta which he keeps only for festivals, for one has to wear something that looks new at least for the two Eids, but he is not ashamed of wearing this light blue shirt and this pair of dark blue denim jeans with the embroidered logo in front, Lewy Jeans, and a leather patch at the back saying the same thing, Lewy Jeans, words Ashraf can decipher, for he has studied up to high school, is fluent in Hindi and can make out words in English, so he can read what the logo proclaims, and he has read somewhere that this is a famous American company, Lewy Jeans, which makes him take particularly good care of this pair of jeans, folding them and the matching shirt away for occasional use, storing them wrapped in plastic in the metal trunk where everything precious is kept and where rats or bugs can't get to them.

The sun has come out now, though the morning is still a bit chilly, and Ashraf thinks of taking the chaddar that he uses when it is cold, but he does not want to carry it back when the sun gets warmer, and he does not like smothering his nice shirt and good pair of jeans with it, so finally he leaves it behind, telling himself that the sunshine will fill with warmth in a few minutes and until then he can simply walk a bit briskly, which is the best way to stay warm in any case, but before he leaves he looks into the shed by the house, where the hens are, retrieves two eggs, takes them back to the house and leaves them where his father will spot them when he wakes up, then latching the door loosely from the inside, by slipping a hand in through a panel, he steps past the threshing floor outside the house, skirting the kathal tree, and into the fields

where the birds are already chirping, a flock of sparrows near the house, around the mehndi tree at the ridge marking the start of the fields, and bigger fowls in the stubbled land, mynahs, pigeons, crows, seven sisters, all fluttering about and chirping, not the crows obviously, undisturbed because the fields are empty, harvest done, which is not the way they would have been this early in the morning two weeks ago, and even further in the village, for the Muslim section outside of which Ashraf lives is at one end of the village, and the Dalit quarter is at another corner, but the main village, largely Yadavs and Kurmis, is to the south, a denser cluster of mud huts and semi-pukka houses, with just two of them over one story, both belonging to the family that runs the village, all *sarpanchs* coming from that one extended family, and on one of the houses, on the roof, Ashraf can see a young man, whom he knows by name, walking around brushing his teeth, and there are two or three men squatting in the fields around the Dalit side, for though the village has enough toilets now, or so claims the government, there are still people who use the fields in the mornings, as do Ashraf and his father on occasion, for the toilet cabinet needs water to flush and they do not always have water.

Ashraf could have gone to the village and taken the road out of it, but it is too early for him to be able to hail a free lift on a tractor, and the road route is longer, so instead he cuts across the fields, he knows which ridges and canal banks to take, what toddy palm or field corner to skirt, he has walked these fields all his life, and this will save him at least twenty minutes, especially now that the fields are bare and no one is around to waylay him with greeting and gossip, so he quickens his pace, partly to stay warm, partly to make up for the hundred or so dands that he has skipped in order to go to Islampur for his favorite breakfast, the thought of which brings water to his mouth, his father loves it too, as had his mother, but they can no longer get it in their village, for it is a mixed village, and that is why Ashraf is walking to Islampur, which is a Muslim village, and bigger too, where there are two or three hotels, hotels is what they call themselves, though they are basically stalls, kiosks, but they serve it, that delicious morning dish, which is known all over that region, from Uttar Pradesh to Bihar, by different names, Payya, Godi, Saweria, Nehari, but which is made in exactly the same way and eaten only by Muslims, mostly by Muslims, and even they don't eat it openly anymore, not in Ashraf's village, for there have again been cases of Muslim men and Dalit men being beaten up and lynched, and you would understand why if I told you the way this dish, this morning soup, you would call it if you were westernized and sophisticated, though Ashraf would not call it a soup, and neither would I, let's say broth then, or stew, yes, broth comes closer to the truth, though the truth, as all our wise men used to say in the days when men could still be wise on occasion, the truth is elusive, and so was this Payya, Godi, Saweria, Nehari, which is why Ashraf is walking almost an hour, with fifty rupees in his shirt pocket, to the only Muslim village in the vicinity, where he is certain that in one of the hotels, those stalls with two benches,

last night a bit before midnight a fire will have been lit, and a cauldron placed on it, and in the cauldron thinly sliced onions fried in ghee until they turned golden brown, then pieces of meat, not the choice cuts as posh recipe books would have you believe but actually the pieces that one finds difficult to cook, such as hunks from the legs, with bones of course, and hence Nehari is also called Goddi or Payya, these pieces are swathed in garlic paste, ginger paste, turmeric paste, all freshly ground, mind you, not dry powder of the sort you would get from Shaan or Pathak's, all this is added to the golden onions in ghee, along with salt, coriander leaves and a freshly prepared mix containing garam masala, nutmeg, peppercorns, cumin and fennel seeds, green and black cardamoms, cloves, and it is stirred thoroughly until the meat is lightly cooked, say for five to eight minutes, and then you add cinnamon sticks, green chilis and bay leaves, stir it once more and add water, at least three times the volume of meat and spices in the cauldron, wait for it to simmer a bit as you reduce the fire, so that finally you have the cauldron, covered now, on low fire, which is the way it has to stay until dawn, when you increase the fire a bit and add, if you want the broth to be thicker, a little flour dissolved in water, stirring all the while, and then the Nehari, or Goddi, or Payya can be served with coriander leaves and lime juice for garnish, usually with thick white bread, freshly baked, which is what Ashraf is dying to eat, because it is impossible for him to get it in his village, because even though sophisticated recipes say Nehari, or Payya, or Goddi is made of mutton, the fact is that it has been made and is still made, or so Ashraf hopes, of beef, and beef has been banned in his state, and in most of India, except in some states where people eat beef, or so Ashraf has been told, and he had said, wouldn't it be lovely to live in a state like that, where you could eat what you wished without being threatened with the law and with lynchings or worse, for mutton is too expensive in any case, and chicken is not cheap either, but beef, ah, Ashraf's mouth waters at the remembrance, and he quickens his pace toward the village Islampur, telling himself that there is nothing I relish more than Nehari, or Goddi, or Payya, early on a morning, it warms you up for the day.

2.

The auto-rickshaw had been more crowded than usual, and his father had to sit in Ashraf's lap, which Ashraf knew his father hated, but there was no option, they had to get to the bank with the money given to them by the contractor, as the harvest had been good this year, the first good harvest in four years, for various blights, flood, drought had destroyed much of the crop in the region year after year for years running, and then the pandemic had destroyed the market when the harvest had been good, but this season had been good again, Allah be thanked, and this time they could make a dent in the loan, the loan they took nine-ten years ago, because they needed money for seeds that had been patented and privatized, and then there were other expenses, and everyone was taking these loans, so why not, if everyone was doing it, surely there was nothing wrong in it, though there was a mullah who had warned against taking or giving loans, for interest is prohibited in Islam, he had said, it is haram, but what interest, all the Muslim farmers had said, and so had all the Hindu farmers, it was not as if they were being given any interest by the bank, why, they were going to pay interest to the bank, so if there was sin in it, surely it fell on the heads of the bankers, may they rot in hell, though there is a chance that hell has five-star hotels too and government bailouts, and Ashraf had laughed at that because it sounded funny despite his having no clear idea what either of them were, and in any case what was the option, now that the government had stopped subsidies and you could not get seeds or fertilizers, what was the option but to mortgage the land against a small loan which, it was obvious, would need just five or six or seven good harvests to repay, what was the risk, and what was the alternative?

The bank is on the second floor, which you reach by a narrow staircase that is partly locked, allowing space only for one person to enter at a time, and upstairs the bank is locked too, or chained in any case, with a guard with a single-barrel, twelve-bore gun standing behind the chain, it is lunchtime he says, five other customers are already standing there in the dark landing, what lunchtime asks one, who is obviously from the town, the sign there says lunch from one to two thirty and it is already three now, well, says the guard, stuffing some snuff between his teeth and lower lip by first pinching his lip and pulling it out like a drawer, well, sir, he says, and the sir is loaded with irony, since you can read signs, you must be reading the newspapers too, and since you can read the newspapers, you should have learned by now that the written word means nothing, it is more fickle than a whore who has been paid, learned sir, surely you do not think that words in print mean what they say, at which the man does not take offense, he is probably used to such banter outside chained banks and other government offices in this little town, and he laughs and says, sir, and this time his sir is loaded with irony too, since you know so much and guard such a great bank, surely you can tell us what to believe and what not to believe, and the guard twirls his mustache and replies, sir, as you know, one should believe only what one sees, and right now you see this chain across the grills of this door . . .

and thus the banter continues, until at around three twenty the guard receives a signal from inside and unlocks the chain, at which the people outside, there are eleven or twelve now, some standing on the stairs, rush in to the counters they need to go to, which is actually not much of a help because the counters are still unstaffed, and they have to wait another ten minutes before the bank starts functioning, though for Ashraf and his Abba the wait is considerably longer, because after they deposit most of the money, which necessitates some filling of forms as the sum deposited is above what can be deposited in cash without query, after having finally had the money counted and accepted, and a pay-in slip issued to them, just as father and son are leaving, a bank official from another section comes up to them and thrusts an official looking envelope at them, and orders them to acknowledge receipt of it, which they do before inquiring what it is about, and the official informs them that it is about their mortgage, for they have missed many installments, and the bank has issued a legal notice, which must have been delivered to them, and in any case that is another matter, but what does this mean, the father asks, this means that the bank has moved to confiscate and sell your land in order to recover its loan, at which the father collapses in a heap on the floor, and Ashraf has to drag him up by both arms, the bank official shrugs and goes away to his section, but Ashraf, having deposited his father in a chair, as some other customers start helping, fetching water, fanning the old man, Ashraf runs after the bank official and asks him what it means, and the bank official says that he is not authorized to answer such queries, but then who is, well, you could speak to a lawyer, which Ashraf knows would cost money, no, he pleads, I need to speak to someone in the bank, then speak to the bank manager, but sir is not in now, he just left for the day, you will have to come back another day.

It takes Ashraf and his father two visits before they get to see the bank manager, because the next day sir is not in until late, and then leaves early, but when they do manage to get an audience, sir turns out to be a tired-looking man, with gray hair and paunches everywhere, including under his eyes, and he looks sad, and he shakes his head, you lot, he laments, you take on loans and do not pay, and we have to do the dirty work, for we have to recover the money, why do you take loans if you cannot pay, what can I do for you, it is out of my hands, I have to answer to others too, there is pressure on us to recover bad loans, and nothing Ashraf and his father say, though Abba starts weeping, which disturbs Ashraf who has seen his father weep on only one occasion, when his mother was being put into the ground, and then he had wept because the ground appeared so cold and dark to him, and the wood they had bought to cover the corpse was so little and of such poor quality, and his father had sobbed into cupped palms and wept and said I should have taken care of her better than I did, I should have taken care of her better than I did, and now she will be in there, in there, in there, and religious people had consoled him with talk of how the body is made of earth and dissolves into earth, how the soul is immortal and returns to its Maker, how paradise is assured to a woman like her, Allah gives and Allah takes away, but Ashraf's father had kept sobbing, uncontrollably, even when some of the strictly religious chided him for failing to be Islamic, for the true Muslim does not grieve in excess, that is like questioning Allah, so calm down, restrain yourself, your son is here, your relatives are here, but Ashraf's father had sobbed all the way home, and that is what he does that day in the bank, he cups his face in his bony, gnarled hands with two of their fingers deformed from the time they had been crushed while plowing, and he sobs, and sobs, until Ashraf forces him up, there is no point sitting there, the manager is checking his smart phone, and Ashraf guides his father out of the cubicle, to where the mustachioed guard stands with his one-barrel gun, and just as they are passing him the man says, there is a way, if you are smart, there is a way.

The way is this, the guard explains to them later in the evening, in the dhaba where he asked them to meet him after closing time, you see the way is this, I will tell you a story, and Ashraf waits, for he knows the guard loves to banter, and Abba is lost in his thoughts in any case, he has not said a thing, just nodded to agree with Ashraf's suggestions or looked straight ahead, as if he is seeing things no one else can, not this narrow, crowded street, netted with electric wires, hemmed in by small drab shops with colorful boards and advertisements, billboards featuring cars that are larger than any that could enter this street, where there are only autos, rickshaws, cycles, and a tumult of pedestrians, billboards featuring muscular men who are smarter and healthier than anyone on the street, except perhaps Ashraf, who was born well-proportioned and has worked on his physique all his life, so Ashraf lets the guard tell them a story, while Abba looks out into the street and sees something else, something worse or something better ...

There was a fox, says the guard sipping from the glass of tea that Ashraf has bought for him, there was a fox you see who had a hen coop with forty-two hens, forty-two okay?, forty-two, which gave him on an average twenty-three eggs per day, which was enough for him to live on, but then one day the neighboring wolf came to him and said fox, my friend, my little friend, why don't you keep another forty-two hens for me, you have enough space, and all you need to do is give me twenty eggs per day, you can see that on average you will make a profit of three eggs per day on my hens alone, with nothing to do, and the fox thought it all made sound business sense, so he signed the papers, and now he had eighty-four hens in all, okay?, eighty-four in all, and they ought to have produced forty-six eggs per day, on an average, forty-six per day, but the law of averages never works that way, the actual numbers are always lower or higher, and in this case, the numbers were lower, and soon the fox owed the wolf dozens of eggs, and he pleaded give me a few more years, for the average will improve, the law of averages is like that, the fox had learned it the hard way, but the papers he had signed did not allow more time, and neither did the wolf, who was bigger than the fox, the papers said that the wolf could now take over all of the hens, not forty-two, mind you, all eighty-four, okay?, all eighty-four, and the fox had only a day to pay back the wolf, so it all looked bad, don't you think it all looked bad?, but the fox was not stupid, he was clever, so he went to the tiger and sold him all his hens, not forty-two, all eighty-four, okay?, all eighty-four, along with the wolf's papers, and of course he sold them for the price of only forty-two, for how else could he convince the tiger to buy, he needed to make an offer, you see, so he got the price of his forty-two hens, more or less, less or more, and now the wolf had to deal with a tiger …

Ashraf can see his father is not paying attention, he is looking out at the street but obviously not seeing the cart selling peanuts, the cyclists, the women with baskets, the two schoolgirls, the crows hopping from wire to ground and back again in order to peck at the spilled intestines of a rodent between the passage of autos and rickshaws, obviously not seeing all that, obviously seeing something else altogether, and hence it is Ashraf who says to the guard, who has now drained the tea in his glass and is wiping his ferocious mustache with the back of his hand, he says, but guard sahib we do not know any tiger.

That is where I can help you, replies the guard, for I know many tigers, and he gives his mustache a twirl to indicate affinity with the species, and I know a tiger in particular who would be interested in your land, not your hut or whatever it is you have as roof over your heads, that's worth nothing, but your land, for this tiger is buying up land in villages outside the town, but why land in villages, asks Ashraf, you won't understand, do not ask, just go to the tiger, he has been buying up land ever since his brother became a Dep'ty Minister, and more so now after the pandemic, which has left small farmers like you with no option but to sell and this tiger does not want them to starve, he likes helping people, you know, okay?, and you can imagine where the money is coming from, so do not ask questions, just come with me to him, and show him your papers, tell him what you want, he will give you a decent price and deal with the bank, he is a good man, and you won't lose all your land to the bank, you will get 50 percent of what it is worth, maybe even 60, and all you will lose is the 3 percent that I will take as my commission.

3.

It comes about as the bank guard promises and not because Ashraf takes it up but because his father, who appeared to have paid no attention to the guard's story in the tea stall, insists on it, convinces Ashraf that it is the only pragmatic option, though Ashraf pays money to consult a lawyer too, and goes into the village to speak to others, who make no promises, though the lawyer is confident they will win in court, not certain of course, one can never be certain about lottery, life or law, but you should win, at least you could get a stay, though the case itself may drag on for years, banks have deep pockets, selling the land will be illegal too, unless of course the man is powerful and can claim a previous loan, which however would also involve you in a court case, the bank might drag you, or not you, your father, for your father signed these papers, the bank will drag your father to court for fraud, banks have deep pockets, the guy you sell it to, if he is powerful, he is, said Ashraf, if he is powerful, continued the lawyer, will get possession of the land, but believe me the bank will make life difficult for your father, in either case you will have to go to court, as petitioner or defendant, but it is your choice, banks have deep pockets.

When Ashraf tells his father what the lawyer had said they are sitting outside their semi-pukka house on a charpoy, which they had dragged out to the shade of the kathal tree outside, for the days are now filling with heat, and his father is lying in the charpoy, clad in lungi and banyan, while Ashraf is sitting at one end, perched delicately on the wooden frame, dressed in his good clothes which he had put on when he went to town to consult the lawyer, whose consultation fee was 250 rupees, an exorbitant sum, but Ashraf had insisted and Abba had relented, but when Ashraf tells him what the lawyer has advised, Abba's eyes lose their focus as they often do these days, and then he props himself up on one elbow and points with the other hand across their strip of field, and way beyond it, to where a row of toddy palms march from south to north, and he says, our land used to stretch all the way to those palm trees in your grandfather's time, and then he moves his arm to a barren mound at the other corner of the horizon, and all the way to there, it was land inherited by use and deed, but your grandfather had a brother, who left for Pakistan with his family in 1951, leaving his inheritance to your grandfather to overlook, not selling it perhaps because he could not bear to, perhaps because he was not certain he would stay in Pakistan, who was certain in those days, but what he did not know was that his land would be declared enemy property and confiscated by the government, your grandfather, my poor father, fought that case for years, twenty years, thirty years maybe, and his brother finally did not believe he was doing so, he thought my father had just misappropriated the land, in due course he stopped communicating, but my father kept fighting the case, until he lost even in the High Court, and then he gave up, for his brother had given up on him too, and the two families never communicated again, my father wrote letters but never got a reply, it hurt him to the moment of his death, you won't remember for you were only two then, you were born late, our only child, born when I was past forty, when we had finally given up even praying at the *dargahs* for a child, just one child, O Holy One, help us O you sainted friend of Allah's prophet, when even your mother had started telling me to marry again, you were two or three when your grandfather died, you won't remember the old man lying in a bed in that room, just there, and he kept on saying, I wish I could just tell my *bhaijaan* and his family that I tried my best, that I did not appropriate an inch of his land, not an inch, not a twig from it, at which Ashraf's father pauses, and Ashraf does not say anything because he knows there is more to come, he has heard the story before, but he does not have the heart to interrupt the old man who finally stops pointing at the horizon, and slumps back exhausted, then he continues, there was still much more land than what we have now, exactly double, but both your aunts decided to sell their shares, I offered to buy if I could pay in installments, but as you know they had married boys working in towns, and they wanted money now, and both my brothers-in-law were adamant about getting the money now, and so that half too was sold, and what was left was not enough, but Allah in his wisdom had given us only one child, and your mother was a thrifty woman, we managed, you went to school, we fed you well, it would have continued that way, if only the subsidies had not been discontinued, or if only we had not had four-five bad years in a row and then the pandemic, yes, we would have managed, and you would have inherited all this, though your mother and I often discussed this, discussed this behind your back, and we wondered if this land was not a burden to pass on to you, for you are a strong young man, with some education, and without this land holding you down maybe you could go to Delhi or the Gulf and earn much more, but now that decision has been taken out of our hands, and despite the fact that this land is me and I am this land, this soil has run in our blood for generations, despite all this, I sometimes wonder if this curse that Allah has sent to me surely for sins I confess I am not aware of, may He spare me, that this curse might not yet turn out to be a blessing for you, Beta.

We have not lost the land yet, Ashraf says, stubbornly, listen to me, listen to what the lawyer said, but the old man closes his eyes and pronounces, no lawyers, no courts, that is like riding a crocodile into the deep river, you do not know, I do, I recall my father fighting for his brother, who no longer trusted him, and believe me, Beta, I will not bestow on you that inheritance, not for your sake, not for my sake, not for the sake of my ancestors whose blood and sweat have irrigated this land, these few bighas left to us we will sell to that Dep'ty Minister or his brother, we will get what you can, and we will just leave this village, leave this state run by a mad monk, you will go to Delhi, go to Dubai, go maybe to America, and you will make more money than anyone in this village has seen, you will have a future that has not been mortgaged to a bank …

and no matter what Ashraf says, no matter how he argues, the old man stays firm, he has made his decision, and no power on earth can shake his resolve.

4.

Ashraf smells the fire before he sees it, from the auto-rickshaw that is bringing him back to the village after he had purchased his train ticket, second class, three tier, to Delhi, as Abba had asked him to do, he had insisted, do it today, there is no point postponing something you have made up your mind to do, the sooner you get started the better, and in any case tomorrow we have to vacate the house, now I can go and live with one of my sisters in town, and the money will last us four-five years, which will give you time to find your feet in Delhi, maybe even get a job in the Gulf, who knows, and then I can join you for the last years of my life, so go today, Beta, get your booking done, and the booking is done now, with the computerized ticket neatly folded in Ashraf's shirt pocket.

At first, Ashraf just thinks that it is someone clearing the fields of stubble, some farmers still do it despite warnings from officers, it might even be the Dep'ty Minister's brother clearing their fields of stubble, for the smell, and now he can see the smoke is coming from the vicinity of their fields, but it is only after Ashraf turns the corner of Ram Bhajan Yadav's house, which is at their end of the village, and after which the fields begin, that he sees the fire, and after that he runs, he runs faster than he ever has, for he can see that the fire is not in any field, not even their recently sold fields, the fire is in their house, and there are people around the house, people with buckets, people with freshly cut fronds, people from their side of the village who have already run down to the house and are trying to put out the fire, while the hens have fluttered into the branches of the kathal tree, under which there lies the padlocked metal trunk in which Abba keeps everything precious, all cash and good clothes, and the one silver *ittardaan* they still have and use for festivals, it is lying under the kathal tree, locked as always, well outside the reach of the greedy flames, the shrieking fire, someone must have pulled it out before the fire barred all entrance, probably his father, but

where is his father? where is his father? by the time Ashraf reaches the house, some of the roof has caved in and most people have stopped fetching water from the well and the canal and throwing it on the burning house, now they are just standing there, watching the house burn, and when Ashraf pushes his way through, shouting for his father, who is not in sight, nowhere to be seen, people shake their heads, someone says the fire spread too quickly, son, too quickly, the place was burning by the time we reached it, one or two try to grab him by the shoulders to restrain him, calm him down, but Ashraf is a powerful young man and he breaks out of their grip, running to the entrance of the house, Abba, where is Abba, shouts Ashraf, where is my Abba, and when two or three people shake their heads and point at the burning house, before they can restrain him, Ashraf tears off his good shirt, pours a bucket of water standing idle near the house on himself and plunges into the flames which receive him with a welcoming cackle, the crowd screams for him to come out, but he has disappeared and some young men start throwing water in his direction again, as if it is some kind of covering fire for a soldier running into enemy territory, futile as it seems, useless as it is, the older men mutter, some women who have by now reached the scene start wailing, and the flames shoot up again, as if they have received fresh fuel, the smoke billows and swirls, and no one can see anything of Ashraf

who cannot see anything himself, as he gasps, eyes watering, body searing, but he does not need to see anything in this house on whose floors he had puttered around as a child, within whose walls he has grown up, he knows where every door and window is, where there is a step, and where there is a stool and if his father is there, if he is alive, he will carry the old man out, Ya Allah grant me that, Ya Allah, let me bury my father as a Muslim should be buried, do not allow these flames to consume him, for surely he must be dead, or he would have been out, fighting the fire, and as Ashraf plunges, pushes, falls, stumbles his way into the inner room, that is what he keeps thinking, praying in his heart, a prayer that renders him oblivious of the heat, his hair burning, his skin singeing, just give me the sight to spot my Abba, the strength to bear him out before all the roof collapses, but

what he sees in the innermost room, for Allah must have heard his prayer, and suddenly he is there, in the inner room that had been their parents' bedroom and whose roof is still intact, burning but intact, the fire has not fully penetrated its interior yet, what he sees there he will never narrate to anyone for the rest of his life, because he sees his Abba there, still not consumed by the flame, only his lungi burning at the edges, small flames moving up, he is sitting in the old chair, which was said to belong to some ancestor, the only proper chair in the house for years now, he is sitting there, his eyes wide open, and next to him are containers, two of them, and

when Ashraf sees the containers, one of metal, the other of plastic and warping in the heat, melting before his eyes, he knows that his father is dead and he knows that he will not bear his father out, for Allah has granted him only half his prayer, which is perhaps the way of Allah, who can question His wisdom, or it is perhaps the way of the world, for one gets only a portion of what one asks for, if that, and Ashraf turns away, even as the roof makes sounds of collapsing, a beam shrieks, but Ashraf knows he cannot carry his father out, for his father is dead, and the tin containers next to him are empty, and Ashraf knows what they had contained, for he has often used them, one to spray the crops with in order to save them from pests, the other to fill kerosene lamps with, he recognizes them, and he knows what his father has done, and though Ashraf will never judge the old man, he knows the world will judge him, and hence Ashraf turns around and plunges back out of the burning house, fending off a collapsing beam of wood, which hits him partly on the temple, leaving a scar on his left forehead that, even after his singed and burnt hair grows out again, even after the smell of smoke finally leaves his nostrils, and that will take months too, even afterwards the scar remains, but Ashraf is a strong young man, and he manages to stumble out of the burning house, fall on his knees, coughing, and crawl to an open space outside as men beat him with fronds, one throws a blanket on him, but Ashraf goes crawling on, as if he is escaping from something stalking him, or as if he is looking for something he has dropped on the ground, until he comes to a halt at the spot under the kathal tree where the metal trunk stands,

5.

and he throws both arms around the trunk in something like an embrace, not because it holds all that is left of his past but because now he knows who dragged it out there.

GLOSSARY

Anchal: Traditional scarves for women. Usually of thin cloth. Commonly used. It can also be used to describe the loose part of the sari that is pulled up to cover a woman's head.

Banyan: A light cotton vest, usually worn as an undershirt by men. (Note: A similar word also refers to a kind of tree.)

Bhabhi: Sister-in-law, often also used as a formal designation of respect for a friend's wife.

Bhaijaan: Literally "dear elder brother." Can also be used as a formal term of respect for an older person one feels close to but is not related to.

BJP: Bharatiya Janata Party, Hindu nationalist party, currently ruling India at the national level and in some of the states.

Boarsi-fire: A traditional hard-baked earthen-bowl (Boarsi) in which a low fire, usually of embers, can be lit and maintained.

Bodh Gaya: Historical place where Buddha attained enlightenment, and hence the birthplace of Buddhism.

Burka: The full veil worn by some Muslim women.

Chaalu: Street-smart, cunning.

Challan: Invoice, receipt, but used, in the context of police action, to mean an official notice.

Chaddi-wallahs: Dismissive term for Hindu nationalists. Used to mock the uniform short pants they are supposed to wear during their regular martial exercises.

Charpoy: A bed, still used widely, with a wooden frame strung with tightly woven ropes (or, in more modern versions, strips of cloth). In this collection, the reader is urged to imagine it as woven with ropes.

Chowk: It means both "road junction" and "marketplace," and usually, at least in a town, it is a market area around a road junction at its heart.

Chowki: A small police station.

Dhaba: A traditional "café."

Dargah: Venerated Muslim graves, usually of Sufi saints.

Dhanwa A kind of python, usually five to ten feet long.

Eid: Usually used to refer to one of the two main Muslim festivals.

English-medium: Schools where all subjects are taught in English.

Firang/Firangi: Commonly used in many North Indian languages to refer to Europeans and Americans, derived through old medieval routes from "Franks."

Gajar ka halwa: Halwa (sweetmeat) made from carrots.

Gamcha: A traditional long scarf, usually worn by poorer or rustic Indians now, which can also be turned into a turban.

Ghagra choli: Traditional dress for women.

Godhuli: Literally "cow dust," used to refer to a short period of obscured visibility between dusk and night. Time when cattle would return to the village for the night.

Gora: White, white people, Europeans.

Godrej almirah: A particular brand (Godrej) of a metal cabinet.

Gular: A kind of fig tree.

Haveli: A traditional house, usually built around a closed courtyard.

Hindutva: Hindu nationalism. There are various varieties of it, but all insist on some kind of equation between being Hindu and being Indian.

Huzoor: Sir. More common in Urdu-speaking circles.

Inter Exams: The equivalent of high school graduation exams.

Jaadu-tona: Magic-witchery.

Jantar mantar: A historical observatory in Delhi, but the term also means, in popular Hindustani usage, something like "abracadabra."

Jamaat-e-Islami: Muslim sociopolitical and religious organization.

Jholla: Loose cloth bag, to be slung under one shoulder.

Jooda-hairdo: Elaborate hair arrangements for women, common in the middle classes during the 1970s and '80s.

Kafir: Used in Islamic texts to refer to idolaters and unbelievers. Equivalent of "heathen."

Karak tea: Strong (karak) tea, made in the Indian style.

Kathal: Jackfruit tree.

Khaddar: A hand-loomed cotton fabric woven in India, and originally propagated by Mahatma Gandhi as a symbol of self-reliance and freedom from Britain and British imports.

Khap-panchayat: A kind of village or caste council, usually with much local authority in non-metropolitan areas but with little legal moorings.

Kurta: Traditional loose "shirt."

Lakh: 100,000.

Loo winds: Hot gusts blowing through North India in the summer months.

Mai-baap: A rustic expression of respect or alarm, literally "mother-father."

Maida ka halwa: A halwa (sweetmeat) made of fine flour.

Maulvi: An Islamic cleric or priest.

Mian: Literally "Mister." Urdu usage.

Mohalla: Neighborhood or colony.

MLA: Member of the Legislative Assembly. Each state in India has a Legislative Assembly, which is its highest elected body and essentially handles the internal affairs of the state. MLAs, like MPs, who are members of the national Parliament, for which separate elections are conducted, have a lot of clout.

Namaste: The common, both-hands-folded-together greeting employed in India. While also used sometimes by Muslims and others, it is a Hindu greeting.

Namaz: Muslim prayer.

Nasiruddin Chiragh-Dehlavi: Muslim poet-mystic from the fourteenth century, revered as a Sufi saint.

Netaji: Title – "Neta" means "leader" and "ji" is a honorific. It can be used generically but is often used by many Indians to refer specifically to Subhash Chandra Bose, a radical leader who fought for the freedom of India from the British, and, in the process, joined the Japanese. He died in a plane crash, and there are various theories about his death and purported survival.

Nimki: Snacks, a bit like small biscuits.

Niqaah: The religious part of the Muslim marriage.

Nukkad: Street corner.

Nullah: An open, uncovered drain.

Paan: A concoction of betel leaves, tobacco, etc., traditionally chewed across India.

Phalgu: A river in Bihar that is mostly dry.

Phansa: Fictional town that appears, in different ways, in all of Khair's longer fiction.

Phochka-wallah: The seller of "phochkas," also known in other parts of India as "golgappas," a popular spicy snack.

Pranam: A version of "namaste." Hindu greeting.

Puja: Hindu worship. Also used for various Hindu festivals.

P2C2E: An acronym concocted by Rushdie in *Haroun and the Sea of Stories*. Literally: "Processes Too Complicated to Explain."

Qawwali: Devotional Muslim songs, associated with Sufism.

Rafoo: Fine stitching and needlework, done by hand.

Rooh Afza: Traditional drink made of rose extract.

Sa'ab: A version of "sahib."

Sahib: The common equivalent of "sir" or "master," sometimes also used as a term of formal courtesy.

Sarpanch: Head of the traditional, and now revived, village councils of India: the panchayats.

Sewai: A type of sweetened and variously flavored vermicelli; popular in India, particularly among Muslims during festivals.

Shalwar kameez: Traditional and still commonly worn dresses for women.

Tablighi Jama'at: A social and religious Islamic organization focusing on preaching among lay Muslims in a bid to return them to the 'true' essence of their religion.

Thana: Police station.

Tiffin carrier: A metal or plastic container, containing various compartments, that Indians use to take meals ("tiffin") to schools and workplaces.

Zillah: An administrative unit – archaic word for a "district" containing various towns and villages.

ACKNOWLEDGEMENTS ARE DUE TO THE FOLLOWING FOR:

1. "Night of Happiness," first published as a novella in South Asia by Picador India, edited by Teesta Guha Sarkar.
2. "Scam," written for *Delhi Noir*, edited by Hirsh Sawhney and published by Akashic (USA), and reprinted by HarperCollins, India. It was also reprinted in *The Book of Bihari Literature* (HarperCollins, India), edited by Abhay K, and in *Anglofiles*, the journal of the Danish Association of Teachers of English.
3. "The Corridor," first published in *Harvard Review* (USA), edited by Neel Mukherjee (guest editor) and Christina Thompson.
4. "Olden Friends Are Golden," written for *Not Quite Right for Us*, edited by Sharmilla Beezmohun and published by Flipped Eye (UK). Readings from the story were also featured in a video film.
5. "The Last Installment," in *New England Review* (USA), edited by Carolyn Kuebler.
6. "Namaste Trump," in *Massachusetts Review*, edited by Jim Hicks (executive editor) and Corinne Demas (fiction editor).
7. My publisher in USA, Michel Moushabeck, my editor with Interlink, USA, David Klein, and the Interlink team.

ABOUT THE AUTHOR

Born in 1966 in a small town in India and educated there up to his MA, after which he worked as a journalist in Delhi and moved to Copenhagen to do a Ph.D., Tabish Khair is the author of numerous poetry collections and novels including *Filming: A Love Story* (Picador), *The Thing about Thugs* (Houghton Mifflin and HarperCollins), *How to Fight Islamist Terror from the Missionary Position* (Interlink, Corsair, HarperCollins), *Just Another Jihadi Jane* (Periscope and Interlink), which was published as *Jihadi Jane* in India (Penguin), and *The Body by the Shore* (Interlink and HarperCollins in 2022). Khair's articles, poetry and fiction have been included in prominent anthologies and magazines, including *New Left Review, Harvard Review, Wasafiri, Journal of Commonwealth Literature, Times Literary Supplement, American Book Review, Massachusetts Review, London Magazine, New England Review, P.N. Review,* and *Journal of Postcolonial Writing*. He is the author of scholarly studies including *Babu Fictions: Alienation in Indian English Novels* (Oxford UP), *The Gothic, Postcolonialism and Otherness* (Palgrave), *The New Xenophobia* (Oxford UP), and co-edited scholarly works as well as *Other Routes,* an anthology of pre-modern travel texts by Africans and Asians, with a foreword by Amitav Ghosh (Signal Books and Indiana University Press).

Khair's honors and prizes include the All India Poetry Prize (awarded by the Poetry Society and the British Council) and honorary fellowship (for creative writing) of the Baptist University of Hong Kong. His novels have been shortlisted for about 20 prizes in six countries, including the Man Asian Literary Prize, the DSC Prize for South Asian Literature, the Sahitya Akademi Award, and the Encore Award, and translated into eight languages.